FALCONI'S TRACTOR

DAVE LeBLANC

Essential Prose Series 159

Canada Council   Conseil des Arts
for the Arts   du Canada

ONTARIO ARTS COUNCIL
CONSEIL DES ARTS DE L'ONTARIO
an Ontario government agency
un organisme du gouvernement de l'Ontario

Canadä

Guernica Editions Inc. acknowledges the support of the Canada Council
for the Arts and the Ontario Arts Council. The Ontario Arts Council
is an agency of the Government of Ontario.

We acknowledge the financial support of the Government of Canada.

FALCONI'S TRACTOR

DAVE LeBLANC

**GUERNICA
EDITIONS**
TORONTO • BUFFALO • LANCASTER (U.K.)
2019

Copyright © 2019, Dave LeBlanc and Guernica Editions Inc.
All rights reserved. The use of any part of this publication,
reproduced, transmitted in any form or by any means, electronic,
mechanical, photocopying, recording or otherwise stored
in a retrieval system, without the prior consent
of the publisher is an infringement of the copyright law.

Michael Mirolla, general editor
Julie Roorda, editor
David Moratto, interior and cover design
Guernica Editions Inc.
1569 Heritage Way, Oakville, (ON), Canada L6M 2Z7
2250 Military Road, Tonawanda, N.Y. 14150-6000 U.S.A.
www.guernicaeditions.com

Distributors:
University of Toronto Press Distribution,
5201 Dufferin Street, Toronto (ON), Canada M3H 5T8
Gazelle Book Services, White Cross Mills
High Town, Lancaster LA1 4XS U.K.

First edition.
Printed in Canada.

Legal Deposit—First Quarter
Library of Congress Catalog Card Number: 2018959169
Library and Archives Canada Cataloguing in Publication
LeBlanc, Dave, 1968-, author
Falconi's tractor / Dave LeBlanc.

(Essential prose series ; 159)
Issued in print and electronic formats.
ISBN 978-1-77183-335-6 (softcover).--ISBN 978-1-77183-336-3 (EPUB).
--ISBN 978-1-77183-337-0 (Kindle).

I. Title. II. Title: Tractor. III. Series: Essential prose series ; 159

PS8623.E3278F35 2019   C813'.6   C2018-905601-0   C2018-905602-9

*To Shauntelle,
my light and my life*

☞ Contents ☜

The Black Hole *1*
   I **Freddy Flowers** 5
Black Art *39*
  II **Falconi Farm Equipment** 43
Healing the Hole? *71*
 III **Carm and Rosa** 73
 IV **Spadina Avenue** *103*
  V **Dom** *119*
 VI **Gina** *139*
Black Hole and Main Egg *157*
 VII **Kensington Market** *161*
VIII **Small Carm** *179*
 IX **The Ferrari** *205*
  X **Falconi's Tractor** *225*
 XI **The Incident** *235*
Black Into Red *261*

Acknowledgements *265*
About the Author *269*

And in the squalid silence of my room
The melancholy winter night descends.
I sit beside the fire,
Staring in meditation.

This heavy shadow that enfolds my heart
And shrouds the inmost powers of my being,
Gnawing my spirit's vitals—
Ah, will it ever vanish?

—Excerpt from *Winter Night* by Liborio Lattoni, 1935

The Black Hole

I suppose in retrospect it was silly to think my mother died of a broken heart.

Then again, I was nine when it happened and I believed what my big brother told me. Besides, she was barely taller than me, with skin so pale she wore hats and sleeves even in the summer. Her delicate face, punctuated by wide-apart, bright blue eyes, looked tiny underneath that thick pile of red hair, and her small frame didn't look as if it could withstand any more punishment after producing two big boys, a smallish daughter, and an in-between me.

When Dad left us, even I could tell she wasn't the same. She put on a brave face, especially for me, since I was her "Freddy Flowers," but I noticed little things. Her voice was different somehow, and lower. There was dirt under her long, oval fingernails. She'd pause after entering a room, look around, and say quietly: "Now, why did I come in here again?" in her soft, accented English. And of course we kids could hear the hours of crying — more like whimpering actually — from behind her closed bedroom door.

Sometimes I'd put my ear to the door and listen, hoping

to absorb some of her pain, until my oldest brother, Carmelo Jr. (who we all called Small Carm), would come clomping over and shoot me a look from under those dark, caterpillar eyebrows, and then motion for me to scram with his big sausage-thumb. Usually I'd scram right into Dom's room to tell him Mom was crying again, and Dom would quickly change the subject to make me feel better.

It was Dom who found Mom's body. That day, which we all call "The Incident," happened about four months after Dad left.

And it's Dom's emotional explosion last night, which I suppose has been simmering for more than two decades, that's got my head spinning with the truth and my backside warming a blue plastic chair at Fifty-two Division. I've finished reading that old SARS poster for the third time, so now I'm concentrating on the scuffs in the drywall so I can avoid the icy gaze of the turban-wearing cop behind the desk. I've gone over what I'm going to say a hundred times since Dom's freak-out, so I'm doing what I used to do before a big test at school: I'm putting the facts out of my mind because they'll be there when I need them.

Now about that drywall: How can people working here not notice? All those dark scrapes from shoes, long gashes from moving furniture around, it looks just awful. Not to mention, what kind of idiot tapes posters right to the walls and then rips them off? Don't they care about the marks it leaves behind? I could come in here with my guys and have it all fixed and clean in a day. It wouldn't even cost that much. I mean, the terrazzo floors have been scrubbed and polished to look like a sheet of glass, so obviously they still take great care in maintaining the building.

Ugh, my OCD is rearing its ugly head again. Better to think about the architecture. Most people would hate this Brutalist police station if they even noticed it, but I love it. Outside, it's all top-heavy, grey concrete supported by thin concrete posts, and there are these cool, chunky grooves on the walls that look like they were made with a giant comb while the concrete was still wet. I know it's not called Brutalism because it's brutal-looking, but because it was a name architects coined using the French term *béton brut*, which means raw concrete. Toronto has a lot of this stuff from the 1960s and 70s, and I read a lot of books about Toronto architecture when I was growing up in the 1980s. Crazy, I know, but architecture comforts me: It's solid, unchanging, reliable ... unlike a lot of people.

Even the long reception desk in here is made of rough concrete, except it's got all these dark patches where people have touched it over the years to form a patina of human grease. The original desks at City Hall were made out of concrete too, but I don't think they're there anymore. And speaking of desks, there's another cop standing beside the one who was drilling holes into me with his dark eyes a few minutes ago.

"Mr. Falconi?" he says, his big cop voice ricocheting off the hard ceiling. "My colleague, Officer Singh, tells me you've got some information concerning the missing person's report your brother filed in 1984. Your mom, Rosabella, right?"

"Yes, ahem, yes I do, sir. First off, she's not missing, she's dead," I said, breaking the blood oath we'd all made to each other twenty-three years ago and opening the Falconi Black Hole.

"And I can take you to her right now."

CHAPTER I

☞ Freddy Flowers ☜

MY TWO BROTHERS, my sister and I all have two histories: before The Incident, and after.

I was a happy little guy. I grew up above my parent's showroom at 413 Spadina Avenue on the western edge of downtown Toronto. At the top of our block, where Spadina crosses College Street, a massive, overhead latticework of streetcar wires cuts the sky into a hundred blue triangles and makes it feel like a giant outdoor room. From College south, Spadina is a wide, frenetic strip until it terminates at an unceremonious guardrail that prevents cars from plunging into Lake Ontario. Most of the buildings date to the late 1800s, like ours, or the early 1900s, and are two-storey or three-storey, fairly utilitarian warehouse and office buildings made mostly from a red brick called "John Price." For a hundred years, this sturdy brick was formed from the rich, soft mud of the Don Valley, seven kilometres to the east.

The Don Valley is Toronto's psychological divide: One is either an east-ender or a west-ender, since Torontonians never identify themselves as northerners or southerners.

When I grew up, all the cool stuff was in the west end, including most of the immigrant neighbourhoods and their amazing restaurants. Two of Toronto's Little Italy neighbourhoods, for example, are in the west end. And so are Little Malta, Portugal Village, Little Manila, Little Korea, Little Jamaica, and the Polish strip on Roncey. Although my mother lived in Little Sicily in the east end when she first came here with her parents, it was so small it wasn't on the radar like other immigrant neighbourhoods. Well, the east end's Greektown was definitely on the radar. Toronto's Greeks are loud and proud, and they have a big festival every year that jams Danforth Avenue, a.k.a. "The Danforth," with hundreds of thousands of people.

A half-block north of College, Spadina wraps around a ceremonial circle that holds Knox College, an old Gothic building that once housed an independent Presbyterian theological school but now belongs to the University of Toronto. It also sucks ninety percent of the street life into its staid, scholarly void. If I hadn't gone to elementary school across the street from Knox, I wouldn't have walked in that direction at all.

There were kids of all colours in my neighbourhood, and we played hide-and-seek and cops-and-robbers in that big outdoor room at College and Spadina sometimes, but mostly we'd play in the cozy back alleys and little streets of Baldwin Village during the sticky summers of the early eighties. A lot of my friends were Chinese and Vietnamese, since our "house" was at the northern tip of the messy signage and stained sidewalks of Chinatown, and the fishy fragrances and rambling fruit stands of Kensington Market.

Spadina is such a busy street teeming with so many

New Canadians, the Toronto Transit Commission installed a high-capacity, right-of-way streetcar line right down the centre of it in 1997. Then again, that's not surprising; when other cities were ripping out their trolley cars in the 1970s, Toronto was expanding its system. Today, we have the largest streetcar network in the Americas.

My full name is Alfredo Dino Falconi, but everyone knows me as "Freddy Flowers" or "Flowerboy." It's an Italian thing, I guess, to stick a stupid nickname on someone because of one small thing, but my thing—two things, actually—happened when I was so young I never got the chance to fight my nicknames off. My parents owned a farm equipment company that made tractors, mostly, and we had land north of the city near little Buttonville Airport; we called it "Falconi Farm," and Dad would bring us up there on a regular basis to test new tractor models and implements and so on.

One time, while Mom and Dad were talking to our employee and showing him something, me and my older brother Dom, who was about thirteen years old then, wandered off to look for frogs in Beaver Creek. I'm not sure what my other brother and my sister were doing, but I know they were there too, since Italians didn't hire babysitters in those days.

As Dom was dunking his head into the mossy-green creek, I was going nuts over a big patch of black-eyed Susans I'd found near the water's edge. Dazzled by their bright yellow faces, I started picking them and sticking them in my pockets and arranging them into my messy Prince Valiant bowl-cut. I twirled and danced and sang songs to the little flower people (as I was now their king), and then collapsed into a sweaty heap like a tiny, drugged-out Woodstock hippie.

Dom found me, sleeping in the middle of the half-decimated flower patch, so, of course, he started to laugh his head off.

"Hey guys, c'mere, you gotta see this: LITTLE FREDDY FLOWERS!"

So I liked flowers, big deal. About a year later, just as the name was starting to wear out, I was cast into the role that would cement my sobriquet forever. At a big Italian wedding in my mom's old neighbourhood, I was waiting in the church vestibule, pulling at my stiff collar and fiddling with the ring sitting on its little velvet pillow. "Do not do that Freddy, you are going to lose it," my mom cautioned. As the story goes, I became belligerent when I met the flower girl and, after much negotiation, she wouldn't let me trade places with her.

"Why can't a *boy* be the flower girl?" I yelled in frustration, causing two hundred heads to swivel around and laugh.

Ever since then, I've been Freddy Flowers, the Flowerboy.

Despite the Italian nickname, I was the least Italian kid in my family. By the time I was born in 1975, unplanned (or "Mom's favourite mistake" as Dom likes to say), my parents had given up on limiting the onslaught of American television from Buffalo, which is only a little over an hour's drive south, or the Canadian junk food at the grocery store. I ate Wagon Wheels or Vachon Flakies after finishing the squishy peanut butter and jam sandwiches I brought to school. Or, worse, I ate Chef Boyardee Beefaroni at home when there was delicious homemade pasta underneath tinfoil in the fridge. Small Carm (because Dad was Big Carm) and Dom, both born in the 60s, had schlepped big brown paper bags filled with fried pepper, onion, and egg sandwiches and clunky orange Tupperware containers filled with grapes, figs and provolone to school. Four hours later, when they'd sit down to lunch, the bags would be dotted with so much olive oil you could see right through the little grease-windows.

My mom, Rosa, was still sewing when my brothers were small, so they looked like miniature Florida retirees in their snap-button dress shirts, plaid slacks and safari jackets. They wore tight dress shoes — "Imported Direct from Italy" — from a little shop near Mom's favourite textile stores on The Danforth, and their hair was cut military-short by a chain-smoking Italian barber until about 1978. My sister wore old-fashioned, frilly homemade dresses and pantyhose until about then, too, but all I remember is seeing her dressed like a tomboy in jeans and rock band "world tour" T-shirts.

I, on the other hand, never had to wear the weird Italian stuff. I wore *Empire Strikes Back* and *Return of the Jedi* T-shirts, gym shorts, white tube socks and Bata running shoes in summer, and long-sleeved, velour shirts over GWG Scrubbies in winter. I looked like a Canadian kid.

While Small Carm and Dom had been blessed with Big Carm's olive skin, thick chestnut hair and brown eyes, my sister and I looked like mungie cakes: pale skin, blue eyes and light brown hair. Well, that's not entirely true. I did get Big Carm's Roman nose. And when I got older and grew a Van Dyke beard, it came in in a darker shade of my mom's beautiful red hair. Gina and I were short like Mom too. But, while I was just stocky, Gina turned into a pear after age twenty: a tiny head and small upper body with a big butt and huge thighs.

I didn't know how to speak Italian. Small Carm was fairly fluent and Dom was pretty good at it, but Gina and I knew only a few odd words and certainly couldn't put a sentence together. Until my teens, I thought everyone was saying: "Ah, Fungu!" when they got angry. It was only when a friend gag-gifted me a book of Italian swearwords that I learned it was *vaffanculo*.

Around seven, I developed severe allergies. This meant a weekly shot in the arm by Dr. Sheinart, who practised out of a big Queen Ann style home on Madison Avenue in the Annex, just a few kilometres north of our place. The Annex is a dense, tree-lined, downtown residential neighbourhood filled with all sorts of big, historic homes from the late-1800s that, even back then, were starting to enjoy new life as University of Toronto fraternities, sororities, law firms and small boutiques for ladies who lunch.

Because Dad was busy running the business, it was my mother who would take me to get my shot. I could tell she enjoyed herself, because we'd go for walks afterward so she could point to details on the houses: simple things like leaded glass, gables and turrets, since she had never studied architecture and didn't know the complex terminology. Or, she would tell me who had lived in them a hundred years ago, like the one on St. George Street that had been built by a member of the Eaton family (any Canadian born before 1985 knows that department store chain). I think she was homesick for the architecture of Sicily, too, and this was as close to it as she could get in modern Toronto, a city she found ugly and let all of us know it.

I was fascinated with these little stained-glass birds over almost every front door on Tranby Street, and I remember my mother laughing and breaking into an Italian children's song, "The Blackbird Lost Its Beak," the first time I pointed them out with my chubby, chocolate-stained little finger:

Il merlo ha perso il becco
come farà a beccar?
Il merlo ha perso il becco
come farà a beccar?
Il merlo ha perso il becco,
povero merlo mio, come farà a beccar?

Il merlo ha perso i denti
come farà a mangiar?
Il merlo ha perso i denti
come farà a mangiar?
Il merlo ha perso i denti,
povero merlo mio, come farà a mangiar?

So this poor blackbird, the song goes, it's lost its beak, so "how will it manage to peck?" In the next verse, the teeth are gone (so how will it eat?) and in the next it's got no tongue (so how can it sing?) and so forth. This became our little song together, and sometimes she'd hum it to herself when combing my messy hair or helping me get ready for a bath. I never heard her sing it to anyone else. Today, when I think of her voice singing it, a warm rush rises up from the base of my spine and then, like the wings of a Monarch butterfly, it spreads into my chest.

By the time I was eight-and-a-half, these walks had emboldened me to show her some of the buildings I liked. I remember, one time, we were on St. George Street near Bernard Avenue, walking south, and I told her I wanted to live in one of the little apartment buildings lining St. George when I grew up. Ironically enough, these buildings, none taller than about ten storeys, had replaced many of the red brick mansions she loved during Toronto's construction boom of the 1950s.

"But why, Freddy, they are just boxes. What do you see?"

"This one is smart because the roof has holes in it," I said about the long canopy over the front door at number 276, "so the flowers can get sun." Then, contemplating the triangular-shaped balconies of number 250 and rubbing my chin like a scholar, I said: "And this one is pointy, and the people get to sit on that part."

"And this one, my little architect? Number 267?" she asked, clearly enjoying herself.

"Well this one is a little boring. But I like the tile around the front door and that everyone gets little skinny windows to look out of."

Another time, at the corner of Beverley and Cecil Street, I spotted a small concrete building that housed a club for war veterans. "Could someone have this as a house if they wanted?"

"I think so. But the other people on the street might think you are *pazzu*, crazy," she said, smiling. She would often say the Italian word first as a way to pause and wait for the English one to land on her tongue.

Just before Mom died, she took me to see the "even bigger boxes" of the financial district. She had started smoking again then, so one of my last memories of her is watching as she rummaged through her purse for her Zippo lighter, which she'd received as a gift during her honeymoon. Sitting, Buddha-like, on a flat, manicured patch of green between the big black towers of the Toronto-Dominion Centre, she daintily placed a long cigarette between her orange-painted lips, flicked her lighter open and inhaled deeply. She was laughing at how excited I was to see the towers, but all I could see through the cloud of grey smoke was the bright turquoise kerchief holding down that big pile of red hair.

I don't remember much from the day I found out Dad left us. Maybe it's because I had no idea why he'd left or whether or not he would be coming back. I just remember Small Carm waiting at the door to the Falconi showroom as I walked down Spadina from school to make sure I didn't bolt through the building to get to the staircase in the backyard like I always did.

"Come in here. Sit down, I have to talk to you."

"But I want to see Mom and tell her about — "

"Mom's not home, she's with a friend in the old neighbourhood. She's going to be there a few days, so I'm in charge right now, okay?"

"Okay," I said, my little brain trying to process the weird look on his face.

"Dad's gone," he said, staring directly into my eyes, which made me uncomfortable. "And I don't mean on a business trip. You know about Italians and honour, right? Well, he has dishonoured this family and he isn't welcome here anymore."

"You mean like Fredo in *The Godfather*?"

"Yeah, Freddy, something like that."

"Can I talk to him?" I didn't dare tell him that, earlier that day, I'd seen what I now guessed was Mom and Dad's last fight from the third floor window.

"Not right now. Maybe in the future, I dunno. All you need to know at the moment is that Mommy loves you, and I love you, and Dom and Gina love you. And life is going to continue as it always has, okay? You're just going to go to school like always and if anyone asks about *him* — which they won't, you say he's on a business trip."

I remember going upstairs and, finding Dom's room locked and him unresponsive to my soft knocking, retreating to my own room. All of our bedrooms were on the second floor and exactly the same size, and that size was small. Since I was the last one to be born, my furniture was a weird mix of hand-me-downs and stuff Mom had repurposed from other rooms. My bed, painted in groovy colours, was Small Carm's from the late 60s, but my bedside table was an old, weird, ornate thing from the 1930s. On the walls, I even had a hand-me-down *Godfather* poster (the one with the black-and-white image of a standing Don Corleone with the popping, red rose on his lapel) from Small Carm, a photograph of the Toronto skyline I'd cut out of a magazine, and a TTC subway map Dom had found in the garbage.

I plopped down on the bed and tried to figure out what had happened. Since I was eight-and-three-quarters at the time, all I could envision was Dad with a Fredo Corleone-style, pencil-thin moustache, walking into the offices of that big tractor company on King Street and giving them our secrets, and then being found out somehow and coming home to a slap across the face from our mother with a Hollywood-style "How could you? You are dead to me now!" In any case, I was used to them arguing in those last few months.

The day Mom died is a lot more vivid because it was so surreal.

I came home from school that day — I think it was the second-last day of grade four — to the exact same scenario: Small Carm standing at the showroom door looking out for me, but this time his face wasn't just sombre, it had changed to the point where I barely recognized him. His forehead was pale and shiny from perspiration, and around his usual deep-set eyes, a puffiness and sort of alligator scaliness to the skin had popped them out so they looked like two brown marbles floating in *zabaglione*. He hadn't shaved that morning, either, so his five-o'clock shadow was extra-dark. Of course, he still had his trademark golf shirt and pressed dress pants on. His breathing was funny when he told me to come inside and sit down.

This time, however, Dom and Gina were there in the old showroom, too, and they also looked pale, tired and stunned; so stunned, in fact, that Small Carm did all the talking.

"So you know how hard it's been for Mom these past few months since Dad left?"

I didn't answer, I just nodded.

"Well, this morning, while you were in school, Mom died, and —"

I heard the scrape of a metal chair leg on the tile floor as Gina bolted upright, made a tiny mmph noise, covered her mouth and left the room. Dom just sat there like a marble statue.

"What do you mean, she *died*?" I said, my stomach flipping over and the taste of bile hitting my tongue.

"You know that people die, right? I mean, you know that we're not here on this planet forever. Well, some of us are strong and live a long time, and some of us are more, well, delicate, and their bodies can't take it when bad things happen to them. Mom was a very delicate person, and she died because she loved Dad so much her heart couldn't take the strain."

"Where is she?" I managed to stammer. My voice sounded as if was in an echo chamber. "Can I see her?"

"No, you can't, I'm sorry," Small Carm answered quickly.

The rest of the conversation is a blur, but what happened that night is so bizarre I can still picture every single detail. Dom knocked on my door and asked me to come downstairs. It was the first time I'd heard him speak that day. He led me down to the showroom, but I almost tripped on the last stair because the overhead lights had been turned off. Only the red tractor in the window had light on it (and I noticed that the blinds had been drawn, something I'd never seen before) and there was candlelight coming from the middle of the showroom. Both desks had been pushed to the walls to make room for the four of us to gather around the candles.

I thought we were going to say some prayers for Mom, but that's not what happened.

"Dom and Gina, you already know about this, but Freddy, we wanted you to be part of this ceremony too," Small Carm said, his voice steady despite the flickering light giving him two sets of fish-lips. "Well, it was Dom, actually, who said you are old enough to take part and understand how serious this is." Dom nodded gently, like he was in church.

"Today has been a real test for our family," he said, "but I know we are strong enough to get through it." He then pulled out four items: a pin, a small paring knife, a wooden handle with three beaded strings attached to it, and an odd, rawhide necklace with two brown squares on either end. One square had old-looking script on it, and the other had a picture of what looked like a saint. He placed the necklace around himself so that one square lay on his chest and the other was on his back, and then said to me: "You ever have a friend that you liked so much you pricked each other's fingers and became blood brothers, Freddy? Well that's what we're going to do here, and then we're going to promise something to each other, okay?"

I just nodded dumbly.

He then took the paring knife and cut X's into the palms of both his hands. He flinched but didn't say anything. Almost immediately, a little string of red pearls appeared on the clean tile floor, which soon turned into a puddle. Dom then held out his hands, but Small Carm cut an X into only one of his palms. He must've gone deeper, however, since Dom quickly sucked in some air as he watched the blood curl around his forearm. Before I could protest on Gina's behalf, Small Carm switched to the pin and produced a tiny dome of red on one of her palms. He did the same to me: one little prick right in the centre.

"Now hold hands, everyone," he said, scanning all of our faces. He took Dom's bloody hand with his dripping right hand, and Dom took Gina's, and Gina took mine. But it was what he did with his left that was really weird. He picked up the wooden handle with the beaded strings and began striking himself on the back with quite a bit of force. Droplets of blood from his open wound were flinging through the air, hitting walls, windows and furniture.

"Our mother, Rosabella Falconi, is gone," he said in the same kind of tone I'd heard in horror movie séances. "But her love lives inside all of us, and we must protect and cherish that love. There has been scandal, and disrespect, but we must protect our proud family name. FALCONI."

Thankfully, his voice then changed back to something more normal. "And the way to do this is by keeping her death a secret. Dom, Gina, again, you already know this," he said, then turned his gaze to me. "Freddy, if anyone asks about our mother, you tell them that she has gone missing, and we are doing everything we can to find her ... *capisce*?"

Because we were Protestant — well, Dad was, Mom had been Catholic, we went to public school. Dad, who was a second-generation Italian-Canadian, had insisted that *his* kids were not to be brought up Catholic, so despite the scandal it caused with his in-laws, Mom agreed. Mom had always been too soft with Dad.

This meant we all attended this crazy-looking, space age school called Lord Lansdowne, which opened the year before *The Jetsons* came on TV. And it looked like something George Jetson would land his spaceship on. Most of the classrooms were in a nine-sided, three-storey, circular building with a roof shaped like a crown. Inserted into this crown at eighteen different points were tall, tapered, boomerang-shaped posts spaced a few feet away from the building, which I later learned was so the school board could add more floors if babies kept booming into the 1970s. This also made it look like a giant spider that could decide to run away if it had enough of all the screaming children. It was awesome, and I'm sure it had a lot to do with me showing my mom those modern apartment buildings on St. George.

When Small Carm took over the family after The Incident that summer, one of his first proclamations was that I would be transferring to St. Francis of Assisi as soon as my conversion to Catholicism was complete.

To say I was devastated is an understatement.

Grade 5 at Lord Lansdowne was a blur. Not only were both my parents gone, I had to study from a bunch of books the priest at St. Francis had given to Small Carm. Basically, I had double the homework of the other kids. Luckily, we had all been baptized in the Methodist church (Mom insisted), so I didn't have to enter the catechumenate, the complex web of Catholic rites, rituals, reflection and recitals that can take a year or more. All I had to do, Small Carm told me, was learn what was different about the Catholic faith and then convince the priest I was excited to join it. He was aiming to have me out of Lord Lansdowne by Christmas and at my new school in the new year.

He was so excited for me, I'm pretty sure *he* was the one who convinced the priest.

St. Francis of Assisi Catholic School, a twenty-minute walk from our place, was the opposite of Lord Lansdowne: an unexciting, utilitarian, 1950s brick box on Manning Street in Toronto's Little Italy. The only decoration was a big crucifix made from raised bricks on one wall. While some Italians had left that neighbourhood for the larger houses of Toronto's other Little Italy at Dufferin Street and St. Clair Avenue West, and others had gone north of the city to an area called Woodbridge, there were still plenty there to greet me in January 1985 when I arrived, trembling, for the second half of Grade 5. Thank goodness Dom offered to walk me that cold and slushy morning to keep me distracted.

I remember Dom, then seventeen, checking in with the principal, Mr. Agnelli — Small Carm had phoned him a few days before to make him aware that our father was away on business and our mother had gone missing — and how he was treated almost as if *he* was the one enrolling in the school. It wasn't the first time I'd seen Dom treated differently, but this time it made a big impression on me.

"My understanding was that Carmelo Falconi Junior, Alfredo's legal guardian, would be bringing him here today," he said, scanning Dom from head to toe.

"Yessir, I know, but he runs our family business, you see, and he had to take care of some clients this morning. I think you'll find that — "

And that's when he grabbed Dom's hand and Dom grabbed mine with a "whatever" look on his face and we were both pulled down a hallway painted mint green on the bottom half and butter yellow up top.

I guess they didn't get a lot of newcomers at this school, because after Mr. Agnelli efficiently triple-rapped on the big wooden door and I heard my new teacher announce, muffled, "Class, we have a new student joining us now," I also heard a stampede of dress shoes on the hard, terrazzo floor. As

Mr. Agnelli was blocking the door when Mrs. Figueroa opened it, I remember hearing this:

"Is it a boy or a girl?"

"C'mon, lemme see!"

"Are they Italian?"

I think there was a collective gasp when they all saw what looked to be an Irish kid standing there, then a sigh of relief when Mrs. Figueroa said: "Everyone, meet Alfredo Falconi, who likes to be called Freddy."

✐

There was so much going on in my head that half-year, I don't remember much about it. I made a couple of friends, but because I was such a non-Italian Italian, I think they regarded me as a curiosity.

Small Carm decided that a great way for me to meet people that summer was to become an altar boy at St. Francis of Assisi Church. While girls have been allowed to serve the priests since 1994, when I joined up it was still an all-boy clique. In other words, the coolest Italians at the school were altar boys, and they didn't take kindly to the new recruits. They couldn't stop us from signing up, but they could, and did, make our lives miserable. They never really talked to us except to bark orders, and when we got to serve at weddings and funerals, which involved little packets of money given to us for our work, they skimmed off the top like casino bosses. Some of them had started in Grade 5 and were now in high school, and they strutted around like they owned the place. These guys wore the red cassocks, which always seemed cleaner than our white ones, which were all fuzzy with pills and crusty with dried wax. They also got to handle the wine, chalice and ciborium (the gold, trophy-like cup that stores the hosts) behind the scenes, and, when Mass started, walk the big, processional cross up the aisle or swing the smoking, incense-filled thurible. They also helped the priest dress the altar. Cocks-of-the-walk is what we called them behind their backs.

We were allowed to be candle bearers, to hold the sacramentary (a big book) up for the priest because it was heavy, bring him the Lavabo (a bowl of water and a towel) so he could wash his hands before the big offertory, and stand around a lot with our hands pressed together looking pious. After Mass, they made us do most of the clean-up. The most important thing I ever got to do, and this took until Grade 7, was to be the bell boy. This means that, at specific points during the transubstantiation, when the priest turns the red wine into the blood of Jesus and the eucharistic host into his body, you have to pick up the altar bell and ring it. I remember the head altar boy at the time, Bart, who had just finished shaving in the church washroom, told me: "This is a big responsibility, Freddy. Jesus is *standing right there* as the priest is doing this. Don't screw it up."

St. Francis was an intimidating church to screw up in, too. Behind the altar is a fifty-five-foot glass tile mosaic of Jesus nailed to the cross. Imagine having that looking down at you, judging you. Behind the cross are giant flames and, above it, weird stars or galaxies. That's not to mention all of the serious faces in the stained glass, the racks and racks of flickering red candles, and images of the Virgin Mary with her "immaculate" heart floating outside of her chest. Oh, and all of the Italians sitting in the pews with their eyes locked onto all of us.

By Grade 6, I was less numb, and because of my altar boy-ing my little group of friends had expanded to about five: four Italians and one big Portuguese guy who didn't say much. Nunzio, who lived about a block away, had ColecoVision with both Pitfall and Pitfall II, so we'd go over whenever his mother was out shopping and his older sister was at home, and we'd play until our hands cramped. She'd also let us eat whatever was in the fridge.

I do remember one time that really made me feel like an outsider, however. We were in the tiny, cinderblock-walled change room putting on our shorts for gym class and one of my friends, Angelo, pointed at my legs.

"B'oh, Freddy," he said, laughing, "what, do you shave your legs?" Then everyone laughed.

I looked down. At age eleven, my legs were covered in golden peach fuzz. Theirs were already bristling with thick, black, manly hair.

About a year later, when I finally hit puberty, the nightmares began.

But before the nightmares came the insomnia. Almost every night for three months, I'd wake up at exactly one in the morning and not be able to get back to sleep. My bedroom shared a wall with Gina's and she and I were right across a little hallway from Small Carm's and Dom's rooms and I didn't want to disturb any of them, so I'd lie there, alternately staring at the ceiling and at my little bedside clock, adjusting my focus to watch the worm-like floaters drift and fall, jerk upward, then drift and fall again. I'd pray to Jesus and ask if he could send my mom down as a ghost so I could see her one more time. I'd pray for Small Carm, since he was in charge of the family now. I'd pray for Dom, since I liked him best and, once in a while, I'd even pray for Gina.

On the nights that I would be up for more than an hour, I'd start thinking about death. Not my own death, thankfully, since I was too young to consider my own mortality, but that Small Carm or Dom might die soon and I'd be left with Gina or, worse, get shipped off to Italy to be with one of my aunts, and probably the crazy one. I'd feel my heart move into my throat and start to beat wildly. I'd feel a weird electrical pulse shooting through my arms; it got so I could predict where it would go. I'd sweat. I'd pray like mad to make it stop. Later, I'd learn these were called panic attacks but, at the time, I thought my brain was going crazy and that my body was rebelling against it.

I got so worried about these episodes, I made sure there were a lot of books on my little bedside table so I could train my brain to calm down. One of them was *Toronto* by Bruce West. It was an adult book that dealt with the early history of the city. I would read the last few paragraphs about how big Toronto was getting and how tall all the new bank towers were, over and over again. That made me think of my mom, too, but in a good way. Another was about the history of baseball, the only sport I really liked. About a month after the insomnia finally went away, the recurring dream started; it was so bad, I kind of wished the insomnia would return.

The first nightmare was so vivid I think it created its

own neural pathways in my brain, since I can still recall it scene-for-scene today, twenty years later. My mom and I were walking in a neighbourhood that looked like a cross between the Annex and a jerky cartoon-scape from *Sesame Street*, like the one where the little girl forgets what her mom asks her to get at the store ("A loaf of bread, a container of milk, a stick of butter"), or the one where the little kid on his bicycle gets lost and passes all of these psychedelic animals, houses and statues until Yo-Yo Man sings a funk song to help him find his way.

Mom takes me into a phone booth because she's got to make a call. It's one of those older, tall glass ones with the accordion door and the little red sign on top that reads "TELEPHONE" in a simple typeface. While she's dialling, I'm fanning the pages of the heavy, dangling phone book. She's speaking Italian, which is boring to me. After a few minutes, I tug on her skirt and ask if I can go outside and wait there. "It's HOT in here, Mom!" I go outside and shut the door behind me. I try not to look at the buildings because they're painted funny colours and incomplete in some areas, like a sketch. She hangs up and can't get the door open. She's wrestling with it and it's responding with squeaky shrieks. She calls out to me: "Freddy, can you help me with the door, it is *rutta*, broken!"

I start pulling on it, pushing on it. The more I tug at it, the less it seems to move.

"You are making it worse, Freddy. What did you do to it?"

I'm pulling with everything my nine-year-old arms can give. Nothing. I start crying. I look around for help and there are only weird *Sesame Street* cartoon characters walking around.

I'm crying so hard now I can barely see through the tears. Mom, instead of panicking, puts her hand against the glass, her long fingernails clicking against the pane. "It is okay, my little Flowerboy. I can live inside here. Look, I have a telephone, I can call you all the time. Go home now, I will be fine."

In another version, my mom still gets trapped, but a big black crow inside the phone booth begins to fly around when I start wrenching at the door. It's flapping wildly above my mom's head and she's ducking, screaming, and holding her hair. The bird is panicking and slamming into the glass walls, over and over and over again. Blood from the crow's mashed head starts to paint long, red lines down the glass.

Needless to say, when cell phones became popular and those old phone booths started to disappear, I was pretty relieved.

By Grade 7, I had become a rebel: I stopped discussing religion with Small Carm. After I'd first transferred to St. Francis and throughout Grade 6, he'd sit me down once a week to discuss what I'd learned in religion class. Often, it wouldn't be very much, since our religion teacher was an ex-hippie, folk music-loving lady who would ask us to think about Jesus in an abstract way and then draw what we were thinking—she was very impressed when I held up my picture of a rose pushing up through a thick blanket of snow—or we'd analyze the lyrics of *Jesus Christ Superstar* after listening to the soundtrack on the big, canvas-covered, utilitarian record player with the built-in speaker. So, sometimes, I'd just make stuff up like, "Oh, we discussed if a bank robber who needed the money to feed his children was committing a sin or not," just to get the conversation started. His eyes would light up and he'd immediately look for the Bible passage that might contain the answer.

I enjoyed it when Small Carm allowed our conversations to go a little more free-form, like my teacher, and we'd discuss the meaning of life together, if there was life on other planets and if they had our god or their own, or if animals were sentient. Unfortunately, more often than not, Small Carm would yammer on about some parable or other and then just read it aloud from his shiny-covered Bible, which bored me to tears. It was nice spending time with him, but I'm sure he got more out of these debriefing sessions than I did.

That's why, when it was time to choose a high school in Grade 8, I put my thirteen-year-old foot down. After the fight of the century between Small Carm and me — a fight that even gentle Dom got involved in because he knew I was tired of being pious, I was allowed to attend Dom's high school, Central Technical School, rather than the Catholic all-boys school Small Carm had his eye on. Despite the name, Central Tech is a unique high school that, in addition to regular academics, offers classes in everything from fine art to automobile repair to aerospace engineering. The main building, designed in a Gothic Revival style almost a hundred years ago, looks like something one might see on the nearby University of Toronto campus.

The funny thing is, even though Small Carm had started referring to me as "Freddy the Fine Ar-teest" because I had fought to go to a school like this, I didn't really take advantage of those great programs. I did a little art because it was fun, and I tried my hand at some of the drafting programs since I loved architecture so much, but I just didn't have the patience for that kind of exacting detail. I stuck mostly to history, English and, strangely enough, some of the softer sciences like sociology and political science.

I was relieved when I found out that being Italian wasn't a point of pride here like it had been at St. Francis. Kids of every nationality and faith came from all over to attend this school, so the Italians I did meet weren't as inclined to talk about how many times they'd been to Italy or seen *The Godfather*. I'd never been to Italy so I'd always feel left out whenever the discussion at recess would turn to whose hometown was cooler. Small Carm, Dom and Gina had gone to Catania and Campodimele when they turned thirteen — a Wop Mitzvah as Dom called it — but our family wasn't in any shape to send me when I hit that age.

By Grade 11, I knew I wasn't going to get any taller than five-foot-six. So even if, as Small Carm claimed, smoking pot would stunt my growth, I was pretty sure it was okay to try it, so I dabbled between the ages of sixteen and seventeen. Small Carm had been drilling into me since he took over the family: "Italians don't do drugs," he'd tell me, and then he and Dom would rent a video about the Mafia and drugs. Honestly, though, I don't know what all the fuss was about. After laughing a lot, you'd eat a whole pizza and then become either sleepy or worried that you were a failure in life. Hopefully you'd get sleepy first.

I doubt it was the drugs, but when it came time to decide what to study in university I was completely lost. It was expected that I would be the first kid to get a post-secondary education, since Small Carm had gone into the family business long before he'd graduated high school, Dom didn't have the grades, and Gina was already married and living in the suburbs. Everyone figured I'd go up the street to that dusty, former dentistry building that housed the Faculty of Architecture at the University of Toronto. It was as close a walk as my former elementary school, Lord Lansdowne, and I suppose my marks were good enough to get in, but truth be told I wanted to keep architecture at arm's length — I wanted it to remain something to admire like a sculpture or a fine painting.

I also didn't want to be in that neighbourhood any longer. I needed to breathe. So I started talking about the environment a lot, especially when Small Carm was around. I took books out of the library on sustainable technology and water pollution and made sure to leave them on the coffee table where my brothers could see them. I knew there weren't many universities that offered degrees in Environmental Studies, so if my plan worked, I could leave town for a while. I told Small Carm that Trent University, an hour-and-a-half drive away in the small city of Peterborough, had one of the best and oldest programs.

I was playing a role, and it worked. When Small Carm thrust the acceptance letter from Trent into my chest, crumpling it, I jumped for joy.

"Well, Mr. Save the Planet, I guess I should congratulate you?" he said, raising his caterpillar eyebrows and staring at me from over his glasses. Had he figured out my ruse? Then his blubbery fish lips curled upward. "Be sure to come back for Easter mass, eh, Enviro-boy?"

Despite Dad leaving the company in a shambles, Small Carm had worked hard to make sure the family wouldn't go broke. So I decided to live on campus with a full meal plan. I applied for, and got, a little single-occupancy room at Champlain College, the first part of the school to open in 1967. The four-storey residence, with its zigging and zagging walls cradling a little diamond-shaped quad on three sides, looked both medieval and modern at the same time. There was a long wooden trellis over a walkway at the bottom of the quad that reminded me of an abstracted cloister enclosure. And speaking of abstraction, rising above campus was a tall, vaguely Cubist clock tower without a clock that had a plaque inscribed with the name of the architect: Ronald J. Thom. You could see this tower from across the Otonabee River, where the other, non-Thom designed part of the campus was located.

I know it sounds strange, but I chose a room to myself because I had no intention of making friends; I'd had enough of people and I just wanted to turn my brain off. Trent had been dubbed "Oxford on the Otonabee" by many writers since it had been inspired by the older universities of England with their nooks, crannies and pedestrian pathways. This made it the perfect place for hiding.

When I finally arrived that last week of August with exactly two suitcases, I was blown away by my room. While it was tiny like the one I had in the Falconi building, it felt like a reverse monastery: a place where reason reigned supreme. After I'd put my clothes and my toothbrush away, I surveyed my domain. Unlike my mismatched room at home, it was cohesive, all flat planes and nooks for reading and storing books. Through a lovely corner window I could see a rolling, grassy drumlin, and when I cranked it open, a fresh breeze fluttered sensible woollen curtains. Instead of a monk's bed of nails, however, I had a single captain's bed. There was hidden lighting in one of the cabinets that aimed up at the ceiling. On every drawer and cabinet, well-worn finger-pulls made from leather loops had darkened by almost three decades of use. It looked like a smartly designed room for getting smart in; all I needed was a pipe and elbow patches.

To pass time before the semester began, I wandered the campus. Sometimes, I'd sit on the banks of the river with a pile of crisp new textbooks and gaze at the dark, slow-moving water. Sometimes I'd even read the books. More often I'd nap.

I was in awe of Thom's buildings, which looked as if they had been grown underground and then pushed through the topsoil to take their rightful place along the riverbank. They had walls made of something called "rubble aggregate," which looked like big stone cookie crumbles suspended in smooth concrete ice cream, and a few of the buildings had glass stair towers that looked like some of the photographs I'd seen of Frank Lloyd Wright's famous house in Pennsylvania, Fallingwater. There was a beautiful concrete footbridge that crossed the river, but I preferred the vibe of Champlain, so I spent most of my time there.

I remember calling Dom to tell him all about it the day after Small Carm had dropped me off with a quick "Call me if you need anything" followed by a squeal of tires. I guess he couldn't wait to get back to the city.

"It's really cool, man, a lot of the buildings look like that big triangular library at U of T, but smaller," I told him. "You know, the one that looks like a turkey?"

"Yeah, the Stone *Tacchino*!" he said, laughing. "I'm happy for you, Freddy, I know how much you've always liked buildings and stuff, and I'm sure you'll be a big cheese *professore* there one day. And I'll still be stuck on Spadina building my models until I'm an old friggin' man."

Dom's skill with model kits was legendary in our family. "Dom, I keep saying, go to one of those big architecture firms I told you about and show them what you can do. Architects have to make models all the time to show the clients!"

"Ah, that's your thing, Freddy. All those eggheads would intimidate me."

Once classes started, I split my free time among three places: my dorm room; the Bata Library, where I'd set myself up on a stool in front of long windows facing the river; or in the large dining hall, which looked like a place where the Knights of the Round Table would've met. The dining hall had long, prickly, wooden light fixtures hanging from a crisscrossing concrete and wood ceiling, and dozens of communal tables, so I'd choose one of the empty ones and spread a few books around me so people would leave me alone.

My classes were pretty interesting. Most of them were foundation courses explaining the history of the environmental movement and the main issues facing the planet, but by October we were studying specific things like air pollution, climate change and even the unique perspective of Indigenous Peoples. That first year, a lot of time was spent on understanding beavers (which are Canada's national animal, because Canadians are industrious and we have a lot of trees), which I found kinda funny because of how Canadian I've always felt. We even touched on sustainable farming, which also made me laugh, because I'd come here to get as far away from that red tractor in the Falconi window as humanly possible.

Because the campus was beside a river that fed into the glacier-carved lakes of the Kawartha region, there were lots of opportunities for field trips, so we'd be out in our rubber boots taking water or soil samples to analyze back at the lab, or paddling along in a canoe to understand how river systems work. It was at times like these that I really enjoyed being a university student. I felt like I was doing something important, something bigger than Spadina Avenue, and that's a pretty big street. I made it through first year quite easily and with most of my marks in the high eighties. I even stayed on campus over most of the summer after first year and got ahead by taking a few more classes. I know Dom missed me because he said so during our twice-weekly phone calls, but I was so busy I didn't have time to miss him or anyone else. When I finally came home for a few weeks that August, Dom stuck to me like glue. We'd sit in the backyard under the big Black Locust tree for hours eating pistachios and shooting the breeze, or, if it wasn't too hot, up on our flat roof looking down onto Spadina, just like old times.

While I was happy to go back to Trent in September, a funny thing happened a few months later: My panic attacks came back. I was sitting there, content in my dorm room, firing up WordPerfect on the IBM clone that Small Carm had given me that summer, with a bunch of notes and textbooks in front of me. As I put my hands over the keyboard, my heart started beating as fast as the flashing cursor at the top of the screen. Then it started exploding in my chest. The arm pain, which I remembered from a decade ago, returned, and then shot down into my legs, which was new. I had to focus on my little vase of fresh flowers and just breathe in and out, in and out, for fifteen minutes until I calmed down. The assignment wasn't even that hard, but completing it was absolutely excruciating.

I started skipping classes. I handed in a few assignments late. I bought a bike for exercise, but what I would really do is whizz down Rotary Greenway Trail past Riverview Zoo and down George Street into downtown Peterborough. After lunch at Hot Belly Mama's, I discovered a beautiful, gold-tiled, very Modern-looking Bank of Montreal branch at the corner of Water and Simcoe, and that proved to be a gateway drug. Three times a week, I'd ride the twenty minutes to downtown to look at architecture, which I found soothing. I bought a map at a gas station and started colouring in streets I'd ridden down. After a few months, half of the map was dark with ink. I wandered into a little stone cottage on Brock Street one crisp fall morning and met some nice folks from the Peterborough Historical Society. When they found out I liked Modern architecture, they told me that the architect of the Toronto Eaton Centre and Ontario Place, Eberhard Zeidler, had started his career here in the 1950s. From that point on I cycled around town and tried to identify his buildings.

All of this seemed to keep my panic attacks at bay. I did see someone at the Student Wellness Centre to talk about what I was going through, and she brought up the idea of anti-anxiety medication, but I just couldn't bring myself to take a happy pill. At that point I guess I was still Italian enough to think I could fight those feelings of helplessness and fear all by myself.

Once exams came along, my heart just wasn't in my studies any longer and I knew I had to quit. I wrote a few, skipped a few, and went home for Christmas break wondering how I was going to break the news to Small Carm.

I'd been back for three days when I finally gathered up the courage to see my biggest brother. He was at work in the old Falconi showroom, sitting at Big Carm's desk, tapping a pencil to his forehead while going over stacks of investment statements and bank balances and plugging them into an accounting program. (A couple of years later, when the World Wide Web became a thing, he'd still be sitting there, but without the stack of paper.) He had made it clear to all of us over the years that "unless you are bleeding," it wasn't a good idea to disturb him when he was at work, so he was pretty surprised when I came in and noisily pulled up a chair. His nervous leg, always pumping up and down under the desk, came to a full stop.

"You've got something on your mind, Freddy?" he said flatly, his eyes not leaving his work.

"I wanted to talk to you about school," I said. "I'm just not feeling it."

His eyes immediately locked onto me like I was Sarah Connor and he was The Terminator. "Feeling it? Feeling what? You're going to have to be more clear, because you can't be saying what I think you're saying."

"Well, yeah. I don't think I'm cut out to be an environmental guy. I just don't know. I feel like maybe I made the wrong choice, and I don't want to waste the family's money until I'm sure."

"It's a little late for that now, eh Flowerboy?" he shot back, his voice becoming lower rather than increasing in volume. "I'm sitting here, every freakin' day making sure this family doesn't go broke, and after you've spent the better part of ten grand you decide *maybe* you've made the wrong choice? That's nice. Very nice." His voice shook a little on the word maybe, but other than that it was steady as a rock, just like the rock he'd become for all of us after The Incident.

"Look, I know this is out of the blue for you, but for me it's been brewing for months," I explained, weakly. "You don't want me doing something for the rest of my life I'm not passionate about, do you?" I didn't dare tell him about the panic attacks.

"You think I love checking the stock market every day, Freddy? You think I love meeting with the bank all the time to make sure we can still eat? You think that's my life's calling?" he said, exhaling at the ceiling and not expecting an answer. "You're the one who told me this environment stuff was your new passion, and I bought it because you're Freddy Flowers, our little nature boy. What do you propose to do if you leave school?"

"I don't know ... yet. But I'll pay the family back, I swear. I'll get a job. I was talking to Giovanni over on Cecil Street and he said his dad is hiring drywallers."

"Drywalling. Huh. Aim high, Freddy, aim high," he said, flatly. A look of profound disappointment registered on his face for exactly one second, then he looked back down at his notepad. His leg started pumping again: Our meeting was over.

Black Art

I'm standing at the corner of Dundas West and McCaul. The Art Gallery of Ontario has had its familiar face ripped off and two dozen, hard-hatted workers are swarming around the controlled ruins like bees. Some are pouring concrete, some are welding, and others are directing traffic as trucks loaded with supplies arrive, all chiming their BEEP BEEP BEEP mantra as they back into the construction site's chain-link gates. Frank Gehry, the most famous living architect in the world, has finally come home and designed this facelift — plus a new titanium-clad addition to the rear — for the country's biggest art gallery, which has been around since 1900.

I've checked the renderings online, and, when this new façade is complete, it's going to look like a big, block-long windshield curving across the front of the building. Behind that windshield, there will be a second floor sculpture court, Galleria Italia, held up by beautiful, curved wooden arches. Tony Gagliano, the seventh of ten kids born to Sicilian immigrants, and the man who helped start the city's artsy Luminato festival, put up some family money and then got twenty more of the city's wealthiest Italian families to donate to the project ... hence the name. When it opens, it'll be a proud moment for Toronto's Italian community, which isn't exactly known as being big on philanthropy.

And despite how exciting all of this is to an architecture nut like me, it's not doing the job of fully distracting me from what I've just done at the police station down the street. My hands are still shaking and icy lines of perspiration are racing down my torso and pooling at the top of my belt.

Luckily, I didn't have to walk the homicide squad over to the Falconi building and point out my dead mother. No, after taking my statement, they asked me to give them a detailed description of our office layout, where to find Rosabella, and then a physical description of Small Carm and Dom so that they can arrest the right person, which they told me will be happening within the next few hours. I didn't bother to tell them Small Carm kicked Dom out of the house after his freak out and that he's now bunking at my place. I guess I'm paranoid that if I say too much, they'll arrest both of them, since Dom was complicit the day of The Incident.

Since the construction workers are now clearly on a break — they must be Italian as most of them are lifting massive ciabatta loaves crammed with cold cuts and thermoses of coffee out of dinged, old metal lunchboxes, I'm done playing sidewalk superintendent. I'm walking back to my little cottage so I can tell Dom what I've done. Even though Dom has been my biggest cheerleader in life and has supported me during all of my harebrained decisions, I'm still nervous as to what he'll think of my breaking the family's blood oath. Then again, after all the crazy stuff that's happened in the past few days, I'm surprised I didn't bump into him at the police station.

It's only an eight-minute walk to Lippincott Street, but I've meandered and made it twelve. I live on the less desirable part, the bit south of Oxford Street that T-bones at the big hospital on Nassau, but I still love it. It's close enough to the old neighbourhood that I can easily meet Dom for our Kensington coffee dates, but far enough that Small Carm chooses to pick up the phone rather than walk over if he needs anything. It's a weird street. There are tall, stately Bay-n-Gable homes that U of T professors live in, one-and-a-half-storey worker's cottages like mine, and those ubiquitous "Toronto Special" houses. Well, that's my name for them, anyway. Just like Vancouver has its "Vancouver Special"—built in the thousands from the 1960s to 1980s these two-storey homes have a low-pitched, flat roof, and a big, floor-to-ceiling window, Toronto had a similar architectural phenomenon. In our case, however, it's as if all the Italian and Portuguese contractors shared the same 1950s blueprint for a tall, boxy, three-storey home with a hip roof and a two-car garage that's down a wide ramp at semi-basement level. Often, there's a public staircase behind a long window so that the owner can live in one unit and rent the others.

As I turn the key to my front door — it was a weird teal-green when I got it so I'd painted it glossy white, Dom snorted and woke up from a nap. I'm glad he'd gotten some much-needed rest after last night.

"Hey Dom, you feeling better?" My keys and my cell phone clatter loudly as they hit the little ceramic dish.

"Yeah, I guess so. I don't know how long I was out." He shakes his head and picks the sleep out of his eyes. Uncharacteristically, he'd slept in his dark blue shirt, which wrinkled it considerably. From the corner of my eye I can see, however, that he'd neatly folded up his cream-coloured blazer and placed it on my Barcalounger. I can still see the angry, dark streak peeking from underneath one of the folds, however.

"Hey, Freddy, you look funny. You okay?"

"Not really. Maybe you should call me Judas instead. I just sold Small Carm, our fearless leader, down the river."

Dom's expression actually softens. "You went to the cops, didn't you?"

I nod. "It was about setting the record straight," I say, my voice hushed. "There have been too many lies in this family."

"I understand," he says, matching my tone. "Remember, I've been walking around with this for twenty-three years. You've only known the whole story for twenty-three hours."

CHAPTER II

☞ Falconi Farm Equipment ☜

MY SISTER, GINA, was big into horses in the early 1980s and actually owned one for a little while. She likes to quote this little poem from one of those "pony books" for teenaged girls:

A horse is such a noble beast
I like to stand beside one
But God and all the Saints forbid
That I should ever ride one

And that pretty much sums up how I feel about tractors.

While Falconi tractors are nicer than most because Italians are known for cool design, I still find them to be big, stinky, dirty, loud shake-mobiles that remind me of the boonies, and I prefer cities. But just like the rest of the Falconi kids, I was propped up against the big, lug-tread tire at the back ("Aww, look how tiny he is!") or plopped onto the driver's seat at numerous stages of my development so my folks could snap a picture, and of course I smiled and waved wildly. When in Rome, right? Truth be told, when I was little and we'd go up to Falconi Farm, the tractors kind of freaked me out. They're just massive engines with a seat on top, really, and the whine of the hydraulics, the smell of the gas, the way they could rip into the soil or flatten weeds taller than I was, was all very unsettling. I know most kids played with toy dump trucks, army jeeps and tractors, but I preferred abstract stuff like marbles, Lego, Tinkertoys, and, if it had to be a vehicle of some kind, spaceships.

While my brothers started driving tractors as soon as their feet could reach the pedals, our family fell apart before I was tall enough, which was just fine with me. I do remember being forced to drive our smaller model, the Falconi Finch, once when I was eight. It was a hot, humid day in late July, and Dad thought it was about time I took the controls. He spread his legs out to the edges of the tractor seat — Falconis were known for having wider-than-average seats — and tucked me in between his linen-clad thighs. He placed my hands on the big steering wheel and showed me the little stalk behind it that controlled the throttle. I looked down, and staring up at me from between the two clusters of gauges was the gleaming, silver face of the Falconi falcon. It had angry, slanted eyes, geometric feathers in the shape of diamonds, and its chrome beak rose from the dashboard like a dangerous hook.

"Now, Freddy, you're just going to have to steer and decide how fast we go," he said. "I'll control the clutch, brakes and gears, okay? So we'll put it into third gear and drive straight along this path and aim for that big patch of weeds."

Now while I knew it wasn't right to correct my dad, I had learned a thing or two about cars from Dom, so I thought I'd impress him. "But Dad, don't we have to start in first gear so we can it get going, *then* go to second, *then* we shift into third when we're going faster?"

"That's true with a car, son," he said. "But a tractor is different. The gears here are more about the strength you need the tractor to work at. If we've got something attached to it that really digs down deep into the dirt so we can put a fence post into it, we'd choose first, because that's got the most strength. But to just drive along or cut weeds, we can start in third. Understand?"

"Okay, I hope you're right," I said as I turned to look up at him and squinted in the brilliant sunlight. Sweat was escaping in long trails from underneath his dark blue, straw fedora. He laughed. I laughed too. Inside, I was petrified.

When he turned the key, the engine roared to life and we started jiggling in unison until the RPMs smoothed out. I should say that we jiggled just a little, since Falconis had a patented engine dampener system that made them shake a lot less than other tractors. That was one of the things that we had built our reputation on, actually. It was part of the whole "CIVILIZED FARMING FOR INTELLIGENT FARMERS" angle that had made the company so successful over the years. Successful for the first forty years, in any case.

"Here we go!" Dad bellowed as he released the clutch with another big laugh. Mercifully, we started off going relatively slowly. Dad asked me to aim us a little to the left, but the steering wheel wasn't very easy to turn.

"Why's it so hard to steer?" I yelled over the roar of the engine.

"It's not, you're just not used to it," he said, putting one hairy, tanned hand over mine on the wheel. "See? Now let's go a little faster. Use that little stick I showed you."

I obeyed. The engine growled and I was pushed against my dad's stomach as we suddenly started moving at a pretty good clip. The weeds were coming up fast. Thankfully, Dad stepped on the clutch and then the dual brakes so we stopped a few feet shy of the thicket.

"Okay, we're going to lower that whack-job at the back, okay?" He was referring to the Bush Hog, which worked like an enormous weed-whacker but looked like a giant vacuum cleaner head as wide as the tractor. It was connected to the back by a hitch but also had a driveshaft that plugged into the tractor to power the long, spinning blade. "You see these levers coming up from the floor by my right leg? This one lowers it. Go ahead, move it back." A hydraulic whine and a slight jerk. "Okay, stop." A big jerk as the device stopped a few inches above the ground. "Okay, let's go on a whack-attack!"

We drove straight into the tall weeds and I decided to steer us in a wavy pattern to deliberately create a crazy-trail that Dom and I could walk through later. I turned my head and watched as the unruly mess got flattened into something that looked like crisscrossed floor-matting. It was the only fun part of the day.

When we were finished carving trails and back in the wide clearing, Dad decided I was ready for fourth gear. I didn't think I was ready to try a gear that was half my age, but I didn't say anything. Dad clunked the tractor into gear and released the clutch and brakes. Again, we started off at a reasonable speed, but when I hammered the little throttle-stick down, we started going really fast. The ground had ruts in it, which were amplified by the speed, so I started to feel nauseous. Dad was jiggling and giggling and having a great time. So great, as a matter of fact, he decided to pull a little practical joke on me.

"Hmmm, the clutch is acting funny," he said. "I don't think I can disengage it." The barn in the distance was rapidly growing in size. "Let go of the throttle, Freddy, or we'll hit the barn!"

I released it. Nothing happened. We were still racing along at the same speed. I started screaming.

"I DON'T KNOW IF WE CAN STOP IN TIME," he screamed back. I grabbed onto the steering wheel for dear life. The chrome falcon looked up at me and its eyes seemed to narrow. Then, Dad started laughing as the tractor jerked to an abrupt stop about two feet away from the barn wall, which looked as big as a drive-in movie screen to me. I was having kittens at this point.

How was I to know tractors have a gas pedal on the floor?

Mom came running over. "What did you do to him?" she scolded as she put a hand through my wet, matted hair. "He is all *impauritu*, upset!"

"Oh, he'll get over it," Dad said with a wave of his hand. "He'll be buzzing around like Carmy and Dom as soon as he's old enough."

I may be scarred for life when it comes to driving tractors, but the story of how Falconi Trattori S.r.l. came to be in Italy, and why Falconi Farm Equipment Ltd. was established in Canada is a fascinating one. I know quite a bit about it, thanks to my grandfather's *diario*. When I was going off to university, Small Carm handed me a stack of beautiful, photo-album-sized, leather-bound books that contained clippings and at least two hundred handwritten pages each: "I know you don't give a crap about tractors, but since you do love history, maybe you should take these with you to Peterborough. When I was about your age I translated them all into English," he said. His big fish-lips curled up at the ends. "Besides, you'll need something to read during all those lonely, country bumpkin nights."

∽

On page four of the August 19, 1938 *Globe and Mail*, beside a story titled "Text of Address Given by Roosevelt at Bridge Opening" — the American president had given a stirring speech in Kingston, Ontario about the friendship between Canada and the U.S. and promised that he would "not stand idly by if domination of Canadian soil is threatened by any other empire" — is the headline "RIBBON CUT AT ITALIAN TRACTOR SHOWROOM." Underneath that is a three-column-wide photo of two men in fedoras shaking hands in front of a sleek new storefront with a big curved window; behind the glass, a pair of headlights and a grille is just visible. The caption reads: "Smiles all around as small crowd gathers at 413 Spadina Ave to-day to witness opening of flashy Massey competitor Falconi Farm Equipment. Red tractor will be permanent fixture in window, says owner. Picture shows, left to right: Joe Falconi, owner, and Mayor Day. — Staff Photo."

That isn't completely true. Had the reporter or photographer asked a few more questions, he (or she, yeah right!) would have learned that Falconi had come to Toronto in large part *because* of Massey-Harris, the behemoth manufacturer that had been belching smoke into the Toronto skies, and tractors into its massive parking lot, since 1879.

Peeking out from behind Mayor Ralph Day's shoulder — two years later he'd announce that families of interned Italian breadwinners wouldn't get welfare because they shouldn't "expect us to spend money for war purposes for the purpose of maintaining alien enemies" — is the part of the Falconi building façade that was long gone when I was growing up. The first floor of our building had been outfitted in large, glass panels called Vitrolite, an ultra-modern, high-gloss material that was immensely popular in the 1930s, 40s and early 50s. The original twelve stations of the Toronto subway, which opened in 1954, were covered in the stuff, with the station names sandblasted right into the glass. (Eglinton Station is the only one that still has it.)

Luckily, our family has photos that show the façade in great detail, since a lot were taken in those early years. The really cool ones are part of a clinical series Nonno Joe had done for the insurance company. A professional photographer took multiple shots of the front and back of the building, and the office space inside, with close-ups of the streamlined counter, rolling stools, and high-tech equipment like the telephone and wax cylinder Dictaphone. Then there are the family photos of various relatives who came over from Italy, like great-uncle Tom, who did the obligatory pose out front on the sidewalk a dozen times. Unfortunately, all of these are in black and white.

By the early 1960s, however, when colour film got cheaper (and just before Dad took over the business), there are photos that finally show what all those sidewalk gawkers witnessed that big day in 1938. Even though it was almost twenty-five years old by then, the Falconi building was still a beautiful thing to behold. While the top two floors looked original to 1890, the ground floor looked as modern as a Raymond Loewy-designed S1 locomotive speeding through one of those Art Deco travel posters.

Underneath the second storey, traditional bay window, a false wall had been built out about a foot-and-a-half from the original brick. This was covered in dark green Vitrolite, upon which raised, stainless steel letters spelling out **falconi** had been pin-mounted. Two thin, vertical speed stripes done in mint green Vitrolite framed the letters on either side. These letters, which survived Dad's renovation of 1967, have always reminded me of something you'd see on the front of a sleek, expensive Italian espresso machine. The sign curved back towards the building and blended into the ceiling over the entranceway.

Like all buildings along the strip, we had two doors: one to access the staircase to the apartments, and one to the showroom. The wooden door to the apartments was painted dark green to match the Vitrolite and had three porthole windows arranged vertically. The shop door beside it was mostly glass, but the door handle was a stylized aluminum F floating over two thin bars set on a slight angle. The shop window beside the showroom door travelled outward toward the street, then curved, gently, to become parallel with it. The speed stripes on the right side of the shiny Falconi letters were applied as decals down the window.

If you ask me, all of that glossy Vitrolite and the sexy curves looked even more amazing because the top two storeys of the building remained unaltered. Above the Falconi sign, that big bay window on the second storey was surrounded on either side by lovely terracotta tiles shaped like diamonds, and inside each diamond was a flower-type shape. (My mother pointed these out to me when I first became Freddy Flowers.) The third floor had the classic, three-window Palladian configuration, and a raised brick course gave this threesome an eyebrow just underneath the building's flat roof.

The building, as a whole, was a craftperson's delight. When Dad ripped off the Vitrolite, squared off the curves, covered everything with boring brown ceramic tile, replaced the windows and painted the aging brickwork bright red, it was almost as if he knew Falconi's glory days were coming to a close.

About halfway between Rome and Naples, there is a tiny hill town nestled between the Ausoni and Aurunci mountain ranges that makes a big claim. Campodimele bills itself as *Il Paese della Longevità*, or The Village of Longevity. Of the seven hundred residents, about ten percent range in age from seventy-five to ninety-five, and studies estimate an average resident today will probably make it to ninety-five. Some say it's the fresh mountain air, some say it's the food, which is all locally grown and prepared, and others say it's because people walk the steep, narrow streets daily rather than drive them, since many are dangerous switchbacks or stone walled dead ends with dizzying and dangerous drop-offs.

This is all fine and good, but my paternal grandfather, Joe, and his brother, Tommaso, who were born on a farm just outside of Campodimele, both died long before their seventy-fifth birthdays.

Tommaso (Tom) Falconi was born in 1908. Giuseppe (Joe) Falconi followed in 1914. There was a sister, Sofia, born in 1910, but she died at the age of ten when she drowned in the Mediterranean. I don't know much about my great-grandparents except that they were peasant farmers. The Falconi Farm Equipment story begins with the 1932 death of Tom and Joe's cousin, Domenic, when he was seventeen.

Domenic Zannella was a year younger than my Nonno Joe, and apparently they were inseparable growing up. Since Joe wasn't keeping a diary then, all I know is the passed-down, family story of the accident. The Falconi farm was far too small and didn't make enough money to afford a purpose-built tractor, so Domenic was converting a British-made, Ford Model T delivery truck into a farm vehicle that could tow implements for the family. He was one of those kids who would take something apart and then, after putting it back together, it would work better than before.

Stripped of its body panels, the naked delivery truck was up on blocks so Dom could work on strengthening the suspension, and that's when it came crashing down and crushed him to death. It goes without saying that the brothers were devastated, but after a period of mourning they put their noses to the grindstone and began sketching out a small, high-performance tractor that would be economical enough for small farmers to afford.

On a fact-finding mission, they drove up to the big farms near Rome. There, they saw a few Fordson tractors, which were made up in Cork, Ireland by Ford's European arm, but found them to be clunky and utilitarian despite their smallish size and cheap price tag. They also saw Fiat 702 and 703 models, and Landini 25/30 models, which used an unconventional engine called a "hot bulb engine" that Giovanni Landini invented in 1910. (All I know about that engine is that it was underpowered.) In those days, tractors were gangly creatures with steel wheels; pneumatic rubber tires wouldn't be introduced until Allis-Chalmers and Firestone in the U.S. got them on a tractor in 1936. When Falconi finally put its tractor into production in late 1936, it would be one of the first in Italy to use them.

The young brothers were smart enough to dream big but start small, so they rented an abandoned machine shop in Campodimele in 1933 where they produced a line of horse-drawn implements, like harrows and ploughs, and human tools like wheelbarrows and rakes. Just like with their dream tractor, the goal here was to make sturdy equipment that small farmers could afford, and it worked. In a year they had two employees and business was booming.

Requiring bigger quarters, they relocated to Fondi, a much larger town twenty kilometres away (I have no idea how big it was then, but there are about 35,000 people there today) and the employee count grew to five. Fondi is known for its fourteenth-century stone castle in the centre of town, the *Castello Baronale*, and a few spectacular churches. Fondi is where three very important things happened: Joe started writing in his diary; the team started to hand-fabricate parts for the first Falconi tractor; and Il Duce came to visit.

When Appius Claudius Caecus was watching his military road, the Appian Way, inch along, stone-by-stone, in 312 BC, he knew that the Pontine Marshes — those vast, malaria-infested swamps that stretched from just south of Rome to Terracina — would present an engineering challenge. Others before him had tried to drain the putrid water but had failed. When he, too, was unsuccessful, a thirty-kilometre causeway and series of bridges were built over the stinking pools, and marching Roman troops quickly learned to hold their noses.

A number of popes, Sixtus V and Pius VI among them, would also try to conquer the marshes. Pius VI would be partially successful and would rebuild the Appian Way in the 1700s, but even as late as the 1920s, the area was still largely uninhabitable.

Until the marshes met Benito Mussolini's Fascist fist, that is.

By 1932, not only had the land been tamed by Il Duce, Littoria, the first of five New Towns, was rising where no town had ever risen before. A logical street grid, orderly piazzas, and an odd architectural mix of Classical Roman and Modernist, International Style was taking shape at the hands of fifty thousand workers. Astonishingly, most of the town would be completed in less than a year. Pontinia would follow the next year, then Sabaudia. In 1937, Aprilia would rise from the former swamp; the last, Pomezia, would take shape in 1939.

Because the New Towns were one of Mussolini's pet projects, he visited often and always made sure photographers and filmmakers were in tow. The reclamation of fertile farmland was part of the government's ruralization policy; farmers, after all, are the backbone of a great nation, and Mussolini's mission was to create a New Roman Empire as powerful as the old one.

So, it should have been no surprise when a uniformed officer showed up at the Fondi workshop of Falconi Brothers Farm Implements with an official telegram in his white-gloved hand. It read (and this is Small Carm's translation):

OPERA NAZIONALE COMBATTENI ANNOUNCE PRIME MINISTER IN FONDI SIX FEB [STOP] FALCONI TRACTOR OF INTEREST FOR INVESTMENT [STOP] WILL ARRIVE PRECISELY 1300 HRS [STOP] ASSEMBLE ALL PRODUCTS & PROTOTYPES FOR INSPECTION [STOP]

Needless to say, disbelief, excitement, and panic followed for Tom and Joe. Their first tractor, which used a modified engine from Fiat, was in the testing stage only. And while they were proud of how it was performing during field trials, there was no real-world data to hand over to the most important man in Italy. There were no satisfied customers to offer testimonials either, unless talk turned to pitchforks, wheelbarrows and horse-drawn implements. The brothers were also a little mystified as to how the Duce had learned of their high-performance, low-cost tractor project, since only about twenty people were privy to that information. Other than a small blurb in the local newspaper about Falconi moving into the via Ponte Gagliardo workshop a year before, nothing had been written about them.

Since Nonno Joe was fairly busy for the next few weeks,

there isn't much in the diary to describe exactly what he and Tom did to prepare for the biggest meeting of their lives. If it weren't for the hastily written entry of February 7, 1935, I would be clueless as to whether Mussolini himself, or a Musso-lackey, showed up that day. However, it reads: "Met 'Our Leader' yesterday —!— Crazy, but he is *interested* in helping expedite tractor project via subsidy for new employee hires and capital investment. Urged us to move to Littoria: low lease on large factory."

In December 1935, the Falconi brothers moved into 16 via Podere, a street in the *Zona Industriale Littoria* along with sixteen employees. The name over the door now read "FALCONI TRATTORI S.r.l.," and the first tractor would roll off the assembly line in less than a year.

Now, to my untrained eyes, the oxblood-red Falconi Primo looked pretty much like any other tractor. However, I'm told that even though it was a match for the Massey-Harris Model 25 or Challenger, which both came out around the same time (my brothers would often compare Falconi models to their Massey equivalent because Massey was Toronto-based), it was smaller, had more horsepower, and sported a few cosmetic refinements. Both Masseys had exposed steering columns: the Model 25 wasn't bad, but the Challenger's attached to a post that came up from the front wheel and travelled across the top of the tractor all the way to the driver. Falconi, on the other hand, had found a way to tuck the steering column completely inside the engine compartment, giving the machine a much cleaner look. Also, the seat on the Massey was bare metal while Falconi's was luxuriously upholstered in horsehair and thick, chocolate-brown leather.

The most important refinement, however, was the reduction of engine-shake, which came about rather serendipitously. In modifying the Fiat engine to fit the more streamlined body of the Falconi, our young designers had created some rather elaborate fittings, panels and spacers. Combined, these created a sort of engineering alchemy that made our tractors run much more smoothly. These things, on their own, weren't revolutionary, but combined they made our tractors a little more civilized.

Civilized enough, actually, that Massey-Harris U.K. decided to send a representative to Littoria to pay us a visit shortly after the release of the Primo. Massey was a giant, so I don't understand why they noticed the flea that was Falconi at that time, but my brothers swear it was so the Massey guys could steal a bunch of ideas from us and put them into their next tractor, the 101 Super.

The 101 Super has been described by at least one author as "one of the world's most strikingly beautiful tractor designs with its chrome striping and fully louvered hood side panels." Albeit smaller, the Falconi Primo did look quite a bit like what became the 101 Super; while it didn't have the chrome striping, it did have indentations to suggest speed stripes in pretty much the same locations, and it had a whole lotta louvers, too. The streamlined nose shape was pretty bang-on as well. However, Nonno Joe wasn't writing much in his diary during those early years in Littoria, so I can't say how accurate this intriguing story of corporate espionage really is. Small Carm and Dom swear by it, however, and still get mad when they talk about it today, seven decades later.

I *can* say two things with confidence: There are ten seconds of footage of the Falconi factory in a 1938 propaganda movie called *July XVI: The Duce Commences the Threshing of Wheat in the Pontine Marshes*, and the Falconi engine dampening system was indeed licensed by Massey eventually.

That licensing agreement is the reason I live in Toronto today.

When the redesigned, second model came out in 1937, this time called Falconi II, it was even better. This was because the company had reached an agreement to replace the drawbar at the back (where implements are attached) with something Irishman Harry Ferguson had patented in 1926: the three-point linkage system. Now, again, I'm not the best guy to discuss the finer points of tractors, but I've been told this revolutionized how implements hooked up, raised, and lowered, and this made things easier for the farmer. This system, by the way, wouldn't be introduced to the North American market until Ferguson and Henry Ford shook hands the next year and it was included on the battleship-grey Fordson 9N model.

Another licensing agreement was being negotiated around this time. This was the one between Massey-Harris and Falconi for the dampener, but talks had stalled for some reason, so there was talk of Tom or Joe flying to either the U.K. or Toronto to meet with a bigwig. Coincidently, this was when another Italian government telegram arrived: Would Falconi be interested in opening a sales office in the U.S. or Canada?

Since they viewed the waves of Italian immigration as a failure of the state and an embarrassment, Mussolini's government had made it extremely hard to emigrate in the 1920s. They made exceptions, however, when it came to exporting Italian culture. As a young company with an innovative product, Falconi, like a number of others, would be given financial aid should it want to expand internationally. They'd even let a few Italian citizens move to other countries to act as emissaries. Tom, married now, appointed his younger, single brother Joe (who could also speak better English) to set up shop in either Montreal, then the largest city in Canada with the largest Italian community, or Toronto, the second-largest city in the country and the home of Massey-Harris.

The Canadian government, however, had put up barriers to Italian immigration at this time, so setting up shop in New York City was discussed for a brief period. The efforts of a Methodist minister, Liborio Lattoni, who was well connected in Montreal and with the Quebec government, saved the day. After a few conversations and letters to the right people, Nonno Joe arrived in Montreal in the summer of 1937.

Lattoni, at that point, was in his early sixties and had been in Montreal since 1908. In his early years, he had run a school for the children of new immigrants, where, officially, his role was to teach them English and French and, unofficially, it was to convert their parents to Protestantism. Because he often secured these immigrants good jobs and places to live, he was largely successful, too. Politically active during the Great War and a born Italo-cheerleader, he convinced many young Italians in the community to enlist. Between the wars, he embraced Mussolini and Fascism (as did many Italians in Canada), and helped set up the Quebec Chapter of the Order Sons of Italy of Canada.

I've hunted around and tried to find out if Lattoni was born Catholic and switched to Methodism, but there hasn't been much written about that part of his life. I do know that it wasn't uncommon for Montreal Italians to switch to Protestantism in the early part of the twentieth century. Since the English population ran most things and Canadian immigration policy at the time favoured Protestant, northern Europeans, it makes sense. Southern, Catholic Italians, many illiterate and unskilled, were lumped in with other undesirables like eastern Europeans, and encouraging them to convert was seen as a first step in "improving" them. By the 40s, 50s and 60s, many Italians were converting also because the perception was that the Montreal Protestants ran better schools.

While he just hinted at it in his diary, I think Nonno Joe preferred Methodism because the interiors of their churches are less cluttered with iconography, the whole razzle-dazzle of actually turning wafers and wine into flesh and blood is absent, there is no confession to attend, and, though I hate to say it, a lot less fawning over the Virgin Mary.

Ironically, the apartment Lattoni arranged for Joe Falconi was located on avenue de Gaspé in Montreal's Little Italy, and from his living room window, behind the big trees of Parc Dante, he could make out the imposing, blocky shape of the Romanesque-style Catholic Church of the Madonna della Difesa. Inside that church, Guido Nincheri's equally imposing ceiling fresco featured a horse-straddling Benito Mussolini — saviour of the Vatican and source of renewed Italian pride — who kept watch over the neighbourhood.

⁂

While Nonno Joe lived in Montreal for only a short time, he enjoyed the close-knit Italian neighbourhood, shopping at Jean-Talon market, and attending events at the newly built Casa d'Italia, a big, curved, brick Art Deco pile at the corner of rue Jean-Talon and rue Berri that had opened its doors less than a year before. Five thousand dollars towards the construction of the cultural centre had come directly from the Italian government, while the rest had been contributed by individuals, local Italian mutual-aid societies, and prominent businessmen, such as shoe factory owner Alfredo Sebastiani, who ponied up a grand. The Fascist government's direct involvement in the building might explain why local architect "Patsy" Colangelo placed multiple *fasces* — those ancient bundle-of-sticks-with-protruding-axe-head symbols that gave the fascist party its name — all over the exterior of the building, and even locked another into the speckled terrazzo floor inside. When I see cars whizzing by it, I often wonder if those people know about the direct link it has to that dark time.

Nonno Joe also enjoyed developing his friendship with Lattoni, a sensitive, interesting man who would go on to become one of the most respected Italian poets in Canada. (A book of his poetry translated into English finally came out a few years ago, *Carmina Cordis: Songs from the Heart*, so

I picked it up.) Because of that friendship, Joe converted to Methodism and, most importantly, through his involvement in the church, met his future wife, Ines Ciccone, who had also come to Canada with the help of Lattoni a few years earlier to work as a church administrator.

Although Ines was older than Joe by five years, they were engaged after two months of courtship. During that time, Joe made arrangements for a storefront at the corner of avenue du Parc and boulevard Saint Joseph, but before he got inside to begin the renovations, he was contacted by Massey-Harris in Toronto.

Massey was massive. While it wasn't the biggest tractor manufacturer in North America, it was certainly the largest in Canada and, as Toronto entered the twentieth century, the city's largest employer. Their multiple factory buildings, which sprouted at least a dozen smokestacks, stretched for almost one kilometre along King Street West from Strachan Avenue to just shy of Dufferin Street. There were also long, low, red-brick administrative buildings that snaked around the site and connected to other buildings. There was a long, glass-walled showroom. Railroad tracks cut through the site at various angles. It was an intimidatingly large complex that had its roots in the simple purchase of an American threshing machine in 1830 by a farmer named Daniel Massey.

After being the first person to import such a machine into what was then known as "Upper Canada," Daniel Massey became interested in labour-saving devices for farmers. It was when he let his son, Hart Almerrin Massey, take over the farm in 1847 that he was able to start designing his own. While poor Daniel would shed his mortal coil in 1856, by 1861 his company, now led by Hart, counted fifty employees.

They'd introduce their first all-Canadian design, the Massey Reel Rake Harvester in 1878, and they'd open the Toronto factory in 1879-80. It boasted two acres of floor space, an automatic sprinkler system, and a network of telephones. The company was so successful, it paid to build Toronto's famous concert hall, Massey Hall, which opened in 1894, and Vincent Massey would complete Hart House at the University of Toronto in 1919 to honour his grandfather.

It was a licensing agreement for Falconi's engine dampener that Massey wanted to discuss, but they also hinted at full design collaboration on future tractor models. Since the Masseys were devout Methodists, they said they were looking forward to doing business with someone who shared their value system. While they didn't outright suggest it, the implication was that Massey-Harris-Falconi was a real possibility, so Joe and his fiancé were put in touch with some of Liborio Lattoni's friends in Toronto, and the move was made.

In 1938, Joe and Ines arrived in Toronto during the snowiest winter in the city's history; while the main sidewalks had been ploughed, some areas required wading through waist-high drifts. Besides the incredibly tall white blanket, when the couple stepped off the train and crunched through the sloppy mess in front of Union Station, they saw the second tallest building in the city at that time: the Royal York Hotel. Two blocks to the north, the tallest building in the British Commonwealth, Commerce Court, dominated the skyline at a whopping thirty-four storeys.

At Toronto's Casa d'Italia on Beverley Street — which

would be raided by police and taken over by the Canadian government in June 1940, they received letters of recommendation to two boarding houses in Little Italy, after which Joe began looking for a location for Falconi.

The diary is patchy for a while, but piecing the various scraps together, what seems to have happened is that Joe asked around for an architect well versed in a sophisticated Hollywood style — he knew that you needed more sizzle than steak to sell in the New World, I guess — so he was introduced to Harold Kaplan and Abraham Sprachman. Kaplan and Sprachman were the kings of Art Deco movie palaces in Toronto, and had just completed the Eglinton, Lansdowne, and Allenby theatres. Since Nonno Joe was living on Clinton Street just north of College Street, the architects met him at Altman's Chop House a short walk away at the corner of College and Brunswick Avenue. After lunch, they showed him the hole in the ground next door that would soon contain their Bellevue Theatre. His brief entry states: "Found the right architects, M&S. For real estate: They recommend WIDE commercial street 'Spadina Av' — they say close to Lt. Itly, a good mix of people, fine bldg. stock. Close to Massey HQ! — Spad & Queen cross-street is 20 min walk to King & Strachan. Will check to-morrow."

"To-morrow" was a good day. Although it was a little farther north than Queen Street, he found 413 Spadina, just below College Street, for sale at a good price. Based on the architectural style and the matching brickwork, 413 looks to me like it had been constructed as part of a block of seventeen, two-window wide, three-storey, red brick commercial buildings in 1890. In fact, 397 Spadina is pretty much a carbon-copy of 413. Back then, our building was also part of a community, since many of the shop owners lived upstairs like Nonno Joe and Nonna Ines. A few doors over, Israel Okun lived over his smallwares store, sisters Mary and Margaret Meighan had their ladies fashion store below their apartment (where Nonna Ines shopped), and Harry Finklestein the barber lived above his shop (where Nonno Joe got his hair cut). Two stores north of Falconi was Sing Kee Chinese Laundry, where everyone brought their shirts. Our building had tenants on all three floors, but Frederick Ingle's bicycle shop on the first floor would be vacating by the end of the month, so Nonno could get inside to renovate. While he'd have to give two months' notice to the third floor residential tenant, he would keep the second floor tenant in place to generate extra income. Maybe he gave the guy a few months free rent to make up for the renovation noise.

While business began to trickle in during the autumn of 1938, public opinion on all things Italian had been declining steadily since Mussolini invaded Ethiopia in 1935, especially because of write-ups in the WASP-y Toronto papers. If it wasn't for the signed Massey contract to use the Falconi dampener in early 1939, I'm sure Joe would have pulled out of Canada. And while it wasn't exactly a design collaboration — Massey said they didn't want to risk releasing something too European-looking in the current climate, they did hire Joe to research small, American-made tractors for them, since their current models, the 101 and 102 Juniors were, ironically, still too big and expensive for farmers who owned farms of less than a hundred acres. The less-than-one-hundred-acre market was now the largest in North America, so Massey didn't want to neglect it any longer. So, Joe did some travelling in the U.S. and found the Cletrac Model GG General in Cleveland, a bare-bones machine with less than twenty horsepower. Massey released it later that year.

Business got pretty bad when the war started in September, but it went from bad to worse when Italy declared war on Britain and France in June 1940, and the Canadian government began sending Italian "enemy aliens" to Camp Petawawa. While his friend Lattoni was arrested in Montreal, Joe was lucky. He had maintained his friendship with Kaplan and Sprachman and, in the three short years he'd been living and working on Spadina, he'd made a number of friends in the Jewish community. And despite receiving money from the Italian government, Joe had never joined any Canadian fascist organizations, even though most of those were places men gathered to play *scopa* and discuss Italian pride and that's about it. While he and Ines were photographed, fingerprinted, and had to report to the Royal Canadian Mounted Police once a month, his support from the community allowed him to continue running his business. And, luckily, Falconi in Littoria was too small to be converted for war production, so the tractors kept rolling out the big doors.

The early morning of December 9, 1941 was particularly stressful, however. Ines, up early to breastfeed six-month-old Big Carm, was startled by the sound of breaking glass. By the time she had roused Joe and he'd shambled, sleepily, down the two flights to investigate, the perpetrators were gone. However, a big rock had shattered the showroom door and, written in black shoe polish on the showroom window was: "PEARL HARBOR MEANS DEATH TO FASCISTS."

⁂

Because Big Carm, my father, caused so many problems coming out of Ines Falconi's womb, he was an only child. He was always a bit of a vain guy, so perhaps this was intentional on his part. From what I can gather, his childhood in the late 1940s and early 1950s was filled with the usual scraped knees, tricycle races, gangs of mostly Jewish friends, birthday parties and doting parents. Like most little boys, he played with toy cars, and it was while scooting around with one on the showroom floor that Falconi tractors got their signature colour.

As a customer from Saskatchewan was shooting the breeze with Nonno Joe, little Carm accidentally rammed his heavy, die-cast Alfa Romeo into the man's shoe.

"Carmelo! Say you're sorry to Mr. Norbraten."

"I'm sorry, Mr. Norb — "

"Let's not make a fuss about it, it's fine. Say, Carmelo, can I see your car?" He took it from Carm's plump little hand and then stroked the big pontoon fender with his finger. "That's a fine shade of red. That's the colour of Italian race cars, is it not?"

"Yes," Nonno Joe said. "It's called *rosso corsa*. It's like the British and their forest green."

"Hmmm," Mr. Norbraten said. "Maybe you should paint your tractors that colour."

It wasn't too much of a stretch, since up until then Falconis had been painted an oxblood red. After a few experiments up at Falconi Farm (which Nonno Joe purchased in 1952), the "Ferrari red" body with "Italian flag green" wheels became the signature look right up until 1986.

With the success of films like *Roman Holiday* with Audrey Hepburn and Gregory Peck, and the rise of Sophia Loren as a sex symbol, Falconi cashed in on the perceived sophistication of Italian culture with its advertisements of the 1950s and 60s. This one, from a 1956 issue of *Progressive Farmer*, was typical: A richly-detailed illustration showed a red sports car that closely resembled a Ferrari 250 Europa whizzing by on an open country road and, just beyond the fence, a Falconi tractor sat in the field, sparkling under dazzling sunlight.

"WHY SHOULD CITY-FOLK HAVE ALL THE FUN?"
City slickers call you a 'hayseed,' a 'bumpkin' and a 'hick.' Politicians call you 'salt of the earth' when they cozy up to you at election-time. But you know the *call* of the Modern Farmer resonates as far into the future as it does the past. That's because today's farming professional works hours as long, faces pressures as great, and handles technology as complex as any Big City Executive. F A L C O N I of ITALY understands that the intelligent farmer of the 1950s is a civilized man with sophisticated tastes. F A L C O N I also understands that just because a tractor is a workhorse, it need not look like a nag. F A L C O N I's 'show-horse' tractors are manufactured in a state-of-the-art facility in Central Italy. Their progressive

CONTOURline™ bodies and patented HUSH-O-Matic™ engines fit the refined mindset of today's Modern Farmer to a 'T.' An extra wide, padded seat with optional backrest, more legroom, push-button ignition, and logical control-panel mean you'll be fresher at the end of your long work-day. See the Yellow Pages to find the F A L C O N I dealer nearest you. In row-crop or standard configurations. Prices start at $1250.00.

"FALCONI of ITALY: CIVILIZED FARMING FOR INTELLIGENT FARMERS"

Falconis got even more civilized in August 1959, when Big Carm got involved in the design process. Then eighteen years old, he'd returned from a visit to the annual Canadian National Exhibition, where he'd seen the new 1960 automobiles on display at the Automotive Building. Ironically, the Ford Falcon had impressed him since it was one of the first American cars to downsize to compete with the Volkswagen Beetle and other small European imports.

While he had been working for the family business since he was around twelve, it was because it was convenient rather than a passion. At this point, however, he asked if he could go to the factory in Latina (the name Littoria had been changed to Latina in 1946) for a few months to work with the designers. Nonno Joe was overjoyed and bought him a plane ticket to Rome the very next day.

On the drawing board at that time was a larger tractor — just as Massey wanted to go smaller, Falconi wanted to go a little bigger to grab a piece of that pie — and Big Carm was able to help with that one. I know he suggested a new place for the battery, which helped create even more legroom, and that he and the team decided to call the bigger tractor the Falcon and the original-but-now-smaller-tractor the Finch. Because of the improved legroom and his love of automobiles, Big Carm came up with something even more civilized: a glove box. The team even figured out how to add one to the smaller model, too. And, because it was novel, the ad campaigns of the early 60s were all over that feature: "FINALLY, A FARM VEHICLE WITH BIG CITY PERKS."

I remember Big Carm bragging to Small Carm some twenty years after he'd come up with the idea: "I just thought, hey, farmers need a place to stash their smokes and their sunglasses, too, right? And even a place to hide the condoms from their wives, ha ha."

Dad was never one for subtlety.

Healing the Hole?

Dom is pacing around my living room, holding the phone a few inches from his ear. I can hear the tinny little screams, but I'm sitting on the leather Barcalounger a few feet away — the only new piece of furniture I own other than my mattress — so I can't make out what's being said. Dom looks over and winces.

"Gina, it's gonna be fine," he says. "Remember, our little Flowerboy is the smart one, he knows what he's doing."

More tinny screaming.

"*Madonn'*, don't say that! Of course he loves Small Carm! That's why he did it!" Dom listens, then covers the mouthpiece and whispers to me: "Now she wants me to put you on the phone so she can rip you a new one for pulling a Fredo."

"That's probably not a good idea," I answer. "Maybe you calm her down, Dom? I mean, you guys have a special relationship."

He nods. "Gina-beana-bumbalina, think of all those years of lies, and how that made Freddy feel. You must be able to understand, since *you* were lied to too, man! By *me*, even! You know how hard it was for me to not tell you guys? I had friggin' nightmares about The Incident for years, and I could've used you and Freddy as my *consiglieri* to get through all of it." His voice is soft, soothing, and when he puts the earpiece back against his head, I know Gina is done with her screaming fit.

"Yes, that's right," he says. "It's time to start the healing process."

CHAPTER III

☞ Carm and Rosa ☜

WHILE THE LICENSING agreement with Massey-Harris on the Falconi engine dampener system would continue when they restructured to become Massey-Ferguson in the early 1950s, a full design partnership between the two companies never did come to fruition. I know from Nonno Joe's diary entries from the late 1950s that he went to a few meetings at their head office, a great 1899 building at 915 King Street West, armed with some facts about the success of Italian designs for cars like VW's Karmann-Ghia, which Luigi Segre of Corrozzeria Ghia designed, and GM's ongoing work with the other huge design house, Pininfarina, but, sadly, nothing ever came of those talks.

It didn't really matter, though, since the 1950s and 60s were boom times for Falconi. In fact, the family joke back then was that, to be a good tractor salesman, all you had to know how to do was pick up the phone, since orders were coming in all the time. It's a good thing, too, because our dad, Big Carm, was in no position to run the Canadian operation when Tom Falconi dropped dead at his desk from a massive heart attack in the spring of 1963.

Joe and Ines travelled to Italy to attend the funeral with every intention to come back to Toronto in a few weeks. However, since there was no real vice president at the Latina operation — Falconi was still a family business run by my grandfather and his brother and that's about it, a group of engineers convinced Joe that he'd have to move to Italy, since a Falconi with experience was needed at the helm. Besides, they added, their son, Carmelo, would turn twenty-two in a few months, and that was plenty old enough to run the Canadian arm of the company. I guess they'd been impressed with his enthusiasm for design and his glove compartment idea back in the autumn of '59.

The thing is, after showing initial interest in design work, Carmelo Giuseppe Falconi, a.k.a. Big Carm, had done diddly-squat since. After graduating from Harbord Collegiate a few years ahead of filmmaker David Cronenberg, Dad had tried his best to coast along with as little responsibility as possible. His favourite movie at that time was *La Dolce Vita* with Marcello Mastroianni, and I seriously think he used it as a model to base his life.

His other hero, and the reason my middle name is Dino, was — and probably still is — Dean Martin. He just loved how ol' Dino made everything he did look so cool and effortless. How he sleepwalked through movie roles. How women swooned and draped off his arm. How he was the only one in the world who could tell Sinatra to bugger off. Dad loved Sinatra, too, of course, and breathlessly waited for each new LP to come out, but when it came to who to emulate, it was Dean, hands down. Sinatra, I remember Dad saying, is "too high-strung, too insecure," while Martin "is his own man." Dad styled his hair like Dino, spoke with a sort of laconic drawl like him, and purchased his Rat Pack-style, sharkskin suits from Lou Myles at Yonge and Dundas, since Myles' real name was Luigi Cocomile and he'd grown up in Little Italy at College and Clinton. Myles would also sell suits to Sinatra and Tony Bennett a few years after Dad started shopping there, which tickled him pink. "You *see* the taste in clothes I had back then?" he'd say. "I influenced *them*."

The thing is, Big Carm had the looks and the charm to pull it all off. While Nonno Joe looked severe, like an Italian version of Abe Lincoln but sporting a bushy moustache instead of a trimmed beard, Dad had more delicate features. He had thick eyebrows over dark brown eyes, long eyelashes, a long, Roman nose, chiselled cheekbones and full lips. He was slim but not skinny, and, at five-foot-ten, fairly tall for an Italian guy in the 1960s. His voice was big and deep and sometimes went into a purr, and when he talked to you, he made you feel like you were the only person in the room that mattered.

So, I can see why he was so successful running Falconi in those early years. Most of what he had to do was take orders, manage shipments, or entertain clients if they came to Toronto to write up their deals in person. Buttonville airport was in full operation by then — it had started as a grass runway the year after Nonno Joe bought Falconi Farm — so some rich cattle farmers from out west, many Royal Canadian Air Force veterans, would fly in themselves and check out the equipment up there. Then, Big Carm would drive them down into the city in his butter-yellow, 1963 Cadillac to sign the papers in the showroom — which he could have just as easily done up at the farm — in order to walk them down to Spadina and Dundas to the old Strand movie theatre, which had turned into the Victory Burlesque Theatre, to have celebratory drinks. After a few, he'd try to get them to double their tractor order, or phone their pals back home and tell them to switch to Falconi from International Harvester or John Deere or whoever they were with. When one of the dancers would sashay up to the table to say hello, like "Cup Cake Cassidy" or "Buxom Babs Bolay," and ask: "Who's your *friend*, Carmy?" while wiggling into the booth beside the unsuspecting farmer, it usually worked, too.

I do think Dad was a good salesman. He probably would've preferred to sell something a lot sexier, but he played the cards he had been dealt. He used to say that the guys he most admired were the Jewish *schmatta* salesmen at Spadina and Adelaide, a kilometre-and-a-half south of our showroom. He'd say to Small Carm, his protégé: "You know, most guys couldn't sell pussy on a troop train, but those guys down there can sell refrigerators to Eskimos," which I take to mean that it didn't matter what the product was — rags, scrap metal, television sets or mink coats — these guys had the charisma and skill to do it. I think he saw a lot of himself in those guys: They didn't grow up thinking: "Hey, I want to buy and sell dresses for a living," but they gave it their all.

He'd then remind Small Carm and Dom that Ferruccio Lamborghini had made his fortune selling tractors first, so there was no shame in what put the roof over our heads, either.

"Okay, but Lamborghini made his first sports car in 1963," Dom snapped back once. "When are we gonna make ours?"

I think he got his ear flicked for that.

One of the other reasons Dad was successful in the 1960s was that, when Nonno Joe and Nonna Ines went back to Italy, they allowed him to hire a secretary and an assistant. Bettina (Tina) Governale was a recent graduate of secretary school and the daughter of the owner of a pizzeria that Big Carm frequented on College Street, so she came aboard in the summer of 1963. It took a few months longer to find an assistant, since he wanted someone young but with business experience, and most of his friends were as much about "the sweet life" as he was. One day, however, while up at Buttonville, he ran into one of the neighbouring property owners, Ralph Whiteway, a nice old guy who ran a farm animal crematorium, and they got to talking. Mr. Whiteway had three sons: Two were already working for him, and the other, Paul, had just finished his business degree. Would Falconi like to "borrow" him so he could live downtown and sow his wild oats before he came to work at Whiteway Cremation Services? Little Paul "Whitey" Whiteway, who was 110 pounds dripping wet, ended up working at Falconi for four years, and became great friends with my dad.

The way the office was laid out, it was pretty easy to add new employees. While Dad would change everything in 1967, when he took over in '63 it was still pretty much 1938 in there. Kaplan and Sprachman had also designed the interiors, so they were quite striking: Two counters, one on each side of the room, curved right out of the wall and were decorated with speed-stripes. One was lower and wider, like a desk, and this is where Nonno Joe had sat in front of his typewriter. The other was bar-height, with those old, rolling, architect-style stools behind it where two or three people could sit. Dad always said that part looked "like a friggin' Hertz Rent-A-Car" and I'm sure it was the first thing that felt the weight of his sledgehammer. Behind this taller counter, there was a water cooler and a bean-shaped credenza built right into the wall with drawers for brochures, spec sheets and contracts. On top of the credenza was the usual office stuff: an in-and-out tray, stapler, rubber-stamp carousel, Rolodex, and one of those neat porcelain disks that, when you spin it, you get a moist surface that licks your stamp. The lighting in the ceiling was made up of fluorescent tubes hidden behind lipped curves in the plaster.

Except for the Ferrari-red tractor in the window — now the re-designed Finch model that Dad had played a part in, everything was white. Well, the one chair for customers in front of Nonno Joe's desk had a chrome frame with swoopy arms and a green vinyl seat, but everything else was white, and it looked like a Buck Rogers movie set. Between the two counters, there was a swinging door that led to a big room that contained a scale model of the tractor's engine (not a Fiat anymore; Falconi had started making their own engines just after the war), a cutaway of the big tractor seat to show the fine European styling and upholstery, a few big implements lying on the glossy white floor like abstract sculpture, and posters of some of our sexier magazine advertising campaigns hanging on the walls. This was, as Dad called it, "The Wow 'Em Room."

Past that room was a teeny-tiny kitchen with a bar fridge and a second water cooler, and, finally, a big storage closet. Upstairs, the second floor apartment hadn't been occupied for some time, so Big Carm let the diminutive, five-foot-four

Paul Whiteway live there for a few years as part of his compensation. Big Carm still lived on the third floor where he'd grown up; it was, and still is, a nice apartment. It has high, loft-like ceilings with exposed beams (before it was cool to have those), a decent-sized living room at the front, a dining room beside it that had been turned into a second bedroom for my grandparents, the real bedroom for Big Carm, and a kitchen in the back that's large enough for a small dining table. The furniture was all somewhat traditional and dark, but here-and-there were a few neat Art Deco pieces, like the china cabinet with curved waterfall sides (that had been pushed into the living room), and beside Nonno Joe's tufted, woolly, wingbacked chair, a chrome ashtray that had a little pelican standing in the middle so the smoker could tuck his or her cigarette into its beak. Since the stairway came up the side of the building, both apartments accessed all rooms from a hallway on the left.

When Dad did his big renovation and added two offices to the front part of the second floor, he also added a metal stairway to the back of the building for the family since he'd blocked off access to the third floor from the internal staircase. He also paved over what was left of Nonna Ines' garden in the backyard, which was pretty large for a commercial property since, unlike neighbouring buildings, a garage had never been attached to the back of ours. While all I remember growing up was the big Black Locust tree and the white clusters of flowers that would appear on it every June, the oil-stained concrete pad, and Big Carm's Cadillac, at one time my grandparents had had a few tomato and basil plants back there, a little bench, and a birdbath. It was quaint, but "too much freakin' work to keep clean" according to Dad.

∽

Dad was a ladies' man when he was young. While he dated girls of all kinds in high school, it was just after he graduated that he started dating Irish girls almost exclusively, especially redheads. Years later, he'd say: "Some guys had Yellow Fever, I craved the Red Menace." He and a buddy would go through the newspaper classifieds and look for ads for Catholic singles mixers in the east end of the downtown core — most of the Irish immigrant families still lived in or near Cabbagetown, Corktown or Leslieville — or to see if there were Orange Order dances anywhere, since they didn't care if the girls were Catholic or Protestant, rich or poor, well-connected or outcasts. During one of these Irish cruising missions, Big Carm met tiny, five-foot-nothing Rosabella Maria Caporuscio.

It was an icy night in January 1963. The full moon was casting ghostly light onto the crusty snow banks and glazed tree branches as the two young men drove along boulevards filled with semi-detached, Craftsman-style homes in search of an old, grey, stone church just north of the Danforth. While everything was tinted bluish-grey by the moon, St. Brigid's Parish was hard to miss: The five-storey Gothic steeple towered over the little 1920s homes. They made their way to the church basement, checked their coats, and paid their fifty-cent admission. In the poorly lit space adorned with faded construction-paper decorations, Big Carm spotted Rosa's cinnamon-red, teased up-do instantly. As he got closer, he took in her round face, pale skin, big blue spaced-apart eyes, symmetrical freckles on each side of her button-nose, and small mouth: an Irish Betty Boop, except she wasn't Irish. Wasting no time, he walked over and started a conversation.

He found out she was barely eighteen; he told her he would be turning twenty-two in a few months. She had been in Canada only five years; he'd been here his entire life. He was confused as to why he was in a room full of Sicilians; she explained that this neighbourhood was becoming something of a Little Sicily, and if he hadn't noticed by now, she was Sicilian also. "Can you not tell by my accent and poor English?" He was so smitten, he hadn't noticed.

It was the fruit trade that brought the first Sicilians here, she told him. This was back in the 1880s, when there were almost no Italians in the city. They came, mostly, from a small town with a big shipping port near Palermo, Termini Imerese. They'd been growing and exporting fruit for hundreds of years, so it was logical to bring these skills "to America." They started with carts in the streets, then upgraded to stores when they could afford it.

"The people in Toronto did not even know the taste of a banana at that time," she told him. "Is fascinating, no? It is if you like history, as I do."

By the time WWII started, most of the city's fruit and vegetable markets were owned by Italians, and many of them worked plots of land just outside the city to grow what could be grown here. What wouldn't come out of the Canadian soil, they'd import. In the 1920s and 30s, she said, there was a Sicilian "farming village" off Midland Avenue between Eglinton and Lawrence Avenues in Scarborough. Everyone there was from three towns in Sicily: Termini Imerese, Vita, and Pachino. These same men were the ones who opened the produce markets along the Danforth before anyone else thought to do so.

"And once they put down *radici*, roots, and buy house, they invite more relations to come over," she said. "They all live in small rooms and save money before they can get their own house. Then the next ones come, and it start all over again."

While she didn't know the term, my mom was talking about something I've read about, chain migration, which basically means these villagers, *paesani*, would subconsciously recreate mini-versions of their hometowns in Canada by all following each other to the same neighbourhood over the years. It made sense: They already spoke the same dialect; they could help each other find work; the men could get wives; and they could even loan each other money. (In fact, the established Italians had already set up official money-lending organizations.) When a guy retired, he'd pass his business to a son or son-in-law, or sell it to someone from the same town. And it worked like crazy: By the 1980s, there were over 300,000 Italians in Toronto.

"So your parents are fruit importers?" my dad asked.

"No, we are from big city, Catania; my dad is shoemaker, my mom stays home to raise me and my sisters. And she do sewing jobs."

She explained that they'd come to Canada for the opportunities she and her sisters, Candida and Anna, would have available to them. Her dad, Calogero, had asked everyone he knew with relatives in Canada which were the good Italian neighbourhoods. While this one was small compared to College Street, he had grown tired of living right downtown in Catania, so he picked it because he could get a house with a little bit of land where he could grow tomatoes and build a trellis for a grape vine.

"And the red hair?"

"There is small amount of us in Sicily," she said. "My great-grandmother also had it. You can give thanks to the Norman people, who conquested us in 1061. They even have name for us, 'Normanni'."

Dad wasn't prepared for the hoops he had to jump through to take Rosabella on a date. He was accustomed to dating second- and third-generation Irish girls who lived downtown. While they weren't "easy" by any stretch, they could leave the house without an escort provided he got them home before curfew. With Rosabella, it was like he'd walked through a wormhole to the Victorian age. At the church dance, he'd been swarmed by the two sisters after they noticed he'd been talking to her for more than a few minutes. He had to endure sitting with the three of them and answering their questions, even from the younger sister, before he could ask to take Rosa onto the dance floor. When they finally did dance, there were two pairs of eyes laser-trained on him the entire time. It was only when a few couples danced into their line-of-sight that Rosa leaned over and whispered in his ear: "I work at cookie factory, Peek Frean, if you want to see me again. I take lunch at 11:30."

So, for the next few months, Big Carm would borrow Nonno Joe's big Buick LeSabre three times a week and drive thirteen kilometres north-east to O'Connor Drive — a wide suburban thoroughfare with a mix of crisp new strip malls, car washes, and large factories — and watch little Rosa eat her lunch. When the spring thaw began, they'd sit outside at the employee picnic tables and hold hands underneath. Once, they even went on a real date. Rosa told her parents there was a little party for a departing employee after work and that she'd be about ninety minutes late getting home. In reality, Big Carm and Rosa walked across the street to the luxurious, twenty-four lane O'Connor Bowl, the same place the CBC broadcast *Championship Bowling* from, and had a dinner of hot dogs and French fries and bowled as many frames as they could before her paranoia got the better of her.

All of this secrecy was necessary so Rosa could work on her parents and, to a lesser extent, her older sister Candida. Once she'd revealed Big Carm's existence, she next had to tell them he'd come to see her at work "a few" times. She had to tell them his entire backstory, how he came from a successful family that made tractors, and that he was in line to run the business one day. Calogero, her father, and her mom, Serafina, agreed that he could come over and meet them and maybe, just maybe, go out with her a few days after that if they approved of him *and if* she brought Candida along. Candida begrudgingly agreed to play chaperone.

At this point, Rosa didn't *dare* tell them he wasn't Catholic.

∽

When Tom Falconi died and Big Carm zoomed into the role of de facto president of the Canadian arm of the company, things turned around for him in the romance department.

This promotion, and the day he showed up on Milverton Blvd. in his new butter-yellow Cadillac to pick her up, impressed his future in-laws so much they loosened their grip. At that point, Big Carm really dialed up the *romanza*. He was a good dancer, so he'd take Rosa to one of the many nightclubs along Spadina and, in those days, there were quite a few. Mostly, they'd walk across the street from Falconi to the El Mocambo, which hosted colourful international acts like "Los Chicanos" from Chile, or walk a block north to the Silver Dollar Room beside the Waverley Hotel. The Silver Dollar's house band, *Tommy Danton and the Echoes*, played rockabilly music and sold their 45s after the show.

The El Mo was the swankier of the two clubs, with its big neon palm tree outside, tropical-themed bar inside, and dance hall on the second floor. It had been a fixture on Spadina since 1948, so when Big Carm was eleven or twelve and able to stay home by himself, he had told us about seeing Nonno Joe and Nonna Ines, then in their forties, go to the El Mo every Friday for exactly two hours to cut a rug and have exactly two drinks each. He'd stand at the showroom door and watch them cross the street — Nonna Ines lifting up her big skirt and crinoline as Nonno Joe took her gloved hand to guide her between the finned cars — and then he'd go off and listen to the radio, since the family wouldn't get a television set until Big Carm turned fifteen. Sometimes, Big Carm would take Rosa all the way over to the neon-drenched strip of nightclubs on Yonge Street and they'd hit the Colonial Tavern or Le Coq d'Or.

The courtship lasted about seven months. At that point, Dad drove over to Calogero's shoe repair shop, a little storefront tucked into a utilitarian, yellow-brick building at the corner of Coxwell Avenue and the Danforth, to have "the talk." He spent a half hour telling his future father-in-law his intentions in order to get his blessing. Poor Calogero still had no idea Big Carm wasn't Catholic, so of course he said yes; besides, by the time they got married, his daughter would be nineteen, and that was plenty old enough to start a family. Dad proposed at the Royal York Hotel in November of 1963. He'd wowed her with tickets to a dinner-dance with Moxie Whitney and his Orchestra followed by Marcelo Ballet Espanol and Vancouver comedian Dave Broadfoot. Little Rosabella Caporuscio from Catania never had a chance: She was literally swept off her feet.

Dad never said much about the blow-up that happened when the happy couple announced their future son-in-law had been brought up a Methodist, and that he'd had no time for religion at all while growing up. All I know is this: The Caporuscio family did freak out; the youngest sister, sixteen-year-old Anna, went off the deep end and started wearing a homemade nun's habit and walking the streets of Little Sicily praying for her sister; and fiery Rosabella ran away from the family home on Milverton and took up residence in a Little Italy boarding house so she could be near her betrothed. It took a month-long negotiation by Candida to get both camps to agree to even talk to each other, and another month to settle on an Anglican Church for the wedding (since it was deemed close enough to Catholic), all while Big Carm watched from the sidelines. I'm not sure, but I think he found the whole thing very entertaining.

My mom and dad didn't have to wait a year to get married like Catholics do, so the wedding was scheduled for May 2, 1964. Big Carm was nice enough to pick a church that was two blocks away from the Caporuscio's home, the Church of the Resurrection at Milverton Boulevard and Woodbine Avenue. There are exactly three photos of the ceremony taken by Nonno Joe and Nonna Ines, who flew in from Latina for the week, so I can't tell you if there was a riot. I am told that when the minister asked if anyone had any objections, Serafina Caporuscio put up her hand, then laughed and pulled it down when the small gathering of twenty guests turned their heads and gasped.

Back then, *the* place to honeymoon was Niagara Falls, even if you lived an hour-and-a-half away in Toronto. So, the Falconis stayed for three nights at the stately Brock-Sheraton Hotel in the same room Marilyn Monroe had lived in while filming *Niagara*. They rode the Maid of the Mist. They took sunshine-y photographs in front of the floral clock. They ate steak and Italian food. And because Dad still wanted to improve the Falconi brand at that time, he arranged for a tour of the Zippo lighter plant while they were there. Apparently, the president himself led them on a long walkabout, introduced them to some of the workers on the line, and even answered Dad's questions about their metal finishing process. They left with a set of his-and-hers lighters that Dad later had engraved with the date of the wedding.

After that, they drove the short distance to Buffalo, New York and stayed at the Statler Hilton for a couple of nights, and hit the jazz clubs: the Kitty-Kat, the Colored Musicians Club, the Town Casino, and the Bon-Ton.

When they got back to Toronto, Big Carm had a contractor come in to restore the dining room in the Falconi third-floor apartment so that his new bride could have more floor space in the kitchen. He had the guys bring Nonno and Nonna's antique dining set — a beautiful carved piece from the 1850s they'd had shipped from Italy back in 1938 — up from the basement and put it back under the modest chandelier. He was able to move the Art Deco China cabinet out of the living room and back into the dining room. He also got rid of his childhood bedroom furniture and allowed Rosa to pick a new set from the Eaton's catalogue. She chose a sleek, contemporary, Danish teak affair that included a headboard with built-in, floating tables on either side of the bed, a highboy dresser for him, a long, low chest of drawers for her, and a little black-wire chair for the corner. She had the walls painted a light coral and wallpaper hung behind the bed. The wallpaper, which I remember seeing removed in the late 70s, had an abstract, Chinese lantern design. It was a lovely, modern room.

About ten months later, they had to cram a crib in there, too, for Small Carm.

A bunch of things happened in 1967: Dom was born in April; Paul Whiteway had to move out of the second floor so Mom and Dad could expand the family's living quarters; Dad decimated the Falconi showroom, inside and out; and both Sgt. Pepper's and the "Summer of Love" happened.

When the Beatles first hit it big and played Maple Leaf Gardens to over thirty thousand screaming fans, I think Big

Carm treated it as a curiosity, as something for teenyboppers that wouldn't last. I don't think he paid much attention to the British Invasion as a whole, either, since most television programs were still geared to adults at that time. I mean, *The Dean Martin Show* was killing it in the ratings, right? And the little shelf-top radio in the Falconi showroom, when it was even turned on, practically had its dial welded to CFRB 1010, a news and issues station (with some really boring adult music thrown in) that still sounded old when I first heard it in the 1980s. But by '67, with Toronto's Yorkville scene starting to make the newspapers, and with U.S. magazines and news reports focusing more and more on youth culture and less and less on Sinatra and the Rat Pack, he really started to think the world was coming to an end. Big Carm even got his fifteen minutes of fame, when his anti-hippie Letter to the Editor got published in the August 24, 1967 edition of the *Globe and Mail*:

No Friend To This Old Man

Is Don Delaplante joking? I read with disgust his "Canada's oldest hippie is jailed with his friends" yesterday and was thankful my oldest son isn't old enough to read. Here is a man of 67 years who has tragically lost his wife and now has bats in his belfry, and Mr. Delaplante describes him as a colourful, fun character named "Pops" who "wears a coat several sizes too large, several wristwatches at once, and numerous rings" and then brags about how he "loves the Yorkville hippies" so much he was jailed with them after participating in their unlawful "sit-ins" and riots on Sunday night. Pardon my harsh tone, but this old man needs to be admitted to 999 Queen Street, a.k.a. the Provincial Lunatic Asylum, immediately. And maybe Mr. Delaplante can be the one to check him in so he can get his head examined too while he's there.

Stories that show these law-breaking, dirty hippies as cute little troll dolls do damage to our youth. They read this sort of thing in your paper and then, after one or two arguments with their parents, think it is okay to run away and live on the street. If they are young girls, how do you think they pay for their lodging or their food? If they are young boys, what are they doing to earn their keep? If they see "Pops" breaking the law for his beloved freaks, maybe they think it's not so bad to break the law also and steal stuff for the older hippies to sell. Or maybe they sell drugs for them.

I'm not much older than these greasy welfare recipients, but I can tell you that I will be raising my two boys to have respect for law and order. I will teach them that society only works if you don't take advantage of it. And if these hippies are still around when my boys are older, and I hope for society's sake they are not, I will tell them that today's hippie is tomorrow's mental patient.

— Carmelo G. Falconi, President,
Falconi Farm Equipment Canada

Dad was no doubt blowing construction dust off his angry letter after he'd typed it; the Summer of Love was the Summer of Construction at Falconi. By day, there would be a work crew on the second floor ripping out the kitchen and replacing it with bedrooms, and in the evening he'd have the same guys ripping out every last piece of Kaplan and Sprachman's work in the front showroom, the "Wow 'Em Room" behind it, and all of the shiny Vitrolite panels and Deco curves on the outdoor façade.

When the dust had settled, the Falconi family apartment spread over almost two full floors. The top floor still looked pretty much as it had since the 1964 mini-reno, but the second was completely different. The entire space had been gutted and divided up into three sections: The back section contained two small bedrooms and a bathroom, and the middle contained a big, open playroom. This new part of the second floor and third floor was now accessed by an external staircase that had been attached to the building's back wall. The front section of the second floor contained two small offices that could be accessed from the building's internal staircase.

To maximize space, the two second-floor offices were divided by thin metal-and-panel walls made by a company that specialized in office systems furniture. These walls had opaque sections painted burnt orange that went up to about chest-height, then ribbed glass above that. Each office had a thin mahogany door. The wall that separated the two offices had glass as well, but it was positioned much higher, from the six-foot mark to the top of the ceiling so each worker would have privacy. Inside each office, the metal part of the wall had padded fabric on it so you could pin notes and stuff into it. Both offices had angular metal desks and rolling chairs, and each could look out *half* of the big bay window. It was cool, in a minimalist, sixties kind of way.

As for the ground floor, well, it was bad. On the exterior, all of the curves and speed stripes were gone; in their place was a square box below the bay window covered in brown ceramic tile. Re-mounted on the poo-brown tiles were the graceful, stainless steel Falconi letters. Maybe Dad had taken a ride on the brand-spanking-new Bloor-Danforth subway line and made a mental note that the TTC had chosen ceramic tile over Vitrolite this time around, I don't know. The curved-corner window was gone as well, replaced by two panes of glass that met at a right angle like every other store window in the world.

Inside, the office was now a boring square room with cheap wood paneling on the back wall. There were two teak desks, one on either side of the room. The built-in credenza was gone, replaced by a teak sideboard. The sculptural ceiling with indirect lighting had been replaced by a gridded drop ceiling with built-in florescent lights. The only interesting things in there now were the red tractor — still a 1962 Finch — and two Italian designer chairs Dad had purchased for customers to sit in; these were called Hyaline chairs and were totally futuristic. Each one consisted of two square glass panels that had upholstered cylinders wedged between them. These cylinders, upholstered in red leather, curved in a sort of C-shape to make up both the seat and the backrest.

Behind the showroom, the "Wow 'Em Room" was now a drafting room, since Dad still fancied himself a designer at that point. Out went the engine model and implements, and in came the drafting tables, pencils and big rolls of paper. This room was used exactly one time to create a new tractor design.

⁂

I think Mom was a little concerned at the finality of the 1967 renovation. While she didn't care one way or the other about the Falconi showroom, she didn't like it when Big Carm started to talk about how the playroom on the second floor could be converted into another bedroom if they had a third child, or that, heck, it could even become two bedrooms if need be. And he also started to talk about how downtown Toronto wasn't like those U.S. cities, where there were race riots and buildings burning down almost every week on the news. In fact, a lot of American draft-dodgers were coming here to live because it was so *unlike* where they were from. Yes, the hippies were a problem but, so far, they were sticking to that one old Victorian neighbourhood which, thankfully, wasn't very close.

Mom, you see, wasn't exactly in love with the idea of living in an old, warehouse-y-office building downtown. Sure, as someone who came from a dense, beautiful old city like Catania, she appreciated heritage architecture, but she wanted the kind of home she saw in *Ontario Homes & Living* magazine for her kids. She wanted what a lot of women in the 1960s wanted: a suburban house with a wide picture window, a matching set of low, wide furniture, a "rec room" in the basement, and a big, lush, grassy backyard. It didn't help that Big Carm had just had the Falconi building's backyard entombed in two inches of concrete.

A couple of times, Mom actually got Dad to drive out to one of the new developments in Scarborough not too far away from where all those Sicilians used to farm back in the 1930s. Once I remember her talking about what was called

Midland Park, and although it had been built about five years before, there were still a few houses left for sale. The houses there weren't big, maybe fifteen-hundred square feet, but they had been designed by an architect and had nice, clean lines and rooms that opened to each other. Some were two-storey designs and some were split-levels, but all of them had really big backyards. Like all suburbia, the streets were twisty and turn-y and one of them even backed onto a ravine. Mom loved it, Dad hated it.

"What do we do when we take a walk?" he asked. "Look into other people's windows? There's no place to get a coffee, no action, no food."

"So we make our espresso at home, Carm. And what about the lovely valley with creek? The boys can play there all day long in summertime. I no have to watch them."

"Rosa, we *own* a farm! A huge farm. It *has* a creek, for God's sake. We can go up there any time you want."

"It is not same thing, you do not understand."

Another time, Mom told Big Carm she'd even settle for one of those little saltbox homes just a few blocks north of where her family lived, like the ones near O'Connor Drive. Big Carm said he didn't want to commute to work, that it was crucial for him to be near Union Station for arriving and departing customers, and the rail lines in general so he could inspect the shipping containers from Latina. He did promise her, however, that once Small Carm was old enough to take over the business, say when he was about twenty-one, he'd semi-retire and reward her with a suburban dream-house.

~

By 1969, Calogero and Serafina Caporuscio had had enough with "America." Calogero's shoe repair business wasn't doing well — he and Big Carm agreed it was because the hippies dressed like bums — and their daughter Anna had developed full-blown mental illness. While she didn't dress like a nun anymore, she had been diagnosed with a split personality, which we now call schizophrenia. She'd scream at invisible people; she'd tell anyone who'd listen that the U.S. military was spying on her; and she'd fly into rage-fits and punch the walls until her knuckles bled. A half hour later, she'd be completely normal and wouldn't remember a thing. Her parents were convinced she had done drugs in high school and that was what had caused her behaviour. So they wanted to take her back to the old country where she'd be able to rest and get cured. The older sister, Candida, hadn't found a husband yet, so she threw in the towel too. Before man landed on the moon, the Caporuscios were back in Catania and little Rosabella was left holding down the fort in Toronto.

Luckily, things were still going relatively well at Falconi Farm Equipment. Sales remained steady into the new decade, and Dad's prediction at needing another bedroom had come true, as half the playroom became Gina's room. Paul "Whitey" Whiteway was long gone, but Tina Governale was working on the second floor in one office, and a new employee, a young Chinese accountant from the neighbourhood, Li-Na Cheng, was in the other one. (We called her "Lina," a good Italian name.) The empty desk in the showroom downstairs was technically Mom's, but she wouldn't really start to use it until Gina went to kindergarten in September 1974.

While Dad would go into his new drafting studio on occasion to doodle, the room was used only once for a design that went into production, and it was a colossal flop. Enclosed-cab tractors weren't necessarily new. One had been available in the late-1930s but it was kind of like the Tucker automobile: too weird, too advanced and too expensive. By the early 1970s, however, the public was ready for them, and since they'd already caught on in Europe, Falconi couldn't wait any longer to release one of their own. But instead of letting our designers in Latina come up with something, Dad convinced Nonno Joe to let him take it on. Naturally, he'd fly to Italy first to do some research and maybe throw in a little side trip to Sicily for Rosa. Mom, however, was about two months pregnant with me and having wicked morning sickness, so she refused to go. She hated the faded Fascist buildings of Latina anyway; she used to call it "a place where Vampires would feel right at home." So Dad went alone, and I'm pretty sure he just pouted most of the time and sat in cafés because, when he came back, he designed the strangest thing I've ever seen, especially for a guy who had been so quick to erase Kaplan and Sprachman's curves.

While the logical thing would have been to put a simple, squared-off box on top of the tractor and fill it with niceties like air conditioning and joystick controls like every other company, Dad took the whole stylish thing a bit too far. He created an oblong, glass bubble that sort of rose up, organically, from the body of the tractor like a transparent egg. While it did have a small metal roof so farmers wouldn't bake like ziti in there, the complex curves of the design proved so costly to manufacture they had to switch from glass to Plexiglas. Also, the seat was a bit weird: While it didn't have glass panels on the sides, it looked a lot like Dad's showroom chairs in that it was made up of connected, upholstered cylinders.

When the first one arrived from Latina after countless dollars had been spent on retooling and almost a year had passed, Dad was like a kid on Christmas morning. He sent the '62 Finch (the one we had all been polishing religiously every week) out to pasture at Falconi Farm and stuffed the "Weath-R-Shield Falcon" in the shop window even though it barely fit. Friends and fellow business-owners, like hatter Sammy Taft and the Ladovskys, the restaurant-bakery owners, came over to congratulate him on it, and he felt like a million bucks.

After sales maxed out at about two hundred units and the engineers in Latina had to rip off the complex bubbles from the remaining eight hundred so that they'd actually sell, Dad felt like a he'd cost the company a million bucks. He probably had. He was devastated, and it didn't help that it was around this time that Nonno Joe was diagnosed with advanced lung cancer. So, after a year in the window, the space tractor as Dom called it, went up to the farm and the '62 Finch came back. It's still in the window today and Small Carm still polishes it religiously. Up until we sold the farm, the Weath-R-Shield Falcon was collecting dust in the barn, its Plexiglas bubble scratched and yellowed. Sold for scrap in the 1990s, now it's probably someone's toaster.

Way back when Dad was seventeen, he convinced Nonno Joe to put out a line of Falconi calendars as a promotional tool.

At that time, salesmen were always coming to our door with stuff like that anyway, whether it was pens, paperweights, ashtrays or shoehorns, so the next time one of them showed up, Nonno Joe asked about a cheap calendar. He chose a pin-up one because the young, buxom girl in the stylized illustration had a cowboy hat on over her pigtails and was holding a pitchfork. Why she was also wearing a garter belt and black stockings while doing farm chores is a mystery, but I'm sure Big Carm liked that part of it. Anyhow, this was one of those calendars that featured the illustration on a piece of hard cardboard and a blank space underneath where the company information would get printed; the actual calendar was just a little stapled pad of twelve sheets at the bottom. Ours read:

F A L C O N I FARM EQUIPMENT "CIVILIZED FARMING for INTELLIGENT FARMERS"
413 SPADINA AVE. TORONTO 2, ONTARIO,
TEL: EM2 — 3434. OUR PRODUCTS MADE IN ITALY WITH PRIDE SINCE 1933.

These calendars were well received by our customers and suppliers, so Nonno Joe kept them going into the 60s, and father and son would select a new pinup drawing from the salesman's catalogue each year. When Big Carm took over the business, he upgraded to calendars that had twelve large pages with a different girl for each month, which cost three times as much. When these started to look old-fashioned in the early 1970s, he came up with an even better idea: Falconi would make its own calendar with live models.

As sleazy as it sounds today, it was commonplace well

into the 1980s to drape women over various things in order to help sell them. So Dad didn't meet with any resistance from Rosa or Nonno Joe in Latina. Besides, since the calendar photos would feature Falconi tractors and implements, Dad reasoned that he could use them on brochures, business cards, spec-sheets and magazine ads, so it was, in his words, "a boffo idea." He started out modestly enough by contacting the Miss Toronto Pageant people, and he and Little Whitey Whiteway had a great time meeting all the contestants and doing interviews to select the twelve girls. They hired a photographer and spent a day up at Falconi Farm getting all sorts of 'Aw Shucks' poses that were pretty wholesome by today's standards. This arrangement worked for five years, but by 1979, Big Carm decided he wanted to go bigger and more American. He wanted the Farrah Fawcett-Cheryl Tiegs California-girl-in-a-bikini thing even though this had very little to do with farming. Since Nonno Joe had died the year before (he was in such pain it was almost a relief), Big Carm was now the big — and only — cheese at Falconi, so he could basically do whatever he wanted.

It was when Dad was hiring for the 1983 calendar in the spring of 1982 that he met her. Linda Larson was everything Rosa Falconi was not: tall, blonde, brash, bubbly, American, at least a decade younger, and a bit of a dolt. She was, ironically, from California but not the glamorous part, although she had done some modelling in L.A. She lived near Sacramento, but had come up to Toronto for a bit part in a crappy horror movie called *Spasms*, which starred Peter Fonda and "The King of Kensington" Al Waxman, and she had decided to stick around to pick up more work. The thing that really blew Dad away was when he found out she'd worked at

Harrah's Lake Tahoe from 1977 to 1980 and had gotten to know Sinatra pretty well. Actually, I think she'd gotten to know him *really* well, if you catch my drift.

So of course she made the cover of the calendar that year. He even went on a business trip to California a few months later, which didn't seem suspicious at the time. Ms. Larson came back to Toronto for the 1984 calendar shoot in the spring of '83, and even stuck around the city for a while even though she didn't have any other work lined up. And she stayed in a hotel that was really close to the Falconi building.

That summer was a really bad one for Mom. Not only was Big Carm growing more distant, her parents had been involved in a horrific automobile accident on the Passo San Boldo, a series of stacked roads with hairpin turns located in the southern Alps. They had been spending some time with friends who lived in Treviso and had gone down to Venice for a few days. When they got back, everyone agreed a trip to the mountains would be lovely. The friends were driving their 1960s Fiat 124 Sport Coupé — a great little sedan that was apparently made with cheap Russian steel — and Calogero and Serafina were in the back seat. A motorcyclist in front of them took one of the hairpin turns too fast and dropped his bike onto the road; they swerved to avoid running him over and rolled down the embankment, landing on the road below. The metal crumpled and their friends were crushed to death, but Calogero wouldn't die until a few days later in hospital. Serafina survived, but permanently lost the use of her legs.

To make matters worse, Big Carm was on a business trip when it happened, and he insisted he couldn't make it to Italy for the funeral. Small Carm stepped in and escorted Mom, but that put a huge strain on Mom and Dad's already fragile marriage. The crazy thing is, I know for a fact that Big Carm and Calogero really liked one another. I guess Big Carm had already mentally checked out of our family by then.

It was in the autumn of 1983 that I remember the vicious fights between my parents began. Most of them were in Italian so I don't know what was being said, but thinking back, Mom was the one that started most of them with a brusque comment. Sometimes, to shield us, they'd walk down the back stairway and scream it out in the alley, but we could still hear them. I don't think Mom knew exactly what was going on with Ms. Larson, but she wasn't stupid either. By the winter, Dad was sleeping in his drafting room quite often, and we were waking up to a lot of silent breakfasts.

Here's some hubris: When Mom found out for sure that Dad was cheating and threw him out on his ear, he actually showed up the next morning like nothing happened. He was sneaky enough to ring the business doorbell rather than just barge in, which brought Mom down the back stairs and into the showroom to see who was at the door. Then she called him every Italian cuss word she could think of through the glass and told him to take a long walk off a short pier.

Dad wasn't expecting this. "What the? Frank visits his first wife Nancy all the time! They're still friends — he sleeps on her couch!" he yelled as she stormed into the drafting room, down the hallway and slammed the big metal door behind her. I remember looking down at him from the third floor window as he stood there in the street, his fedora tilted back on his head and a bewildered expression on his face. For a moment, he looked frozen in time as the throngs of workaday pedestrians parted around him as if he were a rock in a stream. He shook his upper body as if he'd just seen a ghost, turned on his heel and walked down Spadina Avenue with renewed purpose.

CHAPTER IV

☞ Spadina Avenue ☜

SAMMY TAFT ONCE said that Spadina Avenue "is the foreignest street in Canada." And he was right: It was brash; it was loud; it was colourful; and it was unapologetically ethnic. While Toronto played second fiddle to Montreal for the first six decades of the twentieth century in almost every way, there was *nothing* like Spadina in Montreal, or anywhere else in Canada for that matter. And, funnily enough, it was when Toronto bested Montreal to become the country's largest city and financial centre in the mid-1970s (after unrest caused by the Front de libération du Québec caused so many businesses and people to relocate here) that the Jewish Spadina my grandparents and parents knew, and even Small Carm and Dom to an extent, began to fizzle out.

But it still stayed the foreignest.

Big Carm was a regular at Sammy Taft's store at 303 Spadina Avenue, about a five-minute walk south of our building. He bought his first fedora from Sammy when he was seventeen after working at Falconi Farm the summer after graduating from Harbord Collegiate, and he had about fifty when he left the family. Sammy was one of those show-bizzy,

Jewish merchants like Sam "Shopsy" Shopsowitz, who ran a big deli a few doors south, or that other Sam, "Sam the Record Man" Sniderman on Yonge Street, or "Honest" Ed Mirvish and his big discount store with the silly signs — "Honest Ed's fulla baloney, but his prices are teeney weenies" — over at Bathurst and Bloor. Legend has it that when Sammy Taft's pals Phil Silvers or Henny Youngman would come to town, not only would they leave with a new (and free) hat on their heads, he'd supply them with one-liners for their acts.

All of that lovely braggadocio came from a little storefront with two, large, symmetrical display windows and a recessed door in the middle. A wide sign ran across the length of the shop over those windows, and it featured a rudimentary, New York Yankees-style font spelling out "Sammy Taft World Famous Hatter." In each window was a hat-tree sprouting head gear; on each wall were framed photographs of Youngman and other Borscht Belt comedians, plus legends like Bob Hope, Joe Louis, Duke Ellington, Louis Armstrong and Sophie Tucker. Oh, and a lot of hockey players, since Sammy had invented the term "hat trick" in the 1940s after he'd promised a Chicago Blackhawks player that, if he scored three goals that night, he'd give him a hat for free. I think he scored four, just to make sure. Just about every other major celebrity who was willing to pose for the camera wearing their "Sammy" — what Torontonians called hats in those days — made it onto the wall eventually.

When Dad took over Falconi in 1963, he started a twenty-year tradition of buying two hats a year from him, a straw for summer and a felt for winter, despite the fact that U.S. President John F. Kennedy had singlehandedly ruined the men's hat industry when he showed up to his inauguration bare-headed in 1961. Small Carm says Dad liked to tell the story of the time a *Globe & Mail* reporter stopped in to do an interview with Sammy in the spring of 1974 and he was the only customer in there. This guy kept prodding Taft to admit that hats were out of style, that the hippies and their long hair had completely killed them off, and Sammy just kept pointing to Dad, who was then thirty-three, and saying: "What about HIM?" and then listing all the movies, such as *The Godfather*, *The Sting*, *The Great Gatsby* and *Bonnie and Clyde* that kept people "galloping into my store." When the reporter left, Sammy laughed and said in his nasally, high-pitched voice: "How many horses do your tractors have under the hood, Carm? Because that'll be the number I'll say galloped in this week if that *putz* comes back, since you're my first sale of the day!"

Mom didn't like deli food ("Oh no, it is too salty for me," she'd protest) but I can remember my sweaty, plump little hand being pulled along by Dad's big dry one as we passed Sammy's store to have lunch at Shopsy's. Taft would often be sitting outside on a little wooden stool watching Spadina go by, and he'd always wave to my dad and say: "Falconi the Farmer, nice to see you!" Dad would always tip his hat in return and say: "Keep the faith, Sammy!" Since I was only six or seven, I don't remember much about Shopsy's except for the big, red neon letters outside, the framed pictures of celebrities inside (most of them the same as Sammy had in his store) and the smell of the place, which was a sweet, steamy combination of peppercorns, moist bread, fried butter and floor cleaner solution. I also remember these two things: One time, as we were leaving, a Ferrari pulled up and my dad said hello to the driver, a man named Marvin Warsh, who he explained to me later was a mover and shaker down in the rag district — which didn't make sense to me because rags were for poor people; and, for some reason, the fact that he'd always point out a round-faced, laughing man with a doughy double-chin and thick, black glasses and then say to me in a loud voice: "Freddy, that's Sam, the man on the hot dog package in the refrigerator at home!" Then, he'd make a big show of waving to him. I guess he wanted me to know that he knew local celebrities and rich people.

In 1983, when Shopsy's announced it was moving to Yonge and Front streets after over six decades on Spadina, Sammy Taft was the last guy to eat a sandwich there.

∽

Of course, the World Famous Hatter and the Corned Beef King weren't the only colourful characters on Spadina. Heck, they weren't even the only Jewish delis or hat shops. From the early 1900s to the 1970s, Spadina was probably the least Anglo-Saxon street in all of Toronto, and the most Jewish street in Canada. I think its uniqueness and unconventional nature are the main reasons my mother put up with living there. There was a Yiddish theatre, the Standard, back in the 1920s, which turned into the Strand, the movie theatre "The King of Kensington," Al Waxman, would patronize as a kid (which became Victory Burlesque in 1961), as well as Yiddish and Hebrew bookstores, kosher grocery stores, and synagogues all over the place.

The other thing to know about Spadina is that it's really wide, like one of those grand boulevards in Washington D.C.

or Paris, but there's nothing especially grand about the buildings. Near the Falconi building, the buildings are a hodgepodge of two- and three-storey, retail-on-the-bottom/residential-on-top buildings from the late 1800s, with a few from after World War Two scattered about here and there. Closer to Queen Street West, there are some bulkier, utilitarian, five- and six-storey warehouses where the *schmatta* trade petered out; south of Queen, where the majority of the needle trade really took place, there are a few really nice buildings by Jewish architect Benjamin Brown. Near Adelaide Street, his twelve-storey Balfour Building and ten-storey Tower Building form a sort of gateway to the once bustling district, and whenever I find myself down there, I stop, look up, and drink in the detail.

The Balfour is my favourite: It's a lovely composition of tan-coloured brick and limestone carved in the Art Deco style (with great lettering over the front door). But what's really interesting is how nice things are at street level, where five Gothic-inspired, arched openings welcome pedestrians into small shops. Up on the roof, an elegant, windowed penthouse once concealed the building's water tower, but is probably empty now or full of HVAC equipment. The Tower Building is not quite as elegant, but it does have similar arched openings at the ground and the little penthouse on top. The two are pretty much the opposite of all those new, slapdash condos that are starting to pop up near the CN Tower which, to my eyes anyway, feel cold and anonymous when you get up close to them ... but that's not to say I'd turn down the contract to do their dry-walling.

It's easier to appreciate good architecture when you can stand a good distance back from it, and it's thanks to

William Baldwin that Spadina allows for this. While most of Toronto's streets were measured by surveyors back in the 1800s using a standard, sixty-six-foot chain called a Gunter's Chain, Dr. Baldwin, like many early Toronto residents, fancied himself a squire. When he inherited 200 acres on the edge of town in 1817, he figured a nice, wide driveway leading to his future house was appropriate, so he asked his surveyors to double the length of chain. He even had that little ceremonial circle just north of College Street — the one with Knox College on it — included into the design.

Completed in 1818, Baldwin called his house Spadina, which means "a sudden rise of the land" in Ojibwe, because it was on top of the hill above today's Davenport Road. Apparently, because of the width and the lack of trees along his driveway, he had a really nice view of Lake Ontario even though it was some distance away. At some point after Baldwin's death, Spadina was widened further to 160 feet, and, about a hundred years later, long after his house was gone, the city's famous tourist-trap Casa Loma (which means "hill house" in Spanish) was built right next door by that eccentric millionaire.

The funny thing is, with all that street width available to me as a kid, I spent most of my time in our hard concrete backyard or the narrow laneway behind it, which connected to a hidden, stubby street called Glasgow (which looked like a laneway with little workers' cottages on it), which connected to Huron Street via another laneway. There was yet another laneway between Huron and Ross streets, and a few others that didn't connect anything but just thrust up between the rows of houses. So why would a kid spend his time on busy Spadina when he had his own private highway system for his Big Wheel?

⁂

Spadina, to me, was for the adults and their serious business. And it had been home to some pretty serious stuff once the needle trade started booming, big time, in the 1930s. While the first factories started out in the old mansions along Spadina, Richmond and Adelaide, by 1927 Benjamin Brown was designing the Tower Building for Superior-Oxford Ltd., and, in 1929, the Balfour for the Schiffer-Hillman Clothing Co., and the workers inside of them were organizing unions and protest marches. It was easy to get consensus, since most Jews had arrived in Toronto in a very short span of time with the help of established relatives, much like the Italian and Sicilian communities. In 1901, for instance, there were a few thousand Jews, but by 1931 there were 45,000. A lot of these immigrants had ties to socialist and communist organizations in their home countries, so they weren't afraid to drop their tools and walk off the job, fists raised, to show their collective strength.

At 10 a.m. on February 26, 1931, members of the International Garment Makers' Union did just that. Dressed in heavy winter coats, woollen caps and fedoras, fifteen hundred workers spilled onto the cold Spadina sidewalk to protest poor wages and unsafe working conditions. They formed a column that marched up to the Labor Lyceum at number 346 Spadina — a building they'd helped build by buying shares in a co-op — to listen to speeches and get fired up.

Two years later, the Cloakmakers' Union did the same thing, but this time with twenty-eight hundred workers.

In July 1933, there was even an anti-Hitler protest that started in Clarence Square, one of the oldest parks in downtown Toronto, which turned into a march up Spadina to the lawn in front of Queen's Park, where the provincial parliament buildings are located. Of the *fifteen thousand* Jews in attendance, most were needle trade workers and union leaders.

And speaking of Queen's Park, because so many working-class Jews lived within a few blocks of the factories, it was no surprise when they elected Joseph Baruch Salsberg, a former union leader and Communist Party of Canada member, as their city alderman in 1938 and, a few years later, as their representative in the provincial government. Salsberg was a Member of Provincial Parliament for a dozen years and, for most of that time, was the only elected Communist in North America.

Unfortunately, the strikes of the 1930s meant that many factories pulled up stakes and moved to Montreal, where young French-Canadian workers, mostly women, were less inclined to organize. By the 1950s, Montreal had taken over the manufacturing sector of the market, making seventy-five percent of the country's clothing, with Toronto dropping to about twenty percent. But Spadina was still the major sales centre for the entire country — "Montreal makes the clothes and Toronto sells them," it was said — and it would reign until around the time I was born in 1975.

That year, when Small Carm was eleven, he was already kind of an old soul. At the beginning of summer vacation and for the next couple of years, he would walk to the little

United Bakers Dairy Restaurant (next door to the former Labor Lyceum, which by then had become a Chinese restaurant) and plop himself down on one of the little round stools facing the pink Arborite countertop. Since everyone from needle trade bosses to managers to workers had lunch there, he'd ask the owner, Mr. Ladovsky, to spread the word that he wanted to do odd jobs for pocket money. Mr. Ladovsky would always say to him: "Five percent talent, five percent luck, and ninety percent hard work, that's how you make money in the *schmatta* business, Carmy." My big brother would leave with a fresh bagel and a promise that there'd be some work for him within the week. And there always was: One summer, he told me he did everything from helping unload trucks and unpacking boxes to helping a leather cutter with the heavy hides. Now this, remember, was on top of the work he was already doing for Big Carm at Falconi. Then again, Small Carm wasn't like other kids; he didn't ride his bike and play street hockey. He worked. And, in his spare time, he brooded.

United Bakers was one of the last Jewish places to leave Spadina in 1986. Well, Switzer's Delicatessen, across the street from Shopsy's, lasted until 1991, but I never went there so I can't say if the food was good. And despite my dad's continued patronage, Sammy Taft split in 1984 to the newer, more suburban Jewish neighbourhood at Bathurst and Wilson.

By the late 80s, when I started walking up and down Spadina by myself, it was still pulsing with life, but that life was Chinese, mostly, with a little Vietnamese thrown in for good measure. I started bringing home *bahn mi* sandwiches and thousand-year-old eggs when I was sixteen, and both Small Carm and Dom would pinch their noses and give me looks of disgust. While Toronto's original Chinatown had started out a fifteen-minute walk east at Elizabeth and Hagerman streets in the late 1800s, the city's appropriation of land for New City Hall in the 1950s forced it to move west along Dundas and then spill onto Spadina just as the Jews moved north. Today, Chinatown *is* Dundas and Spadina in the minds of Torontonians, except for actual Chinese people; many of them have moved up to the suburbs too.

The only Jewish place I've been able to patronize as an adult is Rotman's Hat Shop and Haberdashery, which is just a stone's throw from the Falconi building. Since I'm not a fedora guy, however, I've only been inside twice. The first time I went in there was pretty funny: I think the little bell on the door woke Mr. Rotman up from his nap, since he looked up from his chair, startled, when I entered the dusty shop. He was a nice old guy, however, and when I asked him about fedoras he showed me how to hold one properly — by the brim so you don't stain or dent the crown — and how to brush dust off it. I think he was disappointed when I bought a Kangol cap instead. The second time was about five years ago, in 2002, to inquire about top hats for a buddy who was getting married. My friend had tried to find a contact number for a few days (he was, as you might expect, anxious about his upcoming nuptials), but hadn't had any luck, so I went in and asked him what his phone number was so I could give it to my friend.

"Well, *everyone* knows I don't have a phone," he said, slightly annoyed. "Back in the 1970s, I was getting so many calls from women looking for bright blue, bright green, white and red fedoras, I got rid of it. You can blame that stupid Woody Allen movie."

༄

Despite the efforts and advancements by the unions in the 1930s, some of the *schmatta* district buildings were still considered dangerous rattraps even as late as the 1950s—places not too different than the kind we hear about in the third world today — and more workers would have died on January 20, 1950, if it wasn't for my Nonno Joe.

It was a bright, clear and cold morning. There were still traces of wispy snow nestling against the stately, forty-foot tall limestone columns of Union Station as Joe Falconi led his customer through the doors into the enormous Great Hall.

"The train to Thunder Bay leaves at 12:30, Mr. Duguay," my grandfather said, his voice echoing off the marble floors. "Thank you again for your continued business, but, moreso, I am especially grateful you remembered little Carmelo and brought him the Sleeping Giant carving."

"I have great respect for your company and your family, Mr. Falconi," he said. "And I'd rather deal with a smaller player than the big guys, since I'm a small operator myself, but you already know that. Then Mr. Duguay shouted over the P.A. announcements: *"Au revoir, mon ami."*.

The sidewalks were clear as Joe walked west along Front St., no doubt thinking about the time he'd first gone to Northern Ontario to meet Mr. Omer Duguay to get a feel for his operation and equipment needs, and how he had met so many French-Canadians in what was, otherwise, a very

English province. He walked north on Simcoe Street and turned west when he reached Richmond. When he reached the intersection of Richmond and Spadina, he noticed a thin column of smoke beginning to climb to the west, but due to Spadina's slight curve, he couldn't pinpoint exactly where it was coming from. So, rather than walk north towards home, he jaywalked quickly to the sound of angry car horns and continued along Richmond. When he reached the squat, brick building at number 447, the thin plume had become twin columns of thick, dark smoke belching from two of the four basement windows of the Phillips Garment Company.

In one of the non-smoking windows, Joe saw the top half of a skinny, dark-haired man's face racked with concentration as he pounded on it with some sort of metal rod. In the other, a plump, shiny, round-faced woman was yelling: "HELP US, HELP US" through a tiny hole she'd managed to break through the window's wire mesh. Worse, on the outside of all of the windows there were prison-like bars, which, that night, late edition newspapers would report were put in place by the lessee, Phillip Chikofsky, to prevent robberies.

Nonno Joe, who knew every inch of the area because of his penchant for walking, got down on his hands and knees to address the panicked employees.

"Go to the back! There's an emergency exit!" he screamed.

"Okay, we'll try, but the smoke is very thick!" said a Ukrainian-accented man behind the plump woman.

Nonno Joe ran down the narrow laneway to the back of the building and spotted the door. Then he heard the pounding. The door was padlocked — an emergency exit, *padlocked*. Then, muffled grunts and dry metallic thumps as a half-dozen men crashed into the door with collective shoulder-power as Nonno Joe pulled on the handle with all of his might. Still nothing.

Not sure what to do next, my grandfather ran back towards the street, but stopped when he noticed one thin basement window without bars or wire mesh. Would it be large enough to pull people out of? He looked around, wildly, for something to break the glass. A few feet away, a rock the size of a potato leaned against the wall of the building next door, which looked like a carbon copy of the one on fire. He picked it up and threw it at the thick pane, which broke loudly and instantly. Cutting his hands badly, he cleared as many of the jagged fragments as he could from the frame and poked his head into what was the building's furnace room; now he could hear the screams coming from the north end of the building: bloodcurdling cries that could only come from watching one's own skin melt and slide off the bone.

"Over here!" he yelled into the acrid darkness. "There's a window and I can help you get out!"

As he eyed the oil tank and wondered how long it would take for fire to penetrate it and cause a massive explosion, the plump woman he'd seen at the front window ran into the room, screaming, her hair on fire. She looked up at my grandfather and blinked in disbelief, then froze like a deer caught in headlights. Re-registering the heat against her skin, she began shaking her head frantically while alternately slapping out the flames and trying to reach up to grab my grandfather's outstretched hands. It looked like some sort of macabre dance.

"Get something to raise yourself up and I'll pull you up!"

She looked around in a panic and finally reached under

an industrial sink to produce a metal tub stained with fabric dye. She was crying and her arms were shaking as she positioned the tub and stepped up onto it, but my grandfather's big hands locked onto her soft wrists and he was able to squeeze her through the window.

"What is your name?" he asked as he propped her against the wall.

"Mary," she said, still dazed and holding her singed hair.

"Are there others we can help?" he asked. She nodded. "What are their names? Help me call out to them!"

This unlikely pair saved four more through that window while firefighters at the front of the building worked to cut through the bars with acetylene torches, and District Chief John Shields led his men down the lobby stairs into a wall of flame. When more firefighters arrived, they ordered my grandfather and Mary Oleksiew to get medical attention as they took over and rescued seven more.

Six people, including Phillip Chikofsky and his eighteen-year-old son, died in the fire. Three more died in hospital the next day. Many were Jewish immigrants who had been in Canada for only a short time; a few of them were concentration camp survivors.

While Mary Oleksiew's eyewitness account made it into the newspaper the next day, she had never learned my grandfather's name, so he wasn't mentioned by the reporter ... and that's just how Joe Falconi wanted it. After his write-up of what happened that day in his diary, he closed with this: "Saved some good people today! — Hard workers — They work in disgusting conditions & deserve better. My hands will heal but what they saw will scar them forever."

It was this experience that led Nonno Joe to get involved in the needle trade nine years later. By the late 1950s, tens of thousands of southern Italian peasants had immigrated to Canada — mostly to Toronto — and those with sewing experience ended up replacing the Eastern Europeans in those dingy basements and outdated factories along Spadina, Adelaide and Richmond. Since most didn't speak English and didn't know the rules, workweeks of fifty hours for wages as low as fifty cents an hour were common. (The industry minimum then was $1 per hour and $1.50 for overtime.) Many young women chose to work from home, where even lower wages were the norm and the unions couldn't penetrate.

So, because Joe Falconi was both a prominent Spadina business owner, fluent in English and Italian, *and* someone who didn't have connections to the factory owners, the International Ladies' Garment Workers Union approached him in late 1959. They were looking to appoint two organizers to spread the word about the benefits of unions to newly-arrived Italians, and he agreed to become one of them. So, until Big Carm took the Falconi reins in 1963, Nonno Joe knocked on hundreds of doors and changed a lot of lives for the better.

Our dad, Big Carm, wasn't interested in stuff like that. His Spadina was hedonistic rather than revolutionary: hats, cigars, burlesque, fatty meats, booze and dancing. I guess that's why, when things really heated up, protest-wise, over the proposed Spadina Expressway in the late 1960s — a linear car-crater that would've ripped open our beloved street much like the Decarie Trench in Montreal, Big Carm shrugged his shoulders and said it wouldn't affect our business, since we didn't rely on walk-ins. It was Nonno Joe in Italy who wrote letters of support to the "Stop Spadina" campaign, which included luminaries like Jane Jacobs and Marshall McLuhan.

It was only after Small Carm started running things that a little bit of Nonno Joe's spirit returned; in 1986, when the ILGW launched an unexpected strike to protest proposed pension cuts, Small Carm was waving a placard and chanting in the rain alongside hundreds of women. It was the first full-scale strike to hit Spadina in forty-nine years. And Falconi Farm Equipment, then celebrating its fifty-third birthday, would strike out and go out of business the next year.

CHAPTER V

☞ Dom ☜

PRETTY MUCH EVERY morning after breakfast for the past three years, Dom has swung open the big metal door to the back staircase and placed a bag of apples, pine nuts, or strawberries at his feet. Looking around, he'll raise his long, slim hands to his mouth, clasp them together and turn them sideways, leaving only a small opening for his lips. His top hand flapping rhythmically, his organic amplifier produces sharp kissing noises that are so loud, they echo off the garage doors in the network of alleyways below his feet.

Within minutes, he'll spot that telltale flash of white against the rich, green backdrop of the neighbourhood trees, then hear the rustle of Black Locust leaves followed by the clickety-clack of tiny claws on metal.

"Hi Edgar! How are you today?" Dom will ask as he reaches for the paper bag. Balancing on hind legs a few feet away, Edgar will wait, patiently. As Dom proffers a juicy morsel, Edgar's red eyes will flick back and forth to check for predators, then he'll wiggle his pink nose in approval.

After a few bites, Edgar, one of Toronto's famous albino squirrels, will then scamper up Dom's arm to perch on his shoulder, since he's learned that food gets to his mouth faster that way. This can go on for ten minutes, followed by Dom being rewarded with the privilege of stroking Edgar's tiny furry chest.

The first time he sat on his shoulder was when Dom named him, and I was lucky enough to be there. As I stood there, incredulous at how trusting the little guy was, Dom said: "Hey, I know what I'll call him. Remember that song 'Frankenstein'? Ba-da-da-da-doo-dat-dat-DAA, da-da-da-doo-da!"

"I don't get it, you're going to call him Frankenstein? Dom, he's too cute!"

"No, the song is by Edgar Winter, and he's an albino, remember?"

Dom has always loved animals, but we were raised with parents who thought they were dirty and belonged in a barn or tied up in the yard. Dom said that whenever Mom and Dad would announce that they had to go to Falconi Farm he'd get super-excited because he could play with the barn cats or feed the Canada geese. He never dared to ask Dad, but I know he wanted a dog pretty badly. While our sister, Gina, had owned a horse for about eight months in 1983, it wasn't really the same thing, so it couldn't be used in a pro-pet argument. Even Small Carm, who raised me, discouraged pet ownership, though I, too, desperately wanted a little fur-baby to love. I was about ten when I asked him if we could get something.

"A dog is a lot of maintenance," he said as if we were talking about a furnace. "Even a cat, and remember cats don't really like people, is a lot of work. All birds do is squawk and crap all the time. If an animal gets sick, we'll have to put it down, and we don't need another death in this house."

So I was allowed to have the newts and salamanders that Dom and I caught at Beaver Creek. Until the tank started to smell, of course.

༺༻

Domenic Eliodoro Falconi was scheduled to enter the world during the week of June 25-July 1, 1967, which meant there was the possibility he could be born on Canada's Centennial. So, as the story goes, all during the pregnancy Mom called him her "Centennial Baby." Unfortunately, Dom decided to come out early, really early, at just under seven months. And instead of coming out crying his head off in a nice shade of Canadian red, he came out blue and wasn't breathing very well. I think it was touch-and-go for a while, but the doctors at St. Michael's Hospital had him rushed up to Sick Children's within the half hour and he pulled through.

Despite the early arrival, Mom still called him Centennial Boy until he was about five years old and Small Carm, having difficulty with the pronunciation, rechristened him Centurion Boy. Sometimes, we still call him that when we want to get his goat.

While Dad named him Domenic to honour his dead cousin, Domenic Zannella, Mom was responsible for Eliodoro. There's a statue of an elephant, carved out of lava, in Catania's main square, *Piazza del Duomo*, and the name has to do with that.

Legend has it that, in the eighth century, a red-bearded young man from a noble family wanted to become Prefect of Catania. When his dream started to unravel, Eliodoro, also known as Heliodorus, visited a Jewish necromancer for advice, and learned how to conjure up a demon; the demon, in turn, asked Elio to reject Christ, which he did. This allowed Elio to become a magician and live a life of vice and indulgence, which he apparently enjoyed. He also enjoyed riding an elephant around town while performing his magic.

The one thorn in his side, however, was Bishop Leo of Catania, who was so pure and generous to the poor he was ruining the city for Elio. To combat this, Elio tried pretty hard to recruit disciples to help turn the place into a sort of ancient version of Pottersville, but ended up getting arrested by a group of centurions. He tells the centurions that if they allow him to escape, they'll each find a "mass of gold" where they plunge their sword in the ground. They agree, dig up their gold, and he makes his escape on a magic horse. When the centurions go back to where they re-buried their booty, all they find is a bunch of worthless metal.

Now I'll skip ahead here, but eventually a guy named Heraclides shows up to escort Elio to Constantinople — I can't remember why — where he meets the emperor, and naturally the two of them get into a pissing match. The emperor calls for his head, but just as the sword comes down, Elio changes into marble and the sword clanks onto the ground as his spirit flies back to Sicily. Unfortunately, the shore has been completely blanketed in holy water, incense and other Catholic stuff, so when he lands, his rib cage shatters and his legs break. His nemesis, the bishop, arrives and, seeing him in terrible agony, tells him to repent and ask God for forgiveness. He says: "I die as I have lived — in my sins," and then kicks the bucket.

I'm not sure if my mom knew this story, but I like to think that she did, and she gave one of her kids the name Eliodoro as a tiny form of rebellion towards my dad for raising us as Methodists.

◈

Dom was a strange kid.

When he was really little, he enjoyed staring at the sun. He says it didn't hurt really, but rather he would experience a neat, rhythmic thrumming in his head while he watched. Eventually, the sound would plunge into his chest and pulse away in there. Mom wasn't too far away the first time he did this, so when she saw him standing there, frozen, with tears running down his cheeks, she grabbed him before he went blind. After that, he says he had to sneak in little minisessions when Mom was distracted, which happened quite often once Gina came along on the last day of 1969.

Even today, his big, dark eyes have issues. Oh, he can see just fine, but he has always had trouble with subtle colours like pink and aqua — he sees them as grey — and now that he's hit forty, his night vision has gone straight down the toilet (not that it was ever that good anyway). Recently Small Carm had to put nightlights all over the building to prevent Dom from bumping into walls when he gets up to pee. Because of this, Dom hasn't driven since the mid-1990s. Then again he doesn't really have anywhere to drive to.

Dom also had a thing for insects when he was small.

There's a well-known Falconi family story of the time Mom was doing the laundry and was emptying everyone's pockets to make sure a library card or money didn't get destroyed. Going through Dom's pockets, she fished out one of those black-and-grey 35mm film canisters and opened it.

I think all of Spadina heard her "OH MIO DIO" as the tiny army of beetles, earwigs, big black ants, and worms spilled into her open palm, and then a few brave soldiers scurried up her arm. After that, she refused to look in anyone's pockets ever again, and Dom was encouraged to kill his pets before storing them.

I remember seeing a photograph of Dom, probably from the next year, smiling beside his second-prize science project, "Creatures and Things in Your Yard." It was so detailed with the pinned bugs and leaves all arranged by size and colour, with neat printing below each one. It looked pretty close to the exhibits at the Royal Ontario Museum with the exotic butterflies, except his was about junk he picked up in our backyard. I think there was even a piece of fossilized bubblegum.

Dom's head has always been a little too big for his body. I think this was a concern for the first few years of his life, but he eventually grew into it. He grew pretty tall, too, for a half-Sicilian kid: By Grade 8 he was probably close to his final height of five-foot-eleven, and he's always been skinny, too, which makes him look even taller. He's got a thick mop of glossy, dark brown hair and long, elegant fingers that are so feminine I get creeped out when I stare at them for too long. He is handsome, though: Dom bears a striking resemblance to the silent movie actor Buster Keaton, but without the trademark porkpie hat. He's got the same high cheekbones, long nose and wide-apart, sad eyes, but above those eyes is a big, fat, Italian unibrow. Put him in a black suit, and Dom would make a great undertaker.

※

By about Grade 7 or 8, I think it was clear that Dom wasn't going to be a Rhodes Scholar. He wasn't stupid by any stretch, but the way he processed information was different, and it started to show in his marks. Also, he would go into these mini-trances and his teachers would have to stand right in front of him and shout his name to snap him out of it. He'd lessen the tension by saying: "Sorry, I was visiting planet Xenon again." Dom wasn't the class clown, but when he did come up with a cute line, even the teacher would laugh and forget all about what a weird kid he was.

By Grade 9, his marks had plunged pretty low, so the guidance counsellor at Central Tech switched him to "basic" courses so he'd have a fighting chance. He did okay, but he dropped math and science as soon as he could, and he worked hard to maintain a sixty percent average. I think by the beginning of Grade 11, our parents decided that as long as he graduated, that would be fine.

Dom shut right down after The Incident. Other than on that first night, I don't think he spoke for a month, and during that period Small Carm kept threatening to take him to a shrink, and he kept walking away in defiance. He never cried like the rest of us, which made Small Carm really angry—"What, you didn't love your own mother?!?"—but my theory is that he was just processing this new information in his own way. When he did start speaking again, I remember him telling us he was going to the Eaton Centre a fair bit, which is funny because he's always hated large crowds and loud noises in general and shopping malls in particular. I think he just didn't want to be with us, but he didn't want to be alone, either.

Dom barely made it through Grade 12. I think he was allowed to graduate because he'd always been such a sweet guy and his teachers' hearts were collectively breaking because his mother had "gone missing."

It was Dom who came up with the name The Incident. He had been sick at home one day back in the late 70s and a 1967 movie with that title came on TV. The setting is, rather claustrophobically, a New York City subway car (which looks a lot like a Toronto subway car) and the main characters are two young punks who've just committed a string of petty crimes. One is a sociopathic Italian with big sideburns, played by Tony Musante, who did some Italian movies and then played Pete in *The Pope of Greenwich Village*; the other punk is portrayed by Martin Sheen. They board the subway and basically torment the passengers for half of the movie — one of them is Johnny Carson's sidekick Ed McMahon — until a broken-armed army private played by Beau Bridges beats the switchblade-wielding Musante using his cast as a bludgeon after he tries touching McMahon's little daughter. I know this movie made a big impression on Dom, because years later he'd warn me about the dangers of taking the subway.

"Try and take the streetcar or even the bus if you can, Flowerboy," he'd caution. "In the subway, you're basically trapped in a tin can, and it's easy pickings for psychopaths."

I don't really want to say this, but I think The Incident

dialled Dom's brain back a few years. He's never gone for a mental aptitude test, but my guess is he'd place somewhere between the ages of thirteen and fifteen. And this sounds selfish, I know, but that worked out pretty well for me while growing up: When I was ten and Dom was eighteen, he was a playmate when I desperately needed one. When I was fifteen and Dom was twenty-three, he was my confidant. When I left university and sleepwalked through my early twenties, he was my both my escape and something familiar that I could count on.

When Small Carm took over Falconi and had to fire Li-Na and Tina, Dom moved out of his room on the third floor and into their old offices on the second. They appealed to him, I think, because they were so uncluttered and generic. He pushed the big metal desk from one office into the other and bumped them together to make a big worktable for his model kits, and then he moved his little twin bed from upstairs into the empty office. By then we'd removed the wall that had been put up behind the second landing on the internal staircase. He's lived in those rooms ever since and has been quite comfortable, although during the first few years he didn't pin anything to the walls or bring down his finished model kits.

He did, however, keep right on building them.

He started out like most kids. His first kit, along with a six-pack of Testors paints and a few cheap brushes, arrived in the form of a Christmas present in 1974. It wasn't a muscle car or an army tank; it was a snap-together Monster Scene called "The Pain Parlour," which featured a hanging skeleton, a dungeon floor, a control panel and what looked to be Dr. Frankenstein's operating table, but I think Frankenstein's monster was part of different kit. It wasn't hard to put together, so he had it done pretty quickly; what really blew the family away was how well he had painted it. There were fine cracks on the skeleton, the stone floor was mottled and shaded, and he'd added wood grain to the operating bed. To do this, he'd had to mix complex colours and trim one of the brushes into a fine point using Mom's sewing scissors, and display incredible talent and insight for a seven-year-old.

I don't know if he did another monster scene after that (I do remember seeing a giant monster-insect when I was really small), but he did move to the more complicated kits — the ones with a dizzying array of parts that have to be glued together — soon afterward, despite being geared to children ten and up. He started with cars, building everything from the usual Chevelles, Mustangs and Z28s, to oddities like Czechoslovakian Tetras and Italian Isettas, and then he got into army tanks and jeeps. He went through an airplane phase, too, building everything from a German Messerschmitt with the sky camouflage, which required sponge-painting of clouds onto it, to Spitfires with the toothy mouths around the propeller and, finally, big B-52 bombers with a bunch of little servicemen inside. Aircraft carriers with a dozen tiny planes on deck, and warships with multiple guns and teeny-tiny antenna clusters came next. By that point, he was also painting barnacles and rust onto the ships' hulls and using a small crème brûlée torch to reshape the plastic to show battle damage. One time, he bought two of the exact same kits when they were on sale — a classic car of some sort — and made a driveway scene with the beat up, rusted parts car and the fully restored, shiny trailer queen that had been constructed with the parts car. It was awesome.

When somebody once asked him why he didn't get into model trains, he answered: "What good are those? They're already built. And all the little buildings, you just buy them and stick them there so the train can go around and around. "With this," he continued, holding up a kit of a Porsche 911, "I can make it look however I want. It can have polka-dots, it can have a Cadillac grille on it. You can't do that with a train."

When Falconi went bankrupt, he moved his model-making room into Dad's old drafting studio and installed wraparound shelves to display everything, plus added a few Ikea "Billy" bookcases for even more display. Except for that monster scene, he had saved pretty much everything, so my guess is that he must've climbed those stairs over a hundred times when he first moved down there, and that's if he carried a model in each hand. And within a few years there were dozens more on display. There are always more to come, too: In one corner, beside the golf clubs that Small Carm gave him, is a neatly stacked pile of shiny, cellophane-wrapped kits.

I still remember, in my late teens, checking in with him on nights I'd be going out for cappuccino with friends. "Whatcha working on, Dom?" I'd ask, surveying the forest of plastic "trees" holding hundreds of itsy-bitsy parts arranged under a little conga-line of mismatched desk lamps he'd picked up in thrift stores over the years.

"Oh hey Flowerboy, this one is pretty special," he'd say every time. "It's a big rig, a Kenworth K123 with a tilting sleeper cab. But I'm not going to paint it to look new. I'm going to make it look like it's been across the country a million times, maybe been in a minor accident."

"Cool, I can't wait to see it. Hey, I'm meeting Jennifer for coffee, d'ya wanna join us?" My two closest friends were both non-Italian girls at this point, and I already knew what Dom's answer would be.

"Oh, no, man, this thing isn't going to build itself!" He'd smile and shake his head while looking down at the crisp instruction sheet.

It was kind of comforting to go out for a few hours and then return home to see Dom still sitting there, hunched over his tidy little stacks of parts, dressed in his usual neat outfit: an expertly ironed, second-hand dress shirt, tan chinos, and squeaky-clean New Balance running shoes. Lost in concentration at this point, he'd give me a quick, dismissive wave hello while absentmindedly pushing out his bottom lip to blow a thick lock of hair out of one eye. Wedged into the other eye was a jeweller's loupe he'd picked up at one of those pawnshops on Church Street so he could really get into the fine gluing and painting detail he was known for.

While I doubt anyone else noticed, I know for a fact that every single model kit Dom built after The Incident had nothing to do with death or warfare.

After living like an ascetic in Li-Na and Tina's offices for the first few years, Dom finally decorated. He brought down his ridiculous "Justification for Higher Education" poster with the five-car garage filled with exotic cars (and the Spanish Revival cliff-house in the background), the one little framed photograph of Mom that he had without Dad in it, his yellowed *Toronto Sun* Sunshine Girl cut-outs from the eighties, and his prized possession, a Rush *Signals* poster he'd lined up in the pouring rain to have autographed by Geddy, Alex and Neil at Sam the Record Man back in the early eighties.

Canada's most famous musical export since Gordon Lightfoot and Anne Murray, Rush was, and still is, without a doubt, Dom's favourite band. While he'd had brief affairs with everyone from Led Zeppelin to ZZ-Top, Rush was like a religion to him. That they were from Toronto meant that he was like a Catholic living in Vatican City. If you asked him why he loved them, however, he wouldn't give you a sarcastic isn't it obvious stare, he'd get thoughtful and tell you it was because they weren't mindless rock-ons like AC/DC, with silly lyrics about big balls and TNT, or devil-worshippers like Ozzy and Black Sabbath. He liked Rush because they had songs about black holes and the power of radio and a red sports car, but they could still produce a head-banging riff worthy of the hardest rock when they wanted to, like on "Anthem" or "La Villa Strangiato." He liked that they used synthesizers, and that Neil, the drummer, was a quiet philosopher who wrote the lyrics. He knew every song on every album and had been to see them at Maple Leaf Gardens at least a dozen times despite finding the smell of marijuana nauseating. I know he once tried to smuggle in a painter's respirator, but the security guys confiscated it at the gate.

Rush's "Subdivisions," to Dom, was The. Best. Song. Ever. Written. He could listen to it over and over and never tire of it. When Gina got married in 1993 and actually moved to a subdivision near Woodbridge, he wouldn't shut up about it. He started walking around singing his own version of it with Gina's name inserted into the lyrics:

> *Sprawling on the fringes of the city*
> *Gina's got the order*
> *She's runnin' for the border*
> *In between the bright lights*
> *And the far unrolled strombol'*

After a few days of enduring his off-key stylings, I said: "Dom, you know that song is all about how young people feel trapped and creatively stifled in suburbia, right? When Geddy says: 'Nowhere is the dreamer, or the misfit so alone,' that's what he's talking about."

"Yeah, but he also says: 'Be cool or be cast out,' Freddy, so I think he really thinks suburbia is cool."

"Alright, well, you leave the bright lights of Spadina and go live with Gina and see how long you last, you misfit," I said, laughing.

He didn't leave, of course, but he did start visiting Gina about once a month after she and Rocco got settled in; he'd take the subway up to the end of the line and Gina would pick him up. Gina wasn't exactly in love with the old Falconi building, or Small Carm's rules for living for that matter. A few years later, when they started having kids, Dom had all the more reason to go up there and the kids got the best uncle they could ever imagine.

While Dom hasn't worked for the past decade, he's no layabout. He's actually more like our building's caretaker. He paints the exterior every five years, cleans the gutters in spring and fall, washes the windows, takes out the garbage, sets up the (humane) rat traps, rakes leaves in fall, shovels the snow and spreads salt on the sidewalk in winter, and checks the roof for drainage problems and raccoon penetration in summer. He even walks around with a can of 3-in-1 oil and keeps the door hinges and locks lubricated, inside and out. The place runs, basically, like a Swiss watch. Inside, however, he and Small Carm decided long ago that paying a woman to come in to do the dusting, mopping and most of the laundry was completely justified and, since they are essentially bachelor brothers, I can't say I blame them.

Dom has held real jobs in the past. During the last few years of high school and into his early twenties, he worked for a landscaping company out of Scarborough called Bladerunners Lawncare, and I remember him coming home filthy but happy. He learned all the different species of trees, a little about urban wildlife, weeding, and how to care for various plants. He also did hard, physical labour, which he didn't mind in the least.

"You know the best part?" he asked me once. "You show up at a place with a complete mess of dirt and mud in the front, and then you unload these big rolls of beautiful, living carpet. You instantly make it all good again, Freddy, and there's life there again, and I was a part of making that happen. And then little kids can go out and play on it the next day."

For a few years, he delivered Chinese food menus for the nice man who owned International Noodle House across the street, and then flyers for Gwartzman's Art Supplies a few doors over. He also worked at a carwash up at Bathurst and Dupont for a little while. I don't know if he got fired each time or just moved on himself, but I can't remember him ever having a job for more than two years, tops.

Then again, Dom doesn't really need money the way the rest of us do; other than his model kits, the only thing he likes to do is go into Kensington Market to buy used clothes, which he then irons back at home, and have a coffee, and most of the time he does that with me anyhow, and I pick up the tab. So, most of the money he did make back then was just handed over to Small Carm to put into the Falconi coffers; Dom called it the "Building No-Fun-d." Once in a while, Small Carm would ask Dom if he wanted to buy everyone dinner with his money and then he'd order a big plate of deli food from Shopsy's, but that's about it.

I know Small Carm was of two minds on Dom working anyway, since he told me as much. On the one hand, he wanted Dom to have as normal a life as possible and friends outside of Gina and me, but he had also become extremely protective of Dom since The Incident. They'd gone, ironically, from quarrelling teenage brothers to a couple of men who needed each other more than they ever could have imagined. I remember when we rented that Diane Keaton movie, *Unstrung Heroes*, we were trying to figure out who was more like the bachelor brothers played by Michael Richards and Maury Chaykin.

In fact, Small Carm was so protective, when I finally moved into my own place in 2003, he instituted a new rule. He asked me to stop bringing magazines or the full newspaper over for Dom when I came to visit, which was usually twice a week since I live a ten-minute walk away in a tiny one-and-a-half-storey cottage on Lippincott Street.

"Freddy, you've heard that expression 'If It Bleeds, It Leads' about newspapers, eh? Well I don't want Dom seeing all that violence," he said in his usual monotone. "Also, half of that stuff in there is a pumped-up version of what actually happened, and the other half is lies, so leave that crap at home, okay? If you have to bring him something, bring him the sports or automotive sections, since that's all he really needs to know about anyways ... or the sales flyer from the hobby store, ha ha."

So, I obliged. Except when there were cool stories about the Mafia or about things going on in the immediate neighbourhood that I thought he should know about; in those cases, I'd hide the clippings inside the permitted sections and hand them over to Dom with a wink.

There are two subjects to avoid with Dom: our parents and women.

Well, that's not entirely true. While Dom wants nothing to do with Big Carm, he will talk about Rosa, but only if it has to do with describing what she was like when I was born. And more often than not, that will morph into a description of her old neighbourhood, which was full of Sicilians back then, but isn't really any longer. While Mom didn't go to Coxwell and Danforth as much when I was growing up, Small Carm and Dom were there regularly in the 1970s so she could visit the few friends she'd made before she got married. She also liked shopping for fabric there because it was cheaper.

To hear Dom talk, that neighbourhood was like a Scorsese movie, with tons of middle-aged men pouring out of the men's clubs like T & M Sidewalk Café (EST 1970), Seb's Cappuccino or The Pachino Club, while tiny, four-foot-something ladies dressed in head-to-toe black would walk past tut-tutting while fingering the rosaries hanging from their belts. On Friday and Saturday nights, he says, there would be so many people on the sidewalk, they could hardly get by. Like the Jews of Spadina, the Sicilians of east-end Toronto didn't stay home and watch television. On weeknights, they took a constitutional after dinner and, when the work-week was over, that same walk also included extended socializing. I'm pretty sure I read somewhere that it was the Italians who loosened up the uptight Anglo-Saxon city government in the early 1960s and got a permit for the first sidewalk café.

There was a fruit market selling enormous tomato plants every two blocks (the best were at Prince of Wales, I'm told); there were wedding dress shops and gift shops where everyone bought their *bombonieres*, at least one religious supplies store, and, in the block between Woodmount and Woodbine Avenues, a half-dozen textile stores that Small Carm and Dom would get dragged into almost every time. Mrs. Bonfanti, the woman who co-owned the jewellery store with her husband, also taught French at the elementary school, St. Brigid's, that my Aunt Anna went to. Apparently, Mrs. Bonfanti would just write down the Italian word on the chalkboard and tell the class what to change to make it French, and the whole class would nod, knowingly, while the one poor Irish kid in the class would raise his hand in total confusion.

Parked along every residential street were beat-up 1960s Cadillacs and Lincolns, and in every front window, heavy drapes were strategically parted to reveal prominent cut-glass chandeliers dwarfing the tiny 1920s living rooms. And, underneath those chandeliers there was plastic-covered furniture and a shiny, faux-traditional coffee table with a piece of decorative Murano stretch-glass, usually in burnt orange. Because you had to show the rest of the neighbourhood you could afford these New World fineries, right? That your decision to move to "America" wasn't wrong. But, like the arms race, isn't that a moot point when everyone has the same stuff?

Strangely, while Dom talks with fondness about the Brio-and-pizza combos or the bitter lemon granitas Mom would buy for them from the old street vendors, he also gets excited when he describes visits to the Woolworth's and Kresge's Five & Dime stores that were beside each other near Woodbine Avenue, and had been there since the 1930s or 40s. One of them — if not both — had the classic lunch counter along one wall, complete with a tidy row of mushroom-shaped stools fronting a gold-speckled Arborite counter trimmed in ribbed stainless steel. Spaced evenly along the counter were ramrod-straight menus held aloft by stainless steel bars, shiny napkin dispensers, salt and pepper shakers, and ketchup and mustard squeeze bottles. Wrigley's Juicyfruit, Spearmint Certs, and cellophane wrapped butter tarts clustered near the cash register at one end, and smack-dab in the middle under the big vent hood was the open grill and deep-fryer station. There, taking centre stage, an old guy in a folded paper hat would create the Canadian experience for Small Carm and Dom in the form of burgers, clubhouses, grilled cheeses and diner lingo — "Combo three UP," "Western no smellies!" or "Two sunnies extra hash" — as two matronly women in chocolate-brown uniforms punctuated by shiny change-dispensers at their waists kept watch over their stool-swivelling charges.

"It was so crazy, Freddy, I wish you could've seen this place," he'd say, staring off into the distance. "I'd be eating my crinkle-cut fries and some guy would be right behind me picking up underwear from a bin!"

Now, about the opposite sex. I'm not going to say Dom is asexual, but it's a subject he's never been comfortable discussing. When he was in his mid-teens and Mom or Dad would ask him if he had a girlfriend, he'd blush and say something evasive like: "Yeah, I've got my eye on a few" and then laugh awkwardly, or change the subject altogether. He certainly never brought anybody home to meet them, and when he went to the prom, he went with a group of guys. Later on, when I started to date, he'd tell me how he wished he had been that brave when he was in high school.

When he and I would talk about girls, the conversation would usually go something like this:

"Freddy, didja see *Babe*watch last night?"

"Nah, I was out. Was it good?"

"Oh, man, that Pamela Anderson, I'd like to slip her the salam'!"

"Yeah, that's for sure. What was it about?"

"You think I remember, with all of those golden bozos swingin' around?"

So imagine my surprise when we were getting ready for our regular visit to Kensington Market not very long ago and he said: "Hey, Freddy, I'm going to introduce you to my girlfriend when we get there."

CHAPTER VI

☞ Gina ☜

I'M GOING TO be honest: there have only been about ten years in my life in which I have had pleasant interactions and conversations longer than one sentence with my sister Gina. And I'm thirty-two, so we've been talking less than a third of my life. Five of those years are the earliest years I can remember, from about age three to eight, and the other five are the past five years.

When I was super-little, but walking (so I guess about two?), I'm told Gina used me like a living doll; she'd take Mom's big, bulky stroller (the kind you see in antique stores now), throw me inside of it, wrap me up like a mummy, and then push me all around the alleyways behind our building while having one-sided conversations with me. When I got a bit older, like maybe five, I remember her giving me Ken and saying "you have to be Ken because he's the boy and I'll be Barbie and we'll have this whole game where they're married and going out to buy groceries and then they make dinner together, okay?"

And I'd agree, but then I'd be made to feel stupid because I wasn't making Ken do and say the right things. This would usually end with Gina grabbing Ken out of my hand and ending the game. However, to her credit, she'd usually find something else we could do together, like draw pictures or play hide-and-seek in the dark and scary basement of our building, where all the greasy tractor parts were stacked or crammed into stained plywood cubbies. I don't know if she was starved for playmates or if she genuinely liked me.

There was even a brief period where Gina was part of a group of neighbourhood friends I was in that Small Carm started calling The Glasgow Gang. This was because we all hung out in the long alley stretching between Glasgow Street, which was right behind the Falconi building, and Huron Street, the next street over. He then branched out and started to say things like: "Off to the Glasgow Green to battle it out, eh?" Or: "Who ya fightin' today, the Penny Mob?" which made absolutely no sense to us kids, but I'd later learn was a reference to gang warfare in Glasgow, Scotland, in the 1960s. Because we wanted to defy him, we changed the name to The Epitome Friends after an old, walk-up apartment building right at the mouth of the alley on Huron which had a plaque reading Epitome Apts over the door, and four of the twelve of us lived there. We pronounced it EPP-ah-tome rather than ee-PIT-a-mee, however. Even Dom would hang out with The Epitome Friends sometimes, which was cool because he was older.

We had secret note-drop locations, secret code-words, a secret alphabet, and a code of honour written up (and I'm sure a few other things I forget now) that, if you broke, would bring about severe penalties, like a rapid, burning noogie or someone stepping on your foot really hard. If you upheld the code well or ratted someone out who broke the rules, you'd get rewards, like a Tootsie Pop or a Lik-m-Aid. The best reward, as I remember, was a package of Sailor Tattoos. These came in a yellow, wax-paper envelope and, when you put them on, they looked totally different from other kid's tattoos. Instead of that bright-coloured vinyl that would crack and peel after a couple of hours, these were ink-based pictures of sailing ships and anchors and stuff, and they would move around with your skin, so they lasted for days and days. The older kids, like Gina and the two Chinese brothers who lived in the Epitome, Wěi and Fāng, would ride their bikes all the way over to the one convenience store on Bathurst Street that carried them.

Often, on the way back from those tattoo runs, the bike riders — which we called the Epitome Cavalry — would return with fascinating tales of carnage. There was this lone Yield sign at one of the intersections in Kensington Market, and a lot of the local, immigrant drivers had no idea what that word meant. One time, Gina, Fāng, and Noah Rothpearl watched in awe as a drunk driver ploughed into the side of a garbage truck at such an incredible speed, his car flipped onto its passenger door and slid along the road, sparks flying, for half a block. He was so loosey-goosey from the booze he was completely unhurt, however, so he just pushed against the shattered windshield and crawled out to survey the scene; well, his nose was so severely broken it was almost sideways on his face, Noah told us, but other than that, he was okay. In any case, a few years later there was a stop sign at that intersection.

Now all of this would have been a few summers after Gina stopped being a peaches-and-cream, frilly-dress-wearing little girl, and had become a tomboy. She had been named after Mom's favourite actress, Gina Lollobrigida, an ultra-feminine woman if there ever was one, so I know Mom was disappointed with the dirty hair, hockey jerseys, and boy's jeans. While she was still wearing tomboy clothes the next summer, when she was thirteen, she abandoned The Epitome Friends and became a cowgirl.

I think it was just before her thirteenth birthday — Luigina Rosabella Falconi was born on the last day of 1969 — that she began taking pony books out of the public library. There was the classic, *The Black Stallion* by Walter Farley, but there was also a bunch by Scottish author Patricia Leitch about a girl named Ginny and her horse Shantih, and a pair by an American author named Diana Walker that featured a girl named Joanna, called *Year of the Horse* and *Mother Wants a Horse*. Those last two were her favourites.

In the spring of 1983, with the moral support of our mother, Gina actually bought a horse. If memory serves, the farmer who sold her Becky, a retired quarter horse, was friendly with Big Carm and his farm was called Cachet Woods. It was located about three kilometres north of Falconi Farm, just above the airport.

Since Gina was becoming increasingly sullen, Mom figured a big responsibility that got her outside in the fresh air and outside of her own head would do her good, plus the thought of owning livestock reminded Mom of Sicily. (Even though she grew up in the city, she had cousins in the country.) Gina was so committed to the idea, she worked weeknights in the Falconi office from January until the end of April to raise the $300 to buy Becky. I think she earned extra money to pay for Becky's monthly boarding fees, too, but it's also possible that Mom picked up that tab.

That entire summer was all about Gina. When there wasn't company business at Falconi Farm that she could piggyback on, she would bug Mom and Dad to take her up to see Becky at the stable at least once per week, and, usually, she'd get her way. Small Carm was eighteen that summer, so he'd take care of me on Spadina. She'd come back all hoity-toity and talk about all the tricks she'd taught Becky the Wonderhorse and brag about how, in a few years, she'd probably be winning big competitions. She also thought that by the time she was eighteen she'd probably have to move to Alberta, "where they *really* understand horses." It was nauseating, but at least she was happy.

The whole thing unravelled when Mom got sloppy and Big Carm got a look at one of the monthly statements from the stable. Becky was costing something like $200 to $300 per month to feed, groom and house, and Falconi wasn't exactly doing gangbuster business in the early 1980s. He gave Gina an ultimatum about working for that money, and Gina, losing interest because it was October and riding season was almost over, didn't put in the hours. By mid-November, Becky had been sold to the stable-owner for $200.

Gina was heartbroken. And she was more moody than ever. The next year, when we lost our parents, Gina became a lost cause. After taking a month off school, her grades did settle back to A's and B's, but she had completely transformed herself physically. She went from tomboy/cowgirl to complete Lee Aaron *Metal Queen*. She didn't have a broadsword and loincloth like the heavy metal singer did on her album cover, but she did wear a studded leather arm cuff and had the wispy, feathered hairdo like Ms. Aaron. She also started wearing nothing but acid-wash jeans, dirty sneakers, and rock concert T-shirts. Oh, and tons of make-up, although she put most of it on once she got to school. I think she started smoking then, too, because I could smell it on her during the brief few seconds it would take her to run upstairs and slam her bedroom door.

Gina has always been very pretty. When she was small, she looked like a mini version of Rosabella, but with strawberry-blonde hair and hazel eyes that weren't quite as doe-like and far apart. She had the same porcelain skin, small nose, high cheekbones, and full lips. There are a few photos of the two of them in 1978 and 1979 wearing identical mother-and-daughter outfits that Mom had sewn, and they're as cute as kittens riding a unicorn that's pooping rainbows. Mom was so short, I think Gina had reached her height in those photos, too. However, when Gina hit twelve or thirteen, she shot up to her final five-foot-four.

Gina went to Harbord Collegiate like Big Carm and Small Carm, but I have no idea what subjects she liked or if she did anything extracurricular. Her entire personality was based on music. She got into tons of hard rock and heavy metal, but her favourite band seemed to change every six months or so. Def Leppard. Then the Rolling Stones. (I remember her telling everyone how they'd played this legendary, surprise concert across the street at the El Mocambo in 1977.) Then Girlschool. The Ramones for a little while. Dokken. Bon Jovi. Guns N' Roses, with a particular fascination with Slash. And the Rolling Stones again, which basically became the band she carried into adulthood. I think being part of the almost 60,000 people at the sold-out "Steel Wheels" show at the Skydome in December 1989 sealed the deal for her.

I envy her dedication. She gave all her energy to those bands, in much the same way Small Carm gave his energy to us, religion, and golf. I never got into music with that much fervour; I ping-ponged around. When I was little, I'd listen to Sinatra with Dad and dance around the Falconi office wearing one of Dad's hats and making everybody laugh. When I was a little older, I'd listen to Rush with Dom. I missed the whole New Wave thing in the 80s, although I did like Depeche Mode's *Violator* when it came out in 1990. I liked the Madchester scene of the early 1990s, which produced bands like the Stone Roses, Happy Mondays and Inspiral Carpets — the ones that all used the same drumbeat — but not enough to go to their concerts. Then I got into the swing dance revival of the late 1990s, which included trying cigars and martinis, which made me kind of ill. These days, at work, my crew and I put on Toronto's Classic Rock station, Q107, since that's the one we can all agree on; they play a lot of Rush, and I smile and think of Dom every time.

During Gina's last year of high school, as part of a business class, she interned at a travel agency. She kept meeting these young gals who worked for the big tour operators, like Signature Vacations and Sunquest, and they kept telling her about job openings down in the tropical countries. This sounded pretty good to her: Not only would she be down in the sunshine all the time, it would be a great way to instantly shed all of those rules that apply to Italian-Canadian girls but not to boys. I'm not sure what sort of conversations Small Carm had with Gina when he took over the family, but I'm guessing he wasn't exactly a "go and explore your feelings" kind of hippie-dad with her.

So for the summer of 1987, since she was only seventeen-and-a-half, she waited it out and stayed on at the travel agency part-time. But on Monday, January 4, 1988, four days after her birthday, she came home from work and announced that she would be joining Sunquest's Mexico team as a full-time employee in one week. Obviously, this had been in the planning stages for months, and Small Carm was pissed.

"I've just had the second worst year of my life and now you're leaving us?" He was referring, of course, to the collapse of Falconi Farm Equipment the previous year.

"Well I hate to inform you of this, dear brother, but these past few years haven't been a Walt Disney movie for me either. Besides, what do you need me for here? To cook? Freddy's going to be thirteen this year, so he can lift a finger to feed himself once in a while. And Dom ... well, Dom is kinda useless but he's a sweetie. You'll be fine."

I have no clue how many oats Gina sowed down there, but she was with Sunquest for over four years and eventually worked all over Mexico, so I'm guessing quite a few. The very protective Small Carm couldn't stand not knowing what she was up to, so he decided he was going on a Mexican vacation a few months after she went down there. I don't think it went very well, because there is no photographic evidence of that trip, and he didn't say very much when he got back. He didn't even have a tan. A year later, however, they must have buried the hatchet, because he came back with a tan, beaming, *and* with a sheaf of photos showing brother and sister smiling like old pals at a zip line station in the jungle, the Mayan pyramids at Chichen Itza (which Dom and I called Chicken Pizza of course) and as part of a snorkelling group. She even came back for Christmas break that year.

He skipped 1990 but went again in 1991 and 1992 and brought back even more photos and, surprisingly, a few tales of drinking tequila with Gina and her workmates. Those photos are the only proof I have that Mr. Dress Pants, Small Carm, has a pair of legs. I still have never seen his feet.

When Gina finally came back to Canada in the late spring of 1992, three things were very different. I don't know how to put this first one without sounding insensitive, so I'll just say it: Her butt was absolutely enormous, like a different body had been grafted onto her at the waist. She'd always been a smallish girl on top, with not much of a chest, but other than having slightly pronounced hips, she was pretty proportionate. After four-and-a-half years of Mexican cuisine, however, she looked comical.

The second thing that was different was that she could now speak Spanish, which was pretty cool.

And the third thing was that she had an engagement ring on her finger. A big one. And the big guy who gave it to her was standing beside her when Small Carm arrived at the airport.

Her beau, thankfully, was not an opportunistic Mexican looking for quick citizenship, but rather a nice, albeit slightly mookish, Italian boy from Woodbridge named Rocco Sarli. Rocco, then twenty-seven, looked like a chubby version of the actor Michael Madsen, and one of Gina's favourite movies at that time was *Thelma & Louise*. Rocco had been working as a bartender for five years at a resort that Gina dealt with on a regular basis. This resort also happened to be fairly close to the little apartment building that Gina was living in during her final year in Cozumel. I don't know how many margaritas it took to get Gina and Rocco from friendly to dating to a marriage proposal, but Gina's always been whip-smart, so I don't think she made the decision quickly or lightly.

Rocco was very polite when he met us, and he impressed the crap out of Small Carm when he asked if they could step outside and discuss the upcoming marriage "like men," to which Gina rolled her eyes and said: "You don't need his approval, Rock!" I remember peeking out the back window and seeing the two of them standing in the backyard, underdressed in the cold, smoking cigars and gesticulating with their hands, like they were negotiating a big corporate merger. After they left—they were going to be staying with his parents in separate rooms until Gina found an apartment, Small Carm made his judgment: "He's okay, he comes from a good family. He's got a sister, too, so that will be nice for Gina. I think he really loves her."

Dom, on the other hand, decided he was going to start calling Rocco Sir Mix-a-Lot or Mack Daddy during the year leading up to their marriage, and he would often dance around the room singing "I like big butts and I cannot lie!" Dom did this purely for his own entertainment however, as he was too sweet a guy to ever have done this in front of Rocco or Gina. I did catch him humming it quietly to himself during their very small and very un-Italian marriage ceremony at City Hall. The culturally unplugged Small Carm, during that whole time, had no clue what Dom was talking about: "Mix a lot? A lot of what? Drinks? Of course he does, he's a bartender, you *scemo!*"

∽

Rocco and Gina had both saved up a lot of money working in Mexico, so they were able to put a healthy down payment on a house up in the very Italian suburb of Woodbridge while they waited to get married. After the Big Day, Gina gave up her bachelor(ette) apartment and they just moved right in, since they'd had almost a year to paint, decorate and furnish.

While I figured they'd purchased a four-thousand-square-foot, faux-historic McMansion with plastic columns holding up a Styrofoam pediment like a lot of houses up there, I was actually pleasantly surprised. Their place was an architect-designed home in Seneca Heights, a neighbourhood built in the late 1950s. It was technically in Woodbridge but psychologically separated from it by the Humber River, which was just fine by me. Their house, at the corner of Wigwoss and Monsheen drives, which I'd later learn Gina picked out, was a wide, low, ranch-style with an almost-flat roof held up by thin wooden posts, meaning her indoor floor area wasn't cluttered by big, fat, load-bearing walls. It was an L-shaped home set back nicely on a corner lot, and the garage was perpendicular to the street. In a couple of places, it had almost floor-to-ceiling windows and, even cooler, it had something I'd only seen in the architecture books up until that point, and mostly on houses in California: a semi-sheltered, outdoor courtyard that you had to walk through to get to the front door. I remember pausing there for a few seconds the first time Small Carm, Dom and I drove up to see the place. That sense of being shielded by the building, of controlling and containing a little piece of nature, of having somewhere to be after you got out of the car but before you opened the front door, it just blew me away.

"Hey, Flowerboy, snap out of it," Small Carm said, ringing the doorbell with his right hand while a tapered box of *panettone* dangled from his left. "Is there a naked lady shape in the clouds or something?"

"I thought you'd like this place, Freddy," Gina said after she'd taken our jackets. "We bought it from the original owner, too, and they told us the name of the architect who designed it. Jerome Markson. A Toronto guy. And they said he's still around, still designing things."

"Wow, that's so amazing," I replied. "If you ever want to do an expansion or something, you could call him up so you don't, you know, mess up these great lines. Maybe I should go meet him, see what kind of a guy he is? You know, for research."

"Up to you, but don't promise him anything, okay," she said, laughing. "We just bought the place and we don't even have enough furniture to fill it yet."

I think that was the first time I'd exchanged more than a few words with her since we were kids. It was nice. We even chatted a bit more about architecture that evening. She surprised me by saying she'd really loved going to Lord Lansdowne school because she knew it was special; she also thought it was a drag when Small Carm pulled me out and sent me to that "drag of a bunker" Catholic school. She said she'd completely understood why Dom gave up his room and moved into the empty 1960s offices on the second floor after Li-Na and Tina were let go. She told me that some of the beach towns she'd worked at in Mexico, like Playa del Carmen, had some neat 1950s and 60s buildings, and whenever she'd drive by one of them, she'd think of me. It was all very surprising.

Our newfound friendship, unfortunately, was put on hold for a few years. While Dom began his once-a-month overnight visits, I was finishing high school and applying to Trent. I went over a few times in the summer of 1994 and had some nice conversations, but once I was in Peterborough, I was incommunicado. And that's the way I wanted it.

Dom and Gina, however, who had always got along well because of their mutual love of animals, became tighter than ever. I don't mean this to sound like I'm making fun of Dom, because I'm not, but I think Gina loved spending time with him because he'd changed the least since The Incident. He still cracks the same stupid jokes, still pulls out obscure references from TV sitcoms or movies, still has the same hobbies and interests. When you spend time with Dom, it's like the nightmare never happened. It's comforting.

Around the same time I was dropping out of Trent, Gina was pregnant with her first child. There were some complications with the pregnancy and it was tense for a while, but as I was apprenticing as a junior drywaller, a red-headed Giuseppe (Joe) Domenic Sarli came into the world pretty much on schedule. It was nice that Rocco and Gina had given him Nonno Joe's name, and it wasn't surprising that Dom was over the moon that his name was in there too. He was also asked to be one of the godparents, so he danced around saying: "I'm gonna make Giuseppe an offer he can't refuse" for about a week.

It took Gina and Rocco a while to have their second. Finally, with three weeks left to go in the twentieth century, they produced a beautiful, chubby, brown-haired baby girl. And while she'd always been expected to come out in early December, Gina had been calling this her Millennial Baby, just like Dom had been Mom's Centennial Baby.

Millennia Serafina Sarli was so named because Gina had read in her baby magazines that a lot of German women expecting at the end of 1999 had invented this as a new name. We call her Millie, and, this time, Small Carm got the godparent honours.

With the demands of motherhood, I didn't see Gina very much over the next few years. Holidays and birthdays, of course, but while she and Dom were together quite a bit (and always at her place), I felt pretty detached from the whole uncle thing, at least in those early years. By the summer of 2003, however, when her kids were a little older, Gina started bringing them down to the Falconi building for visits, which was a surprise. When I bought my little cottage on Lippincott, we even had a few big family gatherings there.

Once, Gina left the bambino and bambina with Rocco and came to the old neighbourhood to hang out with Dom for the whole day. I guess Dom had forgotten, but we were scheduled for one of our regular excursions into Kensington Market; no biggie, we made it a threesome. We hit all of the cool used clothing stores — Gina even bought herself a bandana — and went for cappuccinos. She paid. We walked west along College into the heart of the old Little Italy where Nonno Joe and Nonna Ines had lived briefly, and Mom had escaped to before she and Dad got married. We shot the breeze and tried to spot as many of the old store signs from that time as we could.

There weren't many left; the odd shoe store, bakery, bridal store and pizzeria. There were the institutions, like Café Diplomatico, which had been there since 1968, and CHIN radio (which Mom would listen to when she got homesick), which went on the air in 1966 thanks to local legend Johnny Lombardi. Lombardi had started the station after being a musician with the Big Bands, serving in WWII and running his own grocery store.

"Look at this one," Dom said, pointing to a butcher shop sign that had to be from the early 1960s because the phone number was written "LE6-4593" at the bottom. "That drawing of the lamb's head, it's so nice; he looks kinda smart, eh?"

"He does," Gina said. "He looks wise because the Italian and Portuguese people, they came from countries that have always respected livestock. They knew their lives depended on their animals, and they valued them more because of it."

"Yeah, unlike here," I said. "Here, you've got an ad with a cartoon pig holding a plate of bacon saying: 'I'm delicious!' and nobody thinks it's weird."

"That's so true, Freddy," Dom said. "People here don't value the animals that give their lives for us, do they?"

"They certainly don't," Gina said, answering for me.

∽

That fall, I actually went to see the architect of Gina's house. It was a beautiful, sunny day, and I had time off from work, so, on impulse, I looked him up online. His firm, Markson Borooah Hodgson Architects, had a website with pictures of their work — the usual suburban office buildings, art galleries and government buildings — and little bios on each partner. I learned that Markson had been born in Toronto and had graduated from the University of Toronto in 1953 and started his own practice in 1955.

I picked up the phone and called their office, and was soon chatting with him.

"Seneca Heights. Yeah, of course I remember that one. We did that for Jack Grant, who owned the land. He was a childhood friend and one of the great characters of the century," the architect said, laughing. "What are you doing for lunch?"

As red and gold leaves blew across Poplar Plains Road and I downshifted to make pedaling easier to get up to midtown (so I wouldn't be *shvitzing* too badly), I gazed at the big architect-designed houses and let my mind wander. What would it be like working as a journeyman architect in a big office? Just one guy sitting at one of a hundred desks that belong to celebrity architect Zaha Hadid or Frank Gehry, for instance? Unlike a small company like Falconi, the focus wouldn't be on you all the time, but on the big name, and all you'd have to do is work out little details, go to lunch, and then work some more until you punched out for the day and went for beers. It made me think of a funny little jazz song I heard once called "I Want to be a Sideman." I remember the first verse:

I want to be a sideman
Just an ordinary sideman
A go along for the ride man
Responsibility free

Then, you could visit the swoopy Phaeno Science Centre in Germany during your vacation and point to a door frame, or maybe the place where two different materials join together, and say to your wife: "See that? I drew that, and now it's real!"

I met Markson at a Japanese noodle place on Eglinton Avenue across from his office. Not only did he insist I call him Jerry, he'd brought along one of the original sales brochures from the Seneca Heights development.

"You can see the different models in here," the affable, seventy-something architect said, laying the brochure between the steaming bowls. He had white hair trimmed in a Caesar-cut, and small round eyeglasses that framed curious eyes. "The ones I did are called the M-1, M-2 and M-3, and the ones my professor did are B-1, B-2 and so on."

"Your professor?"

"Michael Bach. An Estonian. He had taught me at U of T. I was asked to suggest a second architect for the project and there were almost none at that time that I cared about. Well, except him," he said with a wry smile.

Outside, storm clouds had gathered and it had suddenly become very dark; the rhythmic clicking of rain tapped at the big window that framed the sleek, glass-and-steel building across the street that housed Jerry's practice.

"This is it, the M-1!" I said, stabbing the line drawing of a house with my finger. Above it was another drawing of an ideal 1950s family and the title "FINE CONTEMPORARY HOMES OF DISTINCTION."

"That courtyard before you walk in, it's so soothing," I told him.

"Thank you. It's kind of an enveloping, transitional thing. Then again, if it's raining, you still get wet," he said, laughing. "You like architecture? You seem to be interested beyond just knowing who designed your sister's house."

I told him about growing up loving it, and how I'd thought of studying it, but had decided to keep it at arm's length. I told him how I'd studied environmental science instead, but hadn't completed my degree. I told him about how much I had loved the Ron Thom campus at Trent, and of course Jerry mentioned that he had known him. I told him about the wild school we Falconis had all attended as kids and how much we had loved it. We talked about the Modernist movement of architecture and his personal influences, Alvar Aalto from Finland, the Swiss-French master Le Corbusier, and the legendary American, Frank Lloyd Wright.

When I told him about the Falconi building on Spadina, he surprised me by saying he knew it, since he'd grown up in a big house across the street from the Art Gallery of Ontario, a ten-minute walk away. He was nine years old when my grandparents opened the showroom, and he was one of the many kids in the area who would ask his parents to stop so he could look at the big red tractor in the window.

It was one of the nicest lunch dates I'd ever had, since I hardly ever get the chance to discuss architecture with anyone. I was about to ask him what would be involved in becoming an architect but, typical me, I chickened out at the last minute.

Black Hole and Main Egg

A white triangle is peeking out of my mailbox. As soon as I grab the envelope, I can tell from the teenaged-boy handwriting that it's from Dom. In big letters across the middle is "TOP SECRET" and, at the bottom, there's a tiny little "EF."

Dom and I are not supposed to be talking: We Falconi kids have all been sequestered for the duration of Small Carm's trial. Which means he must be going nuts pacing around the gloomy Falconi building all by himself.

I stuff the envelope down the front of my pants before I open the door. All of this betrayal stuff has me thinking of *The Godfather*, I guess, since I actually look over my shoulder as I unlock my front door to see if there are any telephoto lenses poking out of the tinted windows of drab grey sedans. The coast seems clear. Maybe there are goons waiting for me inside, but they'll just break my pinky fingers as a reminder that I need to testify "right." Thankfully, it's so quiet in here I can hear my own heartbeat. I pick up Nonno Joe's engraved letter opener that decorates the hall table and spear Dom's letter. It slices through the crease like butter. This is all there is:

"Main Egg — 1 Drop — E.F."

It takes a second, but it all comes rushing back. The Epitome Friends would leave each other spy notes around the neighbourhood — "One of Jimmy Caluzzi's balls was hanging out of his shorts in gym class today," that sort of thing — and we had about ten drop locations. I remember one was on Ross Street under the aluminum finial of Mrs. Whiston's left fence post; another was behind a loose brick at the Becker's on Beverly Street. But I forget the others since I don't have the *Rain Man*-like memory that Dom does for these sorts of things. And because he knows that I don't, he's chosen our most popular drop, the Main Egg (there wasn't a secondary egg so I don't know why we called it that), a.k.a. the huge, basic igneous boulder that sits as sentry/sculpture in front of Lord Lansdowne School. Backhoes clanged against this monster back in 1961 when they got to about twelve feet down in the soil, and the theory is that it was carried here by a glacier during the ice age. In any case, there's a thin gap at the bottom that's great for holding notes that I assume is still there.

I walk over immediately. It's there all right. I grab Dom's note and walk into the shade, out of sight of the cars whizzing along Spadina. It reads: "I miss you, man! If it wasn't for the O.J. stuff that we watched together, I wouldn't have a clue what it means that we're being sea-quested from each other. Why have the legal guys decided there's no preliminary inquiry? The wiki entry is too confusing, and they trapped us at home just before I could ask you. I'm not gonna lie, bro, I'm friggin scared as hell: what's gonna happen to Small Carm now that everyone knows about his OPUS DAY thing? I'm on the stand in two days and I'm really worried about those eggheads grilling me and then pouring salmoriglio sauce on me. What should I say??!? Please leave a note here for me by 8 p.m. tonight."

I check my watch. It's already going on seven, so I walk over to the Smoke & Variety store on College and buy a cheap ballpoint pen and notepad from their sad little stationary section. I write:

"Bro, I miss you too. Basically, no preliminary is bad: it means the Crown — that's the lawyers working against Small Carm — feel they have a strong case, and the judge has agreed with them. I'm pretty sure anyway. Don't worry about Opus; remember what Gina said our lawyer is going to do with those special witnesses. I'm on the stand the day after you and I'm scared too! But, listen Dom, don't lie! Tell them exactly what you did that day, step-by-step, and in your own words. I'm sure they won't blame you for anything! You were only 17, which is underage, remember! Did you call P. before we were sea-quested?!? I'll check to see if you've left me a note by noon tomorrow."

It's the next day, and there's another note from Dom.

"Flowerboy: Yes I called 'P' and thank you for not writing her name in case these notes fall into the wrong hands!"

I know it's crazy, but it crosses my mind that maybe Dom is getting a tiny bit of pleasure in playing spies, like the old days. At least it's something to distract us.

He continues: "She and her mother forgive me, even after what happened with the car. After I told them about the whole thing with Small Carm on trial, they say they support us and will help any way they can. I'm having trouble sleeping — I'm writing this at TWO A.M. man! — but I will do what you say and tell the truth. Look, I want to keep writing you but on my way here this morning there was a helicopter and I could swear it was following me! Either we change the drop location or we just stop. Actually, let's just stop, it's reminding me too much like that scene in *Goodfellas* near the end. Oh, and burn this note after you read it. I'm serious."

I'm on my way to the convenience store to buy a book of matches. Seriously.

CHAPTER VII

☞ Kensington Market ☜

WE'D BEEN HANGING out in Kensington Market for an hour and, despite his promise, Dom still hadn't introduced me to his girlfriend. We were in Exile, one of the many used clothing stores on Kensington Avenue, and he was taking his sweet time rifling through men's dress shirts as I grew more and more impatient.

"Shazbot!" he shouted, and it took me a second to dial up *Mork & Mindy* in my brain's Rolodex. "Here's an Armani shirt, beautiful, for just six bucks!" He pulled it out of the long, low rack quickly, even though there was no one else in the store. "Some *coglione*, right now, is at Harry Rosen's paying a hundred and fifty bucks for this. All I have to do is iron it and it'll look as good as his. What a *sacco di doccia* that guy is." He laughed to himself, since the literal translation of douchebag into Italian doesn't actually mean anything.

Dom does get a lot of pleasure from smoothing out his wrinkled Kensington treasures. In fact, he learned his ironing skills from the master, our mother, who also taught Small Carm back in the early 1970s but didn't bother with Gina and me. Dom has told me on more than one occasion that when Rosabella Caporuscio wanted to earn a little money as an adolescent, she took in ironing since it wasn't permitted for a nice Sicilian girl to get a part-time job until her late teens. As the family story goes, she got so good at ironing, a couple of her clients accused her of sending their stuff out to the dry cleaners, so she was forced to pull out the ironing board and set it up right there under the low living room chandelier to give a demonstration.

Since Dom was a much better student than Small Carm (although he does do his pants and they look pretty good), there was no question that Mom's vintage ironing board would become Dom's property when she passed away. He's now got it in his model-making room on the first floor, and sometimes when I come over I catch him in his Zen-like ironing trance. If I don't say anything, he won't notice that I'm standing five feet away from him.

"Dom, that's a great shirt," I said, snapping myself back to reality, "but you promised me you were going to take me to meet your girlfriend, and it's already two-thirty. What gives?"

"Patience, Freddy Flowers. She's only working a half-shift today, so she's on from three until seven. Let's get a little cappuccino at Moonbean and wait it out, okay?"

We walked south to the little café with the big seafoam-coloured sign and, much to our surprise, a nice table right at the edge of the property was available. I parked Dom there (so we could sit like Europeans, facing the sidewalk, and watch the parade of wonderful weirdos go by) while I went inside to order. Alan, the owner, who looks like a sanitized version of Frank Zappa, greeted me when I walked in, so I just held up two fingers to indicate two of the usual. He nodded.

The great thing about Kensington is that there will never be a Starbucks here. I like Starbucks in a pinch, but Kensington has always been an anti-establishment, free-wheeling, no-holds-barred kind of place, and a corporate store would ruin the vibe. Most of the shops are shabby little places that have so many layers of poor quality renovations strangling them, it's doubtful a corporate store would be able to peel away enough junk to feel comfortable here. Kensington signage is often homemade, the outdoor display tables are cobbled together with spit and shoe polish, and the scent of spices, fish, marijuana, and overripe fruit combine with tinny reggae music or live blues bands to overwhelm the senses; in other words, the definition of cool here is different and it always has been. And while I doubt you could legislate against a chain store coming in, there's some kind of unwritten code between property owners that ensures it will never happen. Maybe that's why, last year, Kensington Market became a National Historic Site of Canada.

It's certainly been a historic site for generations of Torontonians. When I was a teenager in the early 1990s, it was the place to buy beat-up plaid shirts if you were into Grunge, knock-off Chuck Taylor running shoes, and a Trinidadian "doubles" for a quick curry lunch; a decade before that, it was where New Wavers and Mods came to buy army jackets, skinny ties and combat boots, since there were (and still are) army surplus depots and tons of used clothing stores, though the owners and store names have changed. You can also buy produce, dried beans, baked goods, every kind of cheese imaginable, and fresh fish — all from specialty vendors, and most from converted Victorian-era houses.

The market started out because Toronto's Jewish population, when it exploded in size, began to move out of a big, notorious slum called The Ward—which is where our futuristic City Hall now stands—and into the much nicer homes on Kensington, Augusta and Nassau streets in the 1920s and 30s, which makes a lot of sense considering many worked in the needle trade just a few blocks south. At first, the entrepreneurial types sold stuff from wheeled carts in front of their homes on Thursdays and Fridays before the Sabbath; this was known as the Jewish Market and I doubt Anglo-Saxon Canadians even knew it existed. Kensington Market was secluded and it had the feeling of a little European village, so people felt safe doing things a little differently, and soon that cozy and safe vibe meant that other New Canadians started shopping there as well.

There were so many Jews living in the area that, by 1927, money was raised to build the beautiful Kiever Shul, which still stands at the corner of Bellevue Avenue and Denison Square and, in 1930, another synagogue known locally as the Minsk opened up on St. Andrew Street.

Eventually, those wheeled carts morphed into large stands set up on the front lawns of the homes, and some merchants were so successful they quit their jobs in the Spadina sweatshops. I'm guessing by the time Nonno Joe started shopping in Kensington in the 1940s, there were actual *inside* stores too. There isn't much about it in his diary since going shopping is pretty mundane stuff, but he does mention a store everyone called Little Eaton's in the 1950s. (The big department store that everyone shopped at downtown was called Eaton's.) It was, naturally, an old house rammed with assorted machine parts, gadgets and other weird items in every room and also in the alleyway outside. The proprietor had, of all things, a bunch of metric-sized bolts that Nonno Joe needed for a customer, and I guess that surprised him enough to jot it down.

There was another swell of Jewish immigrants after World War Two, but by the late 1950s, many had moved up to the greener, more suburban areas along Bathurst Street, which left Kensington open for the next wave of new merchants, the Portuguese.

In the 1960s and 70s, residents and merchants in the Market successfully fought about five different groups that were threatening to change things — an expressway, urban renewal and a university expansion among other things — in order to keep it intact for even more waves of immigration: the Chinese, Vietnamese and South Asians. It also became a place where Bohemian-types, like actors, artists, and musicians, could afford to live in the 1970s, so health food restaurants and used clothing shops popped up beside the fish markets and fruit stands to service them.

Just about the time live chickens were banned from the Market in 1982, live bands started to perform in semi-legal spaces like the Quoc Te restaurant. When the inevitable drugs crept in, residents and merchants were assisted by, of all things, a group of straight edge punk rockers living in the area; they banded together and eradicated the problem.

Kensington Market, despite the myriad changes over the last seven or eight decades, still does feel very much like a village. It's safe, it's weird, it's colourful, and it doesn't apologize to anybody. It's the exact opposite of the Eaton Centre, and I think that's why Dom loves it so much. Small Carm, on the other hand, abhors it; he thinks it's full of neo-hippies and poseurs who "wouldn't know something cool if it fell on them."

Small Carm once asked me: "Why do they all dress like farmers over there? Plaid shirts, CAT Diesel Power baseball caps, dirty ripped pants? Why don't you bring one of your buddies over here, Freddy? I'll put him on the Falconi Finch and see if he can handle it. Now there's something we could make into one of those YouTubes you and Dom are always watching."

"They're not my 'buddies' Small Carm," I said. "And you know I go there with Dom because it's one of his favourite places in the world. And listen, maybe if it wasn't for those hipsters, the fruit markets, bakeries and cheese places would be gone by now, and we'd have to walk a lot farther to get your precious Parmigiano-Reggiano. Hipsters grow up and want to make nice food too, you know. They're what's keeping that area alive."

Knowing he was beat, he just mumbled "dirty hippies" and walked away.

"Hey, I thought I was the space cadet in this family!" Dom said, snapping me out of my reverie as he drained his cup of its second espresso. "It's almost three o'clock. You wanna walk over to Pineapple Head to meet my lady friend?"

Pineapple Head, it turned out, was a lovely little boutique that'd been open for about a year. Just a few doors south of one of the pioneering vintage clothing shops, Courage My Love, Pineapple Head was a combined custom jewellery shop and vintage clothing store with some kitschy knickknacks thrown in to add visual interest and fill the shelves. Like most Kensington shops, it was housed in a Bay-n-Gable home, and it was painted in tropical turquoise with dark orange window trim. There were also little, bright yellow, stencilled pineapples all over the brickwork. Like Montreal with its outdoor-staircase apartments or Cape Cod with its famous cottages, the Bay-n-Gable is a Toronto fixture: a skinny Victorian house, usually semi-detached, with a two-storey bay window stretching up to a gabled roof.

In the front room, which would have been the home's parlour, there was a big ornate table with a dozen mannequin heads sitting by the bay window. Each head — the necks were displaying the necklaces — had been painted yellow and crowned with pineapple leaves instead of hair. In the centre of the room, there were three big glass cases to display rings and bracelets, and overhead there was a light fixture made out of an exploded dressmaker's form. In one corner, a twin stack of vintage, turquoise-painted suitcases supported a piece of cut glass for the cash register and business card holder; in the other there was an actual, beat-up jeweller's bench cluttered with all sorts of tiny tools. An arrow hanging from the ceiling pointed to a hallway leading to what would have been the dining room and kitchen. It read: "HATS AND SHIRTS AND SHOES, OH MY!"

When the floorboards groaned under our combined weight, a short, slightly chubby girl appeared from the hallway. She looked to be about twenty years old, and had dirty-blonde hair styled in a pixie cut. When light from one of the overhead halogens hit her face, a little diamond stud flashed from the side of her nose. Her round face split into a huge smile when she saw us.

"Hiya, Dommy! What's shakin'?"

"Hi Penny! Nothin' but the bacon, as always," he answered with a little chuckle. "This is my little brother, Freddy, the one I was telling you about."

I stuck out my hand. Although hers was a little moist and clammy, she took mine firmly and shook it vigorously.

"You're the one who loves flowers, right?"

"Yes, my nickname is — "

"Freddy Flowers, duh, I know," she said as she released my hand and turned to Dom. "Did you bring me an Italian coffee?"

"Oh man, no, I forgot!" he said apologetically. "I guess being with my brother had me distracted. Next time, okay? Remember I told you it's called a cappuccino."

"Cappuccino, schmappa-beano," she said while screwing up her face and sticking out her tongue.

"Is your mom here?" Dom asked.

"No, she's not back until five. She's out doing errands. I'll tell her you stopped by, okay?"

"Yeah, okay. Smell ya later," he said.

The little bell tinkled and the pane of glass rattled as we closed the door. We walked down the steps, past the racks of funky used clothing in the front yard, and started walking the few blocks to the Falconi building in silence. I could see out of the corner of my eye that Dom was smiling to himself.

"So ...? What do you think?" he asked.

"That was her? I thought maybe it was the mother we were talking about. She looks pretty young Dom, no offense."

"Freddy, she's thirty-five!" he said, laughing. "I asked her one time."

"Really? Wow."

"Maybe it's because she talks funny, like her tongue is too big, that threw you for a loop? I know it makes her sound young. Anyway, I think she has the face of an angel."

I didn't know how to break it to him, but her face, although indeed beautiful and cherub-like, also suggested Down syndrome. As we turned onto Spadina and were jostled by a dozen Chinese elbows, I moved in as close as I could to Dom's ear.

"You know she may have a genetic condition," I said as quietly as I could. "There's this thing called Down —"

"Down syndrome, I know Freddy," he answered at regular volume, then laughed. "D'you think I just fell off the eggplant truck? I asked her about it. So she's got an extra chromosome, big deal. I think it makes her extra-special."

Five hours later, my head was still processing that Dom had a crush on a girl, so I picked up the phone and dialled the familiar Falconi number to get more details. Her full name, Dom told me, is Penelope Keyes, and she'd lived in Toronto all her life. She was raised by a single mom, Deborah, who had her when she was twenty-one. Penny's father, a *sacco di doccia* if there ever was one, couldn't handle having a special-needs baby and hightailed it back to his native Halifax, Nova Scotia, and hasn't been heard from since. Luckily, because of a great family support system, Penny had a village of grandparents, aunts, uncles and cousins who stepped in to share child-rearing responsibilities while Deborah finished school and became an accountant.

Penny went to a regular elementary school with regular kids. While it took her longer to be understood when she spoke, her work with a speech pathologist — who she was meeting with even before she started school — had her ramp up pretty quickly. Like all kids, she was better in some subjects and worse in others. She needed a tutor for some of them to maintain good marks. She graduated, with honours, from a cool high school called the Etobicoke School of the Arts. She went to the prom, with a boy, just like the other girls.

Her mom retired at fifty-five last year and, after a life-long love of thrifting and years of jewellery-making courses at Harbourfront Centre, fulfilled her dream and opened Pineapple Head. Penny, who had experience working retail jobs in her twenties but more recently worked at a day care teaching arts and crafts to little ones, decided to work with her mom.

"That's an amazing story, Dom. Penny sounds really cool," I said. "Have you asked her out yet?"

"Nah, not yet. I think she likes me, though."

"Tell me something I don't know, bro. Her face lit up the room when you walked in. Do you mind if I ask you a personal question, though?"

"Shoot, Freddy."

"Well, it's not like I don't think you, uh, have *needs*, but I don't remember you being all that interested in girls when we were growing up."

"Ha ha, I'm a red-blooded, Italo-Canadian boy just like you! I just don't think about it all the time, like most guys. I tried dating, you know, back in my twenties. Small Carm helped me get set up on this stupid telephone service. A lot of the girls I met on there were single moms, and they were really nice, but I wasn't ready for that sort of thing, and a lot of them were just looking to have phone buddies because they were lonely.

"I did go out on one date, Flowerboy, and I never told you about it because I was so embarrassed. She was a nice Italian girl named Cinzia and she lived out in Bloor West Village. We exchanged numbers and started talking on the phone a lot, sometimes for two or three hours at a time. I made her laugh a lot. I thought I was in love — with a voice, can you imagine? — so after a week, I asked her if we could meet up. I actually had the courage! I was going to tell you all about her after the date, because I thought it would go really freakin' well, you know? I'm so sorry I didn't."

I could hear the regret in his voice. "It's fine Dom, I'm not mad or anything."

"Okay, good. So we meet up at this old movie theatre that's now a bookstore. You'd love it, it's by that guy Art Deco you're always telling me about. She's not a knockout but she's cute. A little chubby but I'm too skinny, so what do I care? We sit down at the Starbucks in there and we start talking. It's a little awkward at first, but it's going okay. She asks me about the models I build, so I start to tell her, and then she interrupts me.

"She puts her hand on mine, and she says: 'Domenic, I don't mean any disrespect, but that's something that, mostly, little boys do, right?' Nice question, eh Freddy? So I say: 'Well, it's like a lot of things, you get into it when you're young, but if you enjoy it, why can't you keep on doing it when you're older?' So we talk some more. It's more like a job interview than a date, if you want to know the truth. All these questions about what I want out of life, do I want kids, where do I see myself in five years, all that rigatoni-marole.

"It's very different than the way we were laughing on the phone before, I can tell you, and not at all like when I talk to Penny. Penny doesn't worry about that kind of stuff, she just lives in the here-and-now, you know, no worries. Plus she's just as funny as I am."

"You *are* pretty funny, bro."

"So, finally, this Cinzia asks me about my job — I was working at the car wash at the time — and if that's my goal in life, to be a *gidrul'* in a dead-end job. I say something like: 'Hey, a job's a job,' and then she puts her hand on mine again and says this, Freddy, if you can believe it: 'Are you mentally retarded? Because it's okay if you are.'

"*Madonn'* I turned red, I was so embarrassed. I didn't know what to do. I just said: 'Excuse me, I have to go to the washroom,' and then I left. I just walked out of there and got right on the subway. And you know how I feel about the subway."

Sixteen hours after that phone call, I had decided that my mission in life was to ensure Dom's heart never got broken again. The first thing I did was a little reconnaissance, so I told my crew — I was a crew chief now at Hogtown Drywall — that I had to go and talk to one of our suppliers at lunchtime. This bought me some time, since we were working on a condo tower at Church and Lombard streets called Spire, and Kensington Market is a fifteen-minute bike ride away. I knew that only the mom would be at Pineapple Head because Dom told me Penny doesn't work Mondays because business is slow.

As I was pedalling and dodging car doors along Richmond Street, I wondered how I'd start the conversation. "Hey, do people with Down syndrome have sex?" is kind of blunt. Plus, I'm pretty sure some do. "Hey, do you think my slow-learning brother would be a good match for your developmentally challenged daughter?" is pretty insulting, too, so I decided to play it by ear.

There was a customer in Pineapple Head when I got there, so I had time to check things out. Not that I know much about it, but the jewellery seemed really good, professional even. There were the usual big silver rings and bracelets, but some of the necklaces, the ones made out of wood, caught my eye. Those seemed architectural, almost, in that they consisted of blocky shapes that looked like little skyscrapers, with resin inserts that could've been windows. Some were layered shapes, like buildings behind buildings, done in contrasting light and dark woods.

"I see you like our Timbertecture line. They're neat, eh?"

I spun around and a very attractive woman with shoulder-length blond hair, green eyes, a long nose with a little, twinkling stud on the side, and a big smile was standing a foot away from me.

"Uh, yeah, I get it. Timbertecture. They're inspired by architecture?"

"Sure, but abstracted a bit. I'm not sure if building shapes can be copyrighted," she said, laughing.

"Maybe the Chrysler Building in New York. Not sure if you can trademark a box shape like TD Centre. The wood is beautiful."

"I'm mostly self-taught," she said, "with wood anyway. The metal stuff I had to learn."

"Yeah, I know, my brother Dom told me. Domenic Falconi, I think you know—"

"Dommy? Sure I know him. He's here all the time," she said with fake exasperation.

"He is?" I asked, genuinely surprised.

"Yeah," she said, then leaned in closer, which made the bangles around her wrist clink together. "I think he's got the hots for my daughter." She laughed again. "You're his *brother*? You don't even look Italian."

"I take after my mom," I said. "She's a rare, red-headed Sicilian. Pale skin. Dom, er, Dommy as you call him, looks more like our dad."

"I'm sorry, we know he likes to be called Dom. Dommy is just what Penny started calling him, so it just kind of stuck."

"Look, can I ask you something?"

"Sure."

"You say Dom's got 'the hots' for your daughter," I stammered, pausing to figure out what to say next. "What if I told you it's no joke, he really does, and he wants to ask her out on a date?"

"I'd say he should go for it because he's an absolute sweetheart. But I wouldn't say that about just anyone." She held out her right hand, palm down, and spread her fingers out. "See that?"

I looked. Tattooed in the triangular space between her thumb and forefinger was a thick letter T with the number 21 going across the shaft; underneath it were three little stars.

"You like playing blackjack in Tahoe?" I asked.

"That stands for 'trisomy twenty-one,'" she said, rolling

her eyes at my lame joke. "Without getting too technical, it's another way of saying Down syndrome, and the three stars represent that she's got three copies of the twenty-first chromosome instead of the two that you and I have."

"Oh." I didn't know what else to say so I just cleared my throat and looked out the window and nodded.

"I had this done just after she was diagnosed. It's to remind me that anything I do with my hands, I do for her. Make food, make money, make jewellery, whatever. I want her to have the best life I can give her. Even in romance." Deborah looked up from her hand and directly into my eyes. "I like Dom very much, and the fact that you're here checking things out on his behalf tells me he comes from a strong, loving family, just like Penny does."

"Thank you, that means a lot. I would do anything for my brother. Can I tell you something?"

Now she nodded.

"Well, Dom is a little different, I guess. He didn't learn like the other kids in school and he's kind of a hermit. It's a big deal for him to ask a girl out."

"I picked up on Dom's uniqueness," she said softly. "You already know Penny is different too, but that doesn't mean they don't deserve companionship, does it?"

"Well, about that," I stammered again and shifted my weight from one foot to another. "What if one of them wants, uh, more than companionship?"

"Oh, it's time for *that* talk, is it?" She pointed to a stool beside her jeweller's bench. "Sit down, please." I felt rather silly as I placed one butt cheek on the tiny, round slab of wood and she checked the door to see if anyone was coming in. She straddled her office chair and looked back down at her hand again. "Penny is an adult woman. She has desires. I learned about that when I walked into her bedroom unannounced when she was a teenager. Know what I mean? She also had a boyfriend once. A nice kid who also had DS. *She* found *him* boring and decided she wanted a man who could keep up with her."

"Well, Dom and I have had some great conversations over the years. He's got a really interesting way of looking at things."

"And so does Penny. Tell your brother to go with his heart. And not that he needs it, but he has my blessing."

༄

After I talked to Dom that night and told him he had the green light, we began Operation Lucky Penny. The success of Phase One was crucial; without the "yes" when he asked her out, there could be no Phase Two. We decided on a low-key approach for Phase One so as not to scare the poor girl off.

Dom would go into Pineapple Head armed with a cappuccino for Penny like always, but maybe he'd have a little chocolate treat for her too. But probably not flowers because that would raise too much suspicion. He'd be wearing slightly nicer clothes, like maybe a blazer, but nothing too formal. Maybe he'd put a little dab of Brylcreem in his hair and a tiny touch of cologne on his neck — but not douse himself like the mooks in Gina's neighbourhood. Real subtle stuff, just like a velvet hammer.

Phase Two was a bit more complicated. Dom insisted that he wanted to dress up for the date. "Not like a Gino, but classy, like Cary Grant or Fred Astaire," he told me. Now he and I were great at finding old clothes, but we thought that this would be too big a job for Kensington Market. So we needed to do more work on that aspect of the plan.

Phase Three was transportation. In 2001, Small Carm finally retired Dad's butt-ugly Seville and bought himself a new car. But it's a white Pontiac Grand Am and Dom thought it wasn't swanky enough. Plus, we'd been debating as to whether or not we should even tell Small Carm about the date, because he'd become really protective of Dom since I moved out. Gina had a minivan, which was even less swanky. So we knocked ideas around. He suggested renting a limo, but I told him that's what teenagers do, and he was a grown man of forty. I thought maybe it might be silly and cool, and match his sense of humour, if he rented a tandem bicycle or something.

"Geez, I dunno," he said. "I'm not even sure if she can ride a bike. But you saying renting gives me an idea." We were sitting in his model-making room and he got up from behind the big table and walked over to the Ikea bookcase. His hand hovered over a dozen tiny cars like a benevolent giant, hesitated for a second, and then selected one and lifted it gingerly.

"I'll tell you what a real man drives," he said as a wide smile formed on his lips. "A Ferrari, that's what."

CHAPTER VIII

☞ Small Carm ☜

I HAVE PROOF that Carmelo Calogero Falconi Jr., a.k.a. Small Carm, has always been an old man trapped inside a young person's body.

Since he was a first-born Italian son, there are about four million curling and fading photographs and slides of him between the ages of zero and sixteen down in the Falconi basement. Like a lot of successful guys in the mid-1960s, Big Carm was a hobby photographer and his new family was his favourite subject, which means there are also three million of Dom and about two million of Gina. By the late 1960s, Dad had also purchased a Super 8 camera, so there are dozens of little movies of Small Carm, Dom and Gina running around and sitting on tractors at Falconi Farm, too, though no one has watched them since our projector conked out in the 80s. By the time I came along, I think Dad was tired of taking pictures: There are only about a hundred photos of my childhood, and maybe two movies. Consequently, I barely know what I looked like growing up. But I was a "mistake" so I'm not complaining.

Anyhow, in ninety percent of those early photos or little

movies, and regardless of whether Small Carm is circling around in a bright yellow fiberglass airplane at the Canadian National Exhibition or blowing out candles on his Italian bakery birthday cake, he's got a combination serious and semi-disgusted look on his face, like he's either trying to solve a difficult math problem or hold in a fart ... or both. And in photos where you just *know* Mom was begging him to smile ("*Vuoi sorridere per favore, Carmy!*"), he's just stretching his big lips over his teeth without really knowing why, like a trained chimpanzee.

I do remember having a family movie night when I was really young, like maybe six years old, and watching some overexposed footage of a lavender-suited Small Carm bursting from the front doors of St. Brigid's Parish and parting a sea of well-dressed, confetti-covered people milling about in front, and then some of him and Dom having a footrace in the alleyway behind our building. I also remember the family bursting into laughter when those clips came on, and Dad teasing him with "There's my salami boy again!" like it was an old family joke. I looked over and, even in the darkened living room, I could make out Small Carm's reddening face, although he was fake-laughing along with us.

But it's true: Small Carm doesn't move his arms when he runs or, come to think of it, even when he walks. It's the weirdest thing, but both arms just hang there, limp, like a couple of big salamis dangling from the butcher shop ceiling.

In later photos, you can see why it was easy for Small Carm to pass for my father after Big Carm betrayed the family. Small Carm is anything but small: At nineteen, he was already a wide-framed, six-foot-two, very Italian-looking man with deep-set, dark brown eyes under thick Abe Vigoda eyebrows. Under those two caterpillars: a wide nose; acne-scarred cheeks; and big fish lips. And his hanging salami-arms were starting to get extra plump at nineteen since I'm pretty sure he'd become a regular at Gold's Gym by then.

Combine all of this with his premature balding and he looked like he was old enough to have a nine-year-old kid. And if that wasn't enough, a year into being my legal guardian, he grew a full beard. Even though he's kind of clumsy and probably wouldn't hurt a fly, he's an intimidating-looking fella, so it wasn't hard for him to stop one of my tantrums with a cold-blooded stare and a raised finger.

Mom told me that when Small Carm exited her womb on March 20, 1965, he didn't cry. He just squinted into the operating room lights and cleared his tiny throat a couple of times. I think if he'd had a watch on he would have looked at it and said: "It's about time, Ma, it was getting stuffy in there. B'oh, where's Pop? I gotta go talk to him."

I say that because Small Carm has always been Daddy's boy. In fact, Small Carm just missed being born on Italian father's day, *Festa di San Giuseppe*, which honours Jesus' father, St. Joseph, every March 19. Since those little Italian donuts, *zeppole*, are eaten at that time of year, he'd always get a box of them along with his birthday cake, and, luckily, Mom and Dad would make him share with the rest of us.

Apparently, Small Carm started helping out in the Falconi office when he was five or six. Dad would give him little jobs to do, like marking documents with the old fashioned RECEIVED stamp with the day's date and the blank line for the person to fill in their name — which he'd do so slowly a pile of twenty would take him an hour — or refilling the long dispenser attached to the water cooler with the triangular paper cups. When he got a little older, he would file orders, take cheques to our bank at the southeast corner of Spadina and College (which happened to be a beautiful Modernist building), or accompany Dad and whatever client was in town up to Falconi Farm to help rig up the implements. And although we all had to dust and buff the Finch in the store window, Small Carm would often trade us for other jobs so he could do it.

Funnily enough, he's still doing it, twenty years after the company went bankrupt. For some reason, it's always on a Friday morning, and usually when the sidewalks are filling with people, that he chooses to park himself in that cramped little window along with a chamois, touch-up wax, chrome polish and leather conditioner. It's wax on, wax off, just as if Mr. Miyagi is behind him supervising, but he's in such a trance I don't think he notices when tourists stop in their tracks, laugh, and aim their digital cameras at him while wondering if the big red Chinatown tractor is some sort of art installation.

∽

I don't know much about what Small Carm was like in elementary school, but I do know what he *wasn't* like. He wasn't a troublemaker, he wasn't a class clown, he wasn't a keener and he wasn't a bully. I think he just quietly went about his work, raised his hand enough to show he had a brain, handed in his assignments on time and got straight

B's. I hate to say this, but I think his teachers probably forgot about him two days into summer vacation each year.

Well, that's not entirely true. Although Small Carm hasn't expressed any interest in acting since, he was the co-star of a play put on by his Grade 8 class in 1978. In *Captain Stormfield's Visit to Heaven*, based on a 1909 short story by Mark Twain, Small Carm played both Sam Bartlett and Sandy McWilliams, two men tasked with educating Captain Stormfield (who was played by a South Asian kid) on what Heaven is really like.

The story goes like this: After commandeering a few comets to tour the universe and even racing with a big one, the recently deceased, salty old sea captain Eli Stormfield of San Francisco has grown lonely, so he makes his way to Heaven. Problem is, he's gone so far out of his way with his comet-sailing, he arrives at the wrong gate; much to his dismay, they've never heard of San Francisco, America, or the World. After examining a map, a clerk determines the good captain is from a speck of a planet they call "the Wart" in an obscure part of the universe. They give him directions to his district of Heaven, where they assure him he'll be outfitted in his expected garb of wings, halo, palm branch, and harp.

Strumming away and singing while sitting on a cloud with a million other folks, Stormfield soon gets bored. He runs into an old friend, Sam Bartlett (who has been dead for a while), who sets him straight by explaining that only new arrivals expect that choir mumbo-jumbo, so they're put on their own, isolated cloud where they won't bother long-time inhabitants like Bartlett: "Singing hymns and waving palm branches is pretty when you hear about it in the pulpit," he tells him, "but it's as poor a way to put in valuable time as a body could contrive. It would just make a Heaven of warbling ignoramuses, don't ya see?

"Eternal Rest sounds comforting in the pulpit, too. Well, you try it once, and see how heavy time will hang on your hands. Why, Stormfield, a man like you, that had been active and stirring all his life, would go mad in six months in a Heaven where he hadn't anything to do."

So the captain sheds his harp and settles down to ponder something meaningful to do for all eternity. He meets up with the second character Small Carm plays, seventy-two-year-old cranberry farmer McWilliams, and the two have a rich conversation about silly mortal misconceptions of Heaven. Such as: Being in a young body and hanging around with young people is boring if you have the wisdom of age; finding a lost child may be a disappointment if that child chose to grow up in Heaven; getting around using angel's wings is cumbersome (they're really more of a dress uniform); a common man doesn't get to meet the patriarchs and prophets of Heaven, such as Abraham, Isaac or Adam right away, and possibly never; an undiscovered tailor from Tennessee who was ridiculed on earth but wrote better prose than Shakespeare will get more respect in Heaven; and, finally, white people are certainly in the minority. (This went over big with Small Carm's very ethnically diverse class.)

It ends with Stormfield and McWilliams attending a lavish ceremony for a new arrival, an average barkeeper who had found God at the end of his sinful life.

Twain's story is a brilliant takedown of humanity's egocentric view of the universe, and I know Small Carm enjoyed himself, especially since his roles required more listening than speaking.

Six years later, however, he'd drastically change gears and vehemently disagree with Twain's thesis.

※

The only thing I know about Small Carm's time in high school — he was a Harbord Collegiate "Harbordite" just like Dad — is that he played football in Grades 9 and 10 because the coach had spotted him standing a head higher than his classmates and pegged him as a good lineman. I think Small Carm was so surprised to be noticed and asked to do something, anything, that he said yes despite knowing little about football.

Because his player nickname was "Thumbs" Falconi — as in he was all thumbs, I don't think he was regarded as a star, but his size meant he could bowl opponents over easily, and that was good enough to stay on the team. Also, having a football jacket helped him to fit in, and I think Big Carm liked that his first-born was being a manly man, unlike Dom, who was, well, kind of sensitive and weird. I'm sure Big Carm would have preferred to see Small Carm on a soccer team, but soccer wasn't on many high school sports rosters in the late 70s. Back then, the only way to even *see* European soccer was to go to the Italian men's clubs on College Street or St. Clair Avenue, or the much farther ones in Mom's old neighbourhood, where they had enormous satellite dishes on their roofs. Luckily, the year of the massive World Cup win, 1982, was the same year the Canadian Broadcasting Corporation picked up the games, so I remember the two Carms sitting on the living room couch for that first big match with Brazil (I think Big Carm was letting Small Carm drink beer, much to Mom's chagrin) and the two going nuts again a few days later when Italy eliminated Poland in the semi-final. When they saw on the news that a 100,000 Italians had partied all night long on St. Clair, they decided to watch the final game on a big projection television at a College Street pizzeria where Big Carm was friendly with the owner.

While the celebration wasn't as big as the one on St. Clair, where an estimated 300,000 Italians went absolutely ballistic and shut down twenty city blocks (and there were reports of a donkey being led around), the two Carms partied with tens of thousands of *paesans* well into that Sunday night, and Falconi had to close that Monday so the pair could nurse their hangovers.

By Grade 11, Small Carm had grown tired of the jock life and switched his efforts to academics. Most of his electives were in the areas of business and accounting because his plan was to get a degree in business administration and take Falconi Farm Equipment to the next level. While he didn't have the marks for the University of Toronto, he was accepted at a small university in Northern Ontario, Lakehead, which was so far in the hinterland you had to take an airplane to get there.

The Incident took place right at the end of Small Carm's high school career, and that changed everything. Then again, everything changed for Small Carm when Dad ran off with the very photogenic Ms. Larson four or five months before. I was young when Dad left, so I was shielded from a lot of what went down, but when I was in my mid-twenties we finally had a conversation about it.

"How do you think I felt, Freddy? He didn't just betray Mom with what he did, he betrayed his best friend, me, and his whole family."

"You held yourself together well," I said, trying to console him. "I mean, you didn't go crazy — well, except for trying to turn me into a priest — and my life was pretty normal, considering."

"Thank you, Flowerboy. It wasn't easy. And I'll remind you that I'm still a devout Catholic so don't make fun of it, please."

"I know, I'm sorry," I said. "Have you ever wished you could've talked to Dad after he left?"

"I did talk to him, once."

"What?" I asked, completely surprised. "How come I don't know about this?"

"Dom knows. I didn't tell you because it was just before Mom died, and it doesn't matter because our dear father is a rat."

Apparently, it was on a random Tuesday morning that Dad phoned his old extension at Falconi, knowing Small Carm would pick up.

"Hello, Falconi Farm Equipment, how can I help you?"

"Carmy, is that you? Don't hang up, okay?"

Silence, then: "You better have something important to say."

"I, uh, I just wanted to check up on you guys. Little Freddy Flowers, especially. He's not too messed up, is he?"

"Gee, what do you think, you *menefreghista*? You steal the company's money and you leave all of us without saying goodbye? Yeah, he's fine. Real well adjusted. Thanks for asking."

"I earned that money, Carmy! And I know you think I don't give a crap, but I do. But you have no idea what your mother is like. You're a man now, so you can hear this. She's a cold fish. She's got a lot of mental prob—"

Small Carm's eyes were aimed at a random spot over my shoulder, and his nervous leg had started bouncing up and down. "And that's when I hung up the phone on him, boom, just like that, Freddy. And I thank God he never called again, because the things I might have said would not have been very Christian," he said, his big lips lifting at the corners.

Small Carm started wearing a crucifix around his neck about a year before Mom died, but nobody really questioned him on it; a lot of mooky Italians wear them because they've seen them on Mafia movie characters, or on Tony Manero or Rocky Balboa, and they think it looks cool. And while Small Carm isn't exactly a mook, he can come close.

The thing is, Small Carm had been discussing Catholicism with Mom for a few years, and the two of them had started going to church together in secret. Maybe Small Carm could sense Dad drifting away and knew this brought comfort to Mom; maybe it brought comfort to both of them, I don't know. Obviously, when Nonno Calogero died on the San Boldo Pass and Nonna Serafina became a paraplegic, church was very necessary. A lot of the time they'd go to St. Francis of Assisi, the church affiliated with the Catholic school I would be forced to attend halfway through Grade 5, and other times they'd walk east for a half-hour to St. Michael's Cathedral on the other side of Yonge Street to attend Mass there. I can see why, too: It's ground zero for Catholicism in Toronto, and the pre-Confederation building is a pretty spectacular piece of architecture.

Our Grade 7 class went there on a field trip, and had to sketch it. Rising up from a rubble-stone foundation, long stained glass windows lead the eye to a bunch of prickly little spires and dormer windows along a long, slate-tile roof. Over the big, wooden double doors at the front is a thick, tall, square steeple. Inside, it's pretty much what you'd expect: A big, ornate chair behind the altar for the priest, a super-high ceiling decorated with all sorts of crests and murals that's held up by thick stone arches, and twin rows of cast iron light fixtures above the orderly rows of pews.

Small Carm's conversion to Catholicism began in earnest when Dad left. I guess that was the straw that broke the camel's back: Dad was a sinner and Small Carm was starting the path to salvation. He began working with the same priest at St. Francis, Father Trivisonno, who would be enlisted to help me convert later that year. When Mom died a few months later, that was like one of those old-school tests of faith to him, the same as those missionaries we learned about in Grade 8 who came to Canada in the 1600s to convert the "savages." The unlucky ones got out with their lives and a thousand blackfly bites, while the *lucky* ones were tied to stakes as Iroquois leaders slashed their skin and drank their blood in front of them, poured boiling water over their heads in a mockery of baptism, and then performed a few more bizarre rituals before they finally killed them. And while I'm sure Small Carm didn't think he'd become a Catholic rock star like those missionaries for what he was going through, the tragedy did strengthen his resolve and justify his decision.

Once he'd officially become a Catholic, he held a family meeting. I could tell it was a big deal for him because it was (and still is) a rare thing to see him nervous. It was Labour Day weekend, just before school started, and he waited until we all sat down to dinner. Some sort of baked pasta dish was in the oven, so he knew it would stay hot.

"I'm a Catholic now — I converted," he said, fiddling with the wine opener in his big hands, "and I know you guys aren't very religious but I hope you'll respect that I am now. *Very* religious. I'd also like to start doing a couple of things here at home. I'd like to put up a crucifix, and I'd like to say grace before we eat. It's not a lot, but it would mean a great deal to me."

Gina was the first to speak. "Why can't you just be a Methodist like Nonno Joe was, and just get into that, big time? I mean, you already are, technically."

"That's a good question, and you're not going to believe me but I'll tell you anyway. I have felt the Holy Spirit. In my body, and I have seen — "

"Whatchoo talkin' bout Willis?" interrupted Dom, who looked up from the fingernail he'd been picking at. Dom would often use television catch phrases when he didn't know what else to say. "You've been visited by a friggin' ghost?"

"Look, Dom, I'll ask you to wait until I'm done," Small Carm said. "And I am head of this family now if you remember, so I can tell you to shut your trap, too. I'm not asking you to join the Catholic Church, okay, I just thought you might like to know why things are going to be slightly different around here."

"All right, all right, go ahead, Father Sarducci."

"It wasn't *seeing* something, by the way, it was *feeling* something. It started when Dad left. I was nervous, I had butterflies in my stomach, my brain was in a fog. I know you're just going to say it was stress but I've had a little bit of stress in my life before, and this was different. It felt like something inside of me was trying to give me a message.

"And then, one day, earlier this summer when it was really, really hot, I think I got that message. I was sweating a lot, so I lay down on the bed, and had the fan blowing directly on me. I closed my eyes, and, eventually, the buzzing noise from the fan got really loud. Pretty soon it was like I was hearing one of those marching bands that have just drummers. Thurrrrr-up, thurrrrr-up, thurrrr-UP-UP-UP, like that. Then, the sounds of a choir, all men, singing a bunch of scary notes, like the ones that always play whenever Darth Vader walks into the room. I know, Dom, laugh if you will. It wasn't exactly that song, but it reminded me of it, okay? Anyway, after warming up with that, they exploded into two phrases that they just kept singing over and over: HERE ARE THE CATHOLICS OF GOD. HERE ARE THE CHANCES OF GOD. Then there was this big crash of a gong at the end.

"That was it. It scared the crap out of me if you must know." He took a swig of wine. "I sat up in the bed and my heart was beating a million miles an hour."

"Whoa," I said. "That's freaky."

"I know, right? Some of you know I was going to church

with Mom before," he said, scanning our faces to challenge us. "Well, I talked to one the priests and he said that the Holy Spirit will use dreams or visions to talk to someone when they're in trouble. He wrote down this bible passage for me."

Small Carm fished his wallet from his back pocket and took out a neatly folded piece of paper, then cleared his throat. "'And it shall come to pass in the last days that I will pour out of My Spirit on all flesh; your sons and your daughters shall prophesy, your young men shall see visions, your old men shall dream dreams.'

"I know it's not last days but it's felt like that for our family, right? Anyway, since I've done this — converted that is — most of my stress is gone. I mean, I'm still going nuts about what happened, but I have some perspective now. And I don't know about you guys, but I want to go to Heaven when I die."

Small Carm had come a long way from Captain Stormfield. Of course the thing that stuck with me most from that day took place after dinner, when he announced that I was going to become a Catholic too. Maybe he shouldn't have told that scary story about Darth Vader's choir.

I know that Small Carm met with a lawyer a number of times after Mom's death, and it had to do with getting custody of us kids, (even though Dom would be a legal adult in less than a year), but I don't think it was a very hard case. The lawyer, who had been recommended by one of Mr. Ladovsky's kids at United Bakers, was able to prove that Dad had

had an affair and was now living in California with the new woman. (He may have hired a private investigator to get photos.) And once our one sane aunt had been interviewed and it was determined she didn't want to come back to Canada to raise us while Mom was "missing," I don't think the judge had much choice but to award him provisional custody.

Small Carm adjusted to being the head of the family pretty quickly. It was almost as if he had been waiting for the role, like he knew Dad would mess up eventually; he knew Dad better than any of us, so maybe that's true.

Small Carm wasn't mean, but he immediately established some rules, besides the religious ones, that we all had to follow. We had to do more chores since Mom wasn't around to pick up after us. We had to pitch in at Falconi. I hadn't taken an interest in it like Small Carm had when he was little, but there I was at nine and ten, filing orders and going on sandwich runs. I also had to learn how to cook simple things in case everyone was busy and I was hungry. I learned how to make peppers and eggs, which I hated. I learned how to make a quick pasta sauce called *puttanesca*, which means "lady of the evening" (the story is that prostitutes wanted to eat quickly so as not to interrupt the flow of clients), but most of the time I just used the can opener to get myself some Chef Boyardee.

And speaking of puttanesca, that's what we ate practically every Monday when Small Carm and Gina took over the cooking of dinner. I still can't stand the taste of anchovies because of it. Tuesday, if I remember correctly, was homemade pizza night. Wednesday was some sort of frittata. Thursday was always a meat-and-starch night, like a pork chop with mashed potatoes or veal marsala with risotto, and Friday we would get "Canadian take-out" like subs, Canadian-Chinese food, or hamburgers. On weekends we had more elaborate stuff, like lasagna or a big pot of slow-cooked sauce (which they called Sunday gravy on *The Sopranos* but we never did in Canada) over spaghetti or rigatoni. This menu, by the way, didn't change for at least ten years.

By the way, Tony Soprano, that misunderstood and sensitive patriarch of the fictional Mafia family *The Sopranos*, was a favourite of Small Carm's when that show came out in 1999, but I think the TV character that most influenced him was Captain Jean-Luc Picard from *Star Trek: The Next Generation*. While Small Carm is a bit too young to have watched the original Trek in the late 1960s, I know he became a Trekker in the early 70s when it was in constant re-runs, bought a few of the comic books, and was a big fan of the movies, especially the one with the whales. When *Next Generation* came out in 1987, he went nuts for it and tried to get the family to gather around the old Zenith System 3 Space Command (yes that really was its name) and watch it with him. I think we did for that first year, when the sets looked pretty cheap and had Styrofoam rocks like the 1960s version, but only Dom stuck it out with him into season two and beyond, when it actually got good.

By the second or third season of *TNG*, when women started to go nuts for how sexy Patrick Stewart was, Small Carm purchased a barber-style head shaver and began buzzing his rapidly thinning hair down to a quarter-inch all around, just like Picard. He's done it ever since, even though now all he has to cut is a salt-and-pepper horseshoe down to size. I'm pretty sure he resents Dom, who still has most of his thick, dark hair. At least Small Carm never opted to wear a piece, like Dad did because one of his heroes, Frank Sinatra, had done it.

And about Sinatra: While Small Carm had started to listen to him a little — I remember him buying that gawd-awful *L.A. is My Lady* album a few months after Mom died, it didn't take him long to abandon Ol' Blue Eyes because of the connection to Big Carm. He didn't stray far, however. It had been well documented that, when Sinatra wanted to relax, he cranked up the late nineteenth and early twentieth century Italian composer Giacomo Puccini, who wrote *La bohème*, *Tosca* and *Madama Butterfly*. So Small Carm adopted him as his favourite, then branched out into other composers like his predecessor Giuseppe Verdi, and even earlier dudes like "The Italian Mozart," Gioachino Rossini, who wrote *The Barber of Seville*.

I can still remember, as a kid of ten or twelve, going to ask Small Carm about something. If he wasn't sitting at Dad's old Falconi showroom desk, he'd be in his bedroom on the third floor. Since I could hear the muffled crashing of opera music from behind the door, I'd have to knock really loud or wait until there was that little gap between arias. He'd tell me to come in, but he'd leave the volume up for a little while to make some sort of point. And whenever possible, he'd have a golf game on television (remember this was before golf had its own channel) with the sound turned down so Puccini or Verdi could provide the soundtrack.

"Look at that, Flowerboy," he'd say without turning around (I guess he knew my knock), "it's like ballet — that ball, it just hangs in the air, like it's waiting for the crescendo to hit the green. There's nothing like it."

After Roman Catholicism, the game of golf was the most spiritual thing in Small Carm's life. He'd purchased his first set of clubs at the age of seventeen because a school chum was into the game, and they'd go and play at the cheap par three public courses, like the one at Victoria Park station, Dentonia, and pretend they were the Rat Pack. Ironically, Dentonia sits on former farmland owned by the Massey family, who were so concerned about contaminated milk and children's health they started a dairy farm there, City Dairy, when that part of the city was all farmland; the milk was processed, bottled and delivered by milkmen at a facility just up the street from Falconi, where Spadina curves around Knox College.

Small Carm and his buddy were so obsessed with the game, they even went to driving ranges in winter so they could continue to practice their swings. Because golf wasn't something Dad ever got into, I think it really helped Small Carm zone out and think things through after The Incident.

Golf became so important to him, as a matter of fact, he actually convinced Dom to take up the game when he hit eighteen or nineteen, and it wasn't easy to get Dom to try new things. To entice him, he gave him his old set of clubs and upgraded to a pretty expensive set. I think Dom lasted about two years before he abandoned it and went back to his model kits.

This means that, even today, Small Carm's wardrobe consists of nothing but golf shirts in every colour (in the mid-80s, when I was timidly knocking on his door, they were all Yuppie pastels like salmon pink and butter yellow), which he leaves unbuttoned at the collar so you can see the gold crucifix against his hairy chest. And then there are the crisp dress pants, and those slip-on loafers that have the golf-shoe-like tassels on them.

He'll often ask me why I think it's okay to wear T-shirts with stupid slogans and jeans all the time, and I always answer the same way: "Because it's the twenty-first century."

He'll usually give me a piercing look from over his bifocals and say something like: "Okay Peter Pan, have it your way."

✧

No one blames Small Carm for Falconi going out of business in 1987.

Not only had Dad stolen money to finance his dalliances, he'd neglected some of our key accounts for so long they'd pulled their business and gone elsewhere. And then there's the fact that Big Carm secretly took out a mortgage on Falconi Farm to get some cash flow in the late 1970s, so Small Carm was making big payments on that. The Falcon with Weath-R-Shield bubble notwithstanding, the company had failed to keep up with the times, and our tractors were starting to look a little antiquated for modern farming needs by the 1980s. Because the behemoth Massey-Ferguson was in financial trouble at this time *and* had begun using another Italian manufacturer, Landini, to produce models for them (a real blow to Falconi after the decades-long relationship we'd had with them), the licensing agreement hadn't been renewed, so that income stream dried up. Massey, in fact, would be operating with a skeleton staff on their twenty-seven acre site at King and Strachan by 1985, and it would shut down completely a few years after that. Today, there's one building left of that incredible complex, and it's part of a condominium.

I think it took Small Carm about six months after The Incident to really understand just how bad things were, then it took him another six to figure out what to do. He waited until Dom turned eighteen so he could legally take care of me, and then he packed his bags for Latina and stayed a month to see if he could straighten things out. By then, however, I think the writing was on the wall.

Poor guy. At twenty-one, the family company he was now responsible for was haemorrhaging money. He was working with the City of Markham's municipal planning department to get a plan of subdivision to sever Falconi Farm to pay off Dad's mortgage (he first had to fight to get legal control of it); he was raising Gina and me; and he was wondering if he would be able to keep possession of the Falconi building on Spadina so we'd all have a place to live.

It's understandable, then, that he didn't have a lot of time to date women. The family joke had always been that, when Small Carm would marry and have a son of his own, he'd have to change his own name to Medium Carm in order to free up the name Small Carm for his boy. Mom used to say: "I don't understand your jokes: small, medium, big, what are they, fountain drinks at the Seven-To-Eleven store?"

For a while, he was seeing a nice Jewish girl he'd met after he'd gone to the new United Bakers restaurant up at Lawrence Plaza a couple of times. She was a waitress there and lived in the immediate area. I think Small Carm liked the familiarity of the place and the people, but also that it was in a new location and this girl had never worked at the

Spadina one. Not a connection, but a connection, right? At the time, Small Carm was still driving Dad's 1981 Cadillac Seville, which I think is one of the ugliest cars General Motors ever produced. It had this weird, sliced-off back end that they called a "bustle back" and, if that weren't enough, it had a diesel engine. I think Small Carm actually liked the two-toned champagne and dark brown paint job, fake wood interior and spoke hubcaps; then again, he's always been a lot more Italian in that regard than I'll ever be. Since this girl, Rebecca, didn't like coming downtown, Small Carm would drive almost a half-hour up to her neighbourhood in his pimpmobile a few times a week when I was about fifteen and sixteen — so much so that Dom started calling them the Jew-Wops and singing Doo-wop music, like "A Teenager in Love" by Dion and the Belmonts, whenever he would announce he was going to see her.

Rebecca came over for a home-cooked dinner and to meet us exactly once, and by that time Gina was working down in Mexico, so it was just Dom and me. Small Carm asked us to dress up and then pre-approved our choices, which was ridiculous, so Dom and I went to Kensington Market and bought two of those tuxedo-printed T-shirts and surprised him by changing into them just before he walked in with her. We said stuff like "Hello, M'lady" and pulled out her chair and unfolded her napkin for her, which made her laugh, but I don't think Small Carm was too impressed. I'm not sure if it was geography or chemistry, but after about a year and a half they broke up.

Since then, he's kept his dating cards close to his chest, and if it wasn't for seeing a receipt from Telepersonals back in the mid-1990s and then, in the early 2000s, overhearing him on the phone talking to a buddy about a Lavalife date he'd been on, I would have decided that he'd given up on women.

∞

Even though Falconi is dead, Small Carm still works full-time. Every day, he gets up at 7:30 a.m., makes himself an espresso in his ancient, stove-top Bialetti, sits at the dining room table in his bathrobe and eats a couple of those Italian breakfast cookies with Nutella or cherry jam spread on them; then he showers, shaves, and gets completely dressed, including socks and shoes.

He goes downstairs to the showroom and sits at Dad's old desk, which, actually, has been *his* desk since 1984. The only new things in there are his computer and, on the wall, the fake-wood Falconi family crest he ordered from one of those mail-order heraldry places a few years after Mom died — "We were proud Falconers and our name entered the official records in the year 1000," I remember he told me — that hasn't been dusted since it was hung up.

He starts his day by reading the newspaper online because he doesn't want Dom to see it, then he takes a look at our family's investments. After Falconi's assets in Latina were sold and debts were paid off in the late 80s, he put the leftover money in the bank while he taught himself how to play the stock market. One of the books he really relied on was *The Intelligent Investor* by Benjamin Graham, which is apparently the same book Warren Buffett used to make himself rich way back when. He bought others, too — they're still up on the shelf behind his desk—but that's the one he always told me to pick up and read, which I never did because I find financial stuff about as interesting as watching paint dry.

Small Carm, however, found it very interesting and became rather good at it. He bought a fair bit of Apple stock just before Steve Jobs came back in 1997 and made some money that way, and he bought Dell Computer stock even earlier than that for a pretty low price, and of course those were worth a hundred times what he paid for them by the end of the 1990s. I'm sure he bought some dogs, too, but he doesn't brag about those, so I don't know what they were or how much he lost.

About ten years ago, Small Carm had a professional sign made up for the front door of the Falconi building. It reads: "THIS IS THE PROFESSIONAL OFFICE OF C. FALCONI INVESTMENTS, INC. THERE ARE NO LOFTS AVAILABLE. PLEASE NO AGENTS OR SOLICITORS." This is because, starting in the mid-1990s, Kensington Market hipsters and Ontario College of Art students were ringing the doorbell about three times a week looking for artist's lofts. Since my two brothers go to bed so early, there was very little light or activity in the windows, so these poor kids assumed there was space available upstairs. Dom was disappointed when Small Carm put the sign up because he loved answering the door and freaking out these pierced and tattooed kids with things like: "What are you talking about, good sir? We manufacture tractors upstairs!" Or: "Yes, we have loft space available, if you don't mind sleeping on stinking piles of bat guano!"

The other thing that kept Small Carm busy, up until the mid-2000s, anyway, was the selling off of Falconi Farm. The last piece went to Seneca College so they could build their

Markham Campus, which opened a couple of years ago. I always smile when I look at a map and see Centurian Drive, which was a name selected by Small Carm as a tribute to Dom. Why the town planners changed the spelling by one letter is beyond me. Other pieces he sold off over the years went to Allstate Insurance, a church and even an Italian restaurant.

And lastly, Small Carm manages the big inventory of greasy parts stacked into stained wooden crates down in our building's basement. We've been here since 1938, so even though we never manufactured the tractors in Canada, we have a cornucopia of out-of-production engine components, fenders, tires, and cosmetic stuff like chrome trim and badging. There's also a small warehouse full of stuff in Latina, so when e-commerce became a thing, he partnered with an ex-Falconi employee there and they launched www.olditaliantractors.com in order to make a little scratch. It did pretty well for them, so they branched out and started representing other vintage Italian brands like Fiat, Lamborghini, Landini and Alfa Romeo.

∽

There's a great quote by Winston Churchill: "We shape our buildings; thereafter they shape us." The thing is, Small Carm never got to shape the Falconi building, yet it's been shaping him since he was born. Big Carm got to re-shape the place a few years after he took over by renovating the office interiors and the exterior façade, and Mom got to decorate the bedroom and a little bit of the second floor. While I understand that renovation was the last thing on Small

Carm's mind while he was running Falconi for that brief time, what strikes me as odd is that, upstairs, he lives in a perpetual 1984: Other than the calendar on the wall, absolutely nothing has changed. The furniture, the books in the bookcase, the framed photos on the wall, the dishes, they're all the same. He hasn't even moved Nonno Joe's pelican ashtray.

I worry that, eventually, the weight of all that family history will crush him to death.

CHAPTER IX

☞ The Ferrari ☜

DOM WAS BUZZING around like a happy little hummingbird. I can't say I blamed him; not only had Penny agreed to the date, she'd given him a peck on the cheek right there in the store. Then she told him: "I'm going to dress real pretty for you, Dommy, because you deserve it!" Had he been wearing a vest, the buttons would have popped right off as his chest swelled on the way out the door of Pineapple Head.

And speaking of vests, we got a great recommendation from Gina as to where to get Dom suited up in style. It turned out a friend of hers used to work in a higher-end vintage store on Queen West near Tecumseth Street called Cabaret. I'd walked past it a few times, but the window always had dresses in it, so I thought it just sold women's stuff. Apparently, there's a guy in the basement who calls himself "the Kingpin," and he sells really well-made vintage men's stuff. He's also an expert at eyeballing a person up and down and recommending the right clothes.

That's the other thing: Gina was in on our plan, and she agreed that it would be best if we didn't tell Small Carm about any of it. Especially about renting the Ferrari. Dom is a regular overnight guest at her place, so the plan was just to say that he'd be going there. If Small Carm called for any reason, Gina would say he went to the park with Rocco and the kids. Dom could then stay out late on his date, make sure Penny got home safely, and then bring the Ferrari to my place when he was done. He'd crash on my living room floor, and we'd both return the Ferrari in the morning, easy peasy lemon squeezie.

When the Big Day of Operation Lucky Penny arrived, there was so much to do I had to call in sick at work. We had an appointment at Kingpin's Hideaway in the late morning, and then we had to pick up the car. And I was sure that renting a $200,000 car wouldn't be quite as lemon squeezie as renting a Dodge Neon.

First, however, we had to clean Dom up a little, so he and I found ourselves cooling our jets in a pair of squeaky orange chairs at Corrado's Barber Shop on Bathurst Street. It's a twenty-minute walk from our place, but it's an absolute time warp, and Dom and I are weird in that we both draw energy from old things that are still useful. Like dial telephones or wind-up wristwatches. Or Corrado Accaputo, an opinionated old Sicilian who got off a train at Union Station in 1957 at seventeen, found a job at this place, and then bought it from Augustino Gentile six years later. He's been walking these five hundred square feet offering his thoughts on every topic under the sun ever since, usually closing with an "Eh, whaddaya gonna do?" And if you want to wind him up, ask him what he thinks of the Beatles. They almost killed the barbering business from 1965 to 1975.

He's never renovated his shop, which Dom and I also love. The plaster walls, from the chest up, are plastered with girlie photos, postcards from customers, pictures of Jesus, and newspaper clippings. There's even a black velvet painting of John Wayne. From the chest down, it's wood paneling behind the orderly line of Formica-lined cabinets and countertops. Three gangly, shiny, now-vintage Belmont chairs take pride of place, and their upholstery matches the bluish-green liquid in the Barbicide bottles.

The morning of Operation Lucky Penny, an old guy had won the race to become Corrado's first customer of the day, so I was flipping through a *Playboy* while Dom fidgeted and bit off his cuticles. Even showing him some vintage 1998 boobies didn't help, so I put the magazine down and engaged him in conversation.

"How long you been coming here, Dom?"

"Oh, geez, probably since the early 1990s, Freddy. You remember Mom used to take Small Carm and me to that shaky old guy on College? The du Maurier Man? He'd blow smoke right in our faces!"

"I remember you talking about it, but I didn't go there. By the time I was getting my hair cut by someone other than Mom, barbers weren't cool anymore. I went to something called a hair stylist and she had to pay three times as much!"

"Ha ha, yeah. What did —"

"Hey, Domenico of Spadina, let's make you look pretty,

uh?" said the round-faced Corrado as he flapped the blue cutting cape and sent a hundred grey tufts fluttering into the air.

∽

"I'm going to tell you something that my grandmother told me a long time ago," said the Kingpin, real name Jonathan, to Dom and I as he shook our hands. "A man in a good suit is to a woman what a woman in fine lingerie is to a man."

That had been an hour ago. The Kingpin was full of entertaining bon mots and one-liners, but he had me worried. Even though we were on a tight schedule, he and Dom had been trying on sailor's hats and Sherlock Holmes' capes and giggling like schoolgirls, when what we needed to do was get a simple jacket and pants and then make like trees. Or, as Dom likes to say: "Make like a horse's *cazzo* and hit the road." We had to return Gina's minivan to Woodbridge after we picked up the Ferrari, and that car was halfway to Niagara Falls in a little town called Stoney Creek, which locals call Stoner Creek. We could've got a Ferrari in Toronto, but Dom's buddy at the hobby store knew a guy who knew a guy, so he got a really good deal. But still.

Now that we knew this place was in the basement of Cabaret, I was sure we'd come back. Jonathan has an impressive collection of vintage cufflinks, bow ties, pocket squares, spats, dress uniforms, loud 1940s ties, and nubby wool suits. He's even got ashtrays, cigar cutters, dirty-picture playing cards, and desk sets on display, which give the store a men's club sort of atmosphere. It's a neat, theatrical environment, so we weren't surprised when he told us he used to work in television.

Jonathan, who looks a bit like Clark Kent's older, accountant brother, was standing ramrod straight in a vintage three-piece suit, crisp white shirt, and floppy, paisley bow tie while he scanned Dom from head to toe. At that point, Dom was wearing what would eventually be part of the outfit we'd walk out of there with. While the pants weren't right, the jacket was a well-fitting, summer-weight, cream-coloured blazer with medium-width lapels and black buttons.

"Oh, that jacket is good!" I said. "What about the pants, Kingpin?"

Kingpin sucked in some air and tapped a knuckle on the tip of his nose. "Well that would depend on the shirt. Are you going with that pink Oxford you've got on," he asked Dom, "or do you want to select a whole outfit?"

"We're here for your eye," Dom answered quickly. "Let's shoot the works."

"Good man!" Jonathan said as he puffed out his barrel-chest and stood back to scan his wares. He clapped his hands loudly. "Let's get to it then, chop-chop!"

The Kingpin was good. In five minutes, Dom was transformed: Below that freshly trimmed mop of hair and dark eyes was a refined gentleman. Underneath the cream-coloured jacket was a crisp, dark blue shirt paired with a striped, baby-blue tie. The cufflinks were sparkly sapphires, the pocket square was turquoise and the pants were a cool grey. The shoes were classic brogues. The clothes fit so well, Dom didn't look like his usual under-fed, mortician self. He looked like a cross between 1940s Humphrey Bogart and 1970s Bryan Ferry. In a word, he was hot.

"The clothes maketh the man," Jonathan said, beaming, as he calculated the cost with a well-sharpened pencil.

Jamming the money into his hand, I said: "Now we must maketh like a couple of trees, and leave."

༄

Dom and I pulled up to a stark, one-storey, concrete block building that had exactly one small window covered in mirrored film, and a single, thin door. If it hadn't been for the Porsche 911, Lamborghini Gallardo and Bentley Continental GT resting in the parking lot, this could have been a welding shop or an injection-moulding factory. Inside Speed Kingz Exotics, I wasn't surprised to see the usual man-cave baloney: a hard, uncomfortable black leather couch, a stack of custom rims in a corner, a bunch of exotic car magazines on a polished-chrome end table, a lunchroom-style cappuccino machine, and posters of exotic cars on the walls, some showing engine schematics.

When our helpful rental agent, Mike, was finished with some paperwork, he asked Dom to fill out a two-page questionnaire, and then checked his driver's license for a full minute. He gave Dom the discounted rate of $600 for the day (usual is $900), but he had to put the whopping $7000 holding charge on his credit card; this, he said, would be refunded when the car was returned.

After that, he took us into the attached garage where the six-month-old Ferrari F430 Spider in Nuovo Rosso F1 red was waiting. It had just been washed, so the sexy Pininfarina-designed curves of the fenders sparkled like the caps of ocean waves in sunlight. When Mike opened the door to the car, the smell of warm, expensive leather wafted out. He inserted the key into the ignition and hit the button that lowered the convertible top.

Then, it was time for Dom to take his place in the cockpit so the tutorial could begin.

"Ooof," said Dom as his butt finally connected with the soft, tan-coloured driver's seat.

"Yeah, you fall into a Ferrari, you don't get in," Mike said, laughing. The seat was about a foot lower than where a butt expects it to be, since these cars sit a mere four inches above the road. I fell into the passenger seat beside Dom so I could listen to Mike's tutorial as well, since Dom had decided he wanted *me* to drive the Ferrari back to Woodbridge. After Gina's minivan was safe and sound back in her driveway, Dom said he'd drive us down to Checkpoint One of Operation Lucky Penny, which was located about a block away from Pineapple Head. I'd already locked up my bicycle at CP-One, so my plan was to ride over to Checkpoint Two and watch from the shadows to see Penny's reaction when Dom pulled up. However, we decided not to tell Mike that I'd be driving the Ferrari since we didn't want to pay extra on the rental contract.

"If you're going to be driving it in fully automatic," Mike said as he hovered over Dom's head and reached out, "you have to use the paddle shifters and click it into first gear, then click the Auto button, and then you can drive it just like any other vehicle."

"Right," Dom said as he nodded and pretended like driving a Ferrari was something he did every day.

"Now, as much as the car is going to feel automatic, it's a hundred percent standard," Mike said. "There's clutches and everything inside of it, it's just all computer controlled."

"Okay, no sweat," Dom said, "but the seat is too close to the steering wheel — where's the button?"

"Well, it's manual and the lever is under the seat. There's no power anything in this car except the windows, and there's only one set of buttons for that. They need to save weight, right, so no little motors to slide the seats around. It's basically a race-car for the street. There's not even any cup-holders."

It was true. For such an expensive car, it was pretty bare bones: basically a giant engine on wheels with a few rudimentary tools to control it. The instrument cluster was about as uncomplicated as the one on a Falconi tractor. Behind the little steering wheel there were five gauges, all analogue: oil temperature, oil pressure and coolant temperature on the left; a big yellow tachometer smack dab in the centre; and, on the extreme right, the speedometer, which went up to 360 kilometres per hour. Jeebus. In the middle of the dashboard was an Alpine stereo with a single CD slot; under that were the fresh air vents and three puny climate control dials. And then there was a glove box above the passenger's knees right where it ought to be. And that was it. There was no back seat since the massive engine took up the entire back third of the car; and, of course, the Ferrari engineers put it under a big window so that the whole world could see what's necessary to produce five hundred horsepower.

Mike reached over again and slapped the two paddle shifters forward to put the car into neutral, then he told Dom to press the big red start button on the steering wheel. "VARROOOOOSHH," the car said in Ferrari-speak. Then it settled into a quiet purr, like a big jungle-cat digesting a juicy gazelle steak. Mike said that we still had to put the car into first gear with the UP paddle shifter on the right before we started driving, even though it would take care of the shifting for us after that. He shook Dom's hand and started to walk back to the sad little door surrounded by cinderblock. I heaved myself out of the car and headed to Gina's sad minivan.

Dom took his foot off the brake. Nothing.

"Hey, Mike, the car isn't moving," Dom shouted. We both turned around.

"You've got to give it some gas," Mike shouted back. "Just like a standard transmission, you'll feel the clutch engage even though you're not releasing a clutch pedal with your left foot. When you do feel it release, just give it some more gas."

Dom gave 'er a little more juice, and the car lurched forward like a cheetah straining against its leash. And with that, he was off on the biggest adventure of his life.

A minute later, we were both pulled over at the side of South Service Road playing musical cars. Even though he hadn't said it, I knew Dom was far more comfortable driving Gina's Honda Odyssey on the unfamiliar highways back to Woodbridge. I told him that if the spirit moved me and I opened up the Ferrari, I'd be sure to pull over so he could catch up with me. We both had cellphones with each other's number on speed-dial in case Dom lost his way, which was a distinct possibility since, after the Queen Elizabeth Way, we'd have to use Ontario's lone toll road, the 407, which he'd never been on before. Thankfully, the 407 would get us most of the way back to Gina's place.

The car performed pretty nicely at lower speeds. The engine wasn't too loud and the steering, as I had expected, was tight and responsive; you could also feel every microscopic pebble the tires rolled over. There were two little dents in the steering wheel at exactly the right place for my thumbs to sink into, and inside each of those was a horn button so I didn't have to move my hands to toot at someone. Not that I had to; when you're driving a red Ferrari, everyone notices you, even on the highway. All those eyeballs were a little off-putting, since I've never been one for the spotlight. I'm also not one of those guys, like Dom, who thinks that owning a car like this means I've made it in life. To me, owning a super-expensive car means I'd just have something else to cause me super-worry. I was also not so sure a girl like Penny was going to care if Dom showed up in this car or sitting on top of the Falconi Finch for the Big Date. Then again, while Dom may not have realized it, it was obvious to me that these cars were all about making *the man* feel confident and have very little to do with the woman. Hey, if Dom needed a little boost to land a good woman, why not? One day he'd figure out that a car like that doesn't prove anything, especially his manhood.

All of my musings, however, didn't mean I was against stomping down hard on the gas pedal to see what that sucker could do for *my* manhood. A few minutes into the drive, the traffic opened up, so I opened up the engine. It roared to life as the car downshifted to deliver raw power to the big back tires. Within two seconds I'd gone from quietly cruising with the pack at 110 to leaving everyone behind, including

Dom, as if they were standing still. I looked down: 230 km/h. Holy crap. Thank goodness there wasn't a speed trap along here. I moved back into the slow lane and brought the Ferrari down to 100; it grumbled its disapproval. Dom was a speck in the rear view mirror. I'm sure he was laughing and shaking his head at his impetuous little brother.

At 4:30 p.m., Dom was taking it really easy with the Ferrari as we drove from Gina's place back downtown. He was acting like we were inside a delicate Fabergé egg and he was an old lady driving to church on Sunday. Other drivers didn't honk at us, however, since they were used to douchebags in expensive cars cruising slowly in order to soak up extra admiration and awe. At a stoplight, I put the top up because I was tired of the gawking. Dom protested. I promised we'd open it again before the big reveal to Penny. Once it was up, we realized that there was absolutely no blindspot-checking ability, so we agreed that unless it was raining, it was going to stay down until he got to the restaurant. He had reservations at Toronto's oldest steakhouse, Barberian's, a little, white-brick place full of crests and Canadiana that is steps from busy Yonge Street. It's a place that Sinatra used to patronize when he was in town playing the Gardens. Also, we'd checked beforehand and they offered valet parking. I didn't want Dom to worry about finding a parking spot.

I knew it was bugging him, but I kept asking if he'd got the hang of the Ferrari's weird automatic gear shifting, which has pauses in it like real shifting. Since I had just driven the car for eighty kilometres from Stoney Creek to

Woodbridge, I had become used to it myself, but for the first little while I'd lifted my foot off the gas when I'd feel the pause, which would make the car buck and lurch. The best way to drive the F430, I'd discovered, was to just press the gas pedal smoothly and let the little Ferrari robots do their thing. When I also suggested that maybe he shouldn't bother fiddling with the CD player that night, he'd had enough.

"Man, Freddy, lay off already!" he said. "I know how to drive a car, and I'm putting on the Rush *Greatest Hits* album — the best car in the world deserves the best band, man! Look, I promise I'll put the CD in and just let it play in a loop, okay?"

"Okay, I just worry too much, that's all."

We had a few hours to kill before Dom's date, so we parked the Ferrari in front of my place and went inside so Dom could freshen up. He was pacing the room and picking up random objects, inspecting them intently, and putting them back down again, so I turned on the TV. He sat for a bit to watch the rerun of *Friends* that was on. But he was up again within a few minutes, so I suggested maybe he could use a disco nap, since he was between events. He started singing "Macho Man" by the Village People and dancing around instead.

Checkpoint Two. That meant it was just before 7 p.m. and I was tucked into a Kensington laneway between two housestores across from Pineapple Head. Yesterday, I'd spoken to the owners of both to tell them I'd be lurking here for a few minutes, so I wasn't worried that they'd call the cops. I could see what I needed to see from this vantage point, and there was a big tree in one of the front yards that I could use as a shield if required. My Motorola Razr vibrated: It was Dom.

"Is she outside yet?" he asked. I could hear that he was nervous.

"Not yet, bro, hold on. Wait, I see someone in the window. It's her, she's flipping over the OPEN sign to CLOSED! She looks good, Dom. Emerald green dress."

"Should I drive over now?"

"Yeah, yeah, you don't want to be late and make a bad impression."

Within seconds I could hear the Ferrari's engine in the distance at CP-One; that's how distinctive it was. Penny had just stepped onto the narrow porch after locking the store door. She had some product in her hair to make it look kind of spikey, and there was a big, silk flower in yellow pinned into it to soften things up. She was wearing a fair bit of makeup but it was really well done; either she knew how to do a smoky eye or she had gone to a professional. The dress was tight but flattering; it had a cowl-neck and a slit up the side of the skirt. She was wearing yellow kitten heels. And she was smiling.

The Ferrari slid around the corner. I had no idea Dom even owned them, but he was wearing the same sunglasses Pacino's Tony Montana wears in *Scarface* — the aviators with the white stripe on top — and he looked as cool as a freakin' cucumber. So cool, in fact, that Penny didn't even recognize him at first.

He shut off the engine and said loudly: "Hey, any hot chicks around here looking for a date? Maybe someone named Penny who likes Italian coffee?"

At the sound of her name, Penny looked over. "Dommy? DOMMY!" It wasn't graceful, but she started jumping up and down at the sight of him. "A RED car?! For me?" She ran down the stairs as he lifted himself up from the seat to greet her. They hugged. She kissed him on the shoulder as he held her. It was absolutely beautiful. Like a real gentleman, Dom lifted a finger to keep Penny back as he trotted around the car and opened the passenger door. He checked for traffic, and then went back over to escort her. He held her hand as she hiked up her dress to lower herself into the car. He closed the door gently. As she adjusted herself, he quickly looked in my direction, pulled down his shades and gave me a wink. I gave him a discreet thumbs-up. As he burbled off to Checkpoint Three, the steakhouse, I started pedaling back to Checkpoint Three-B, my house. It was not like I was going to go to Barberian's wearing a pair of plastic eyeglasses with the built-in plastic nose and moustache. I mean, we had discussed it, but ...

Just as I was sitting down to a what's-in-the-fridge stir fry, the telephone rang. It had been about ninety minutes since I had gotten home, so I assumed it was Dom with an Operation Lucky Penny status report from Checkpoint Three. It was.

"How's it going?" I asked. "Was the car okay to handle?"

"Geez, Flowerboy, stop with the car already. How fast can you drive in this city anyway? Hey, it was so funny: we were stopped at the lights at Dundas and University, and this guy in a Corvette looks over, checking us out. I look over and give him a big smile, then I rev the engine really loud. He just laughs and mouths you win and gives me a thumbs-up. It was awesome."

"Ha ha, that *is* awesome. So how's it going with Penny?"

"Ah, man, she's the best," he said, finally sounding comfortable. "We had a cocktail and an appetizer already. I had the jumbo shrimp and she had something called Cockles Saint Jacques. And before you lecture me, I promise I'm only gonna have one drink. Anyhow, we just ordered our main course: I'm havin' the rib eye, she's havin' the New York strip. Says she can eat the whole thing! I said I had to go to the washroom so I could call you, bro."

"Yeah, that's great, but I'm not talking about the food. How are you getting along? Is there stuff to talk about?"

"*Madonn'* she doesn't shut up!" he said, laughing. "But it's great, I don't mind at all. She's got big dreams, man! She wants to open an art school for children, one that specializes in Down kids or autistic ones. She really wants to make a difference in the world. She's already looking at business models and corporate sponsorships to make it happen. Her mom is totally on board."

"So great, man. Are you getting a word in edgewise?"

"Yeah, yeah, but she already knows about my weird life. I did mention to her that I'd been to Italy and she really got excited about that. I think she used to travel with her mom a little, but now that there's the store they can't get away as much."

"So you'll take her to the Old Country," I said with a chuckle. "Just don't take her to Latina, stick to the tried and tr—"

"Hey, Freddy, sorry to interrupt, but I gotta split soon. First, though, I want to thank you for all your help. Not just with the car today, but for, you know, everything." He paused, and then sighed: "This is the best day of my friggin' life."

∽

The next scheduled contact was to be from Checkpoint-Four, in front of 460 Queens Quay West, Penny's home. Dom was going to call once he'd escorted her inside and she'd stepped safely into the elevator. Penny lives with her mom, Deborah, in a big, two-bedroom condo on the seventh floor of a terraced building from the 1980s called King's Landing. The National Ballet of Canada has a practice facility on the lower level, which is kind of neat. From their balcony, Penny and Deborah can watch sailboats glide across Lake Ontario, contemplate the decaying concrete of the Canada Malting silos at the foot of Bathurst Street, or watch people frolic in the Yo-Yo Ma-designed park, Toronto Music Garden, right across the street. If I lived there, I'd go down into that park and look back up at the building, since it was designed by one of Canada's best architects, Arthur Erickson, who lives in Vancouver and did some ground-breaking houses there in the 1950s.

Anyhow, around 11:15 p.m., just as I was dozing off in front of an episode of HGTV's *House Hunters*, my phone rang, but it wasn't my cell. As soon as I heard Small Carm's deep voice on the other end of the line, I knew it couldn't be good, since he'd usually be sawing logs by that time.

"Freddy, there's been some kind of accident with Dom," he said in his flat baritone. "Apparently he's okay but acting totally spacey, like the old days. Some young girl with a lisp, she sounded about eighteen, just called me. What the frig?

He's supposed to be up at Gina's. Anyways, they're at the bottom of Spadina by the water. I'm going down there right now."

"Oh God, oh God. Okay, I'll hop on my bike and be right there too."

"The cops are on their way," he said. His voice got lower. "Something tells me you might know what this is all about?"

Light rain was falling on Dom as he sat against one of the big concrete columns that holds up the office building at Lower Spadina and Queens Quay West, one building over from Penny's condo. His striped blue tie was still done up neatly around his neck, but his cream-coloured jacket had a big black streak across the front. Like the tourist-trap tall ship rocking in its berth across the street, Dom was cradling his legs as he rocked back and forth like an autistic child. He was mumbling to himself. He was on Planet Xenon and it seemed like he'd be visiting for a while, since my voice didn't register with him when I approached.

The Ferrari was sitting against a thick, black light standard ten feet away. I could see that both airbags had deployed. The moulded front bumper was so lopsided it touched the road, and the aluminum around the front passenger wheel-well was shredded like paper; there were red triangles scattered all over the place. The inner workings of the complex suspension system were visible behind the front tire because it was sticking out sideways. The beautiful and expensive rim was cracked, too. There was a long black gash along the passenger door. Wiggly tire marks ran from the back of the car to the curving, wet streetcar tracks on Spadina.

I walked over to Small Carm, who was towering over Penny. She had an airbag bruise on one cheek and her makeup was smeared. Amazingly, he was keeping his cool and listening to her story.

"... on a bicycle comes out of nowhere. Dommy swerved to avoid him but I guess the car slipped on the streetcar tracks. Then we kind of bucked as the wheels caught again and then the next thing I know we hit the lamp-post. Dom asked if I was okay, and I said yes."

"I'm glad you're okay. Penny, was it?" he asked.

"Yes, Penny Keyes, Dommy's *girlfriend*," she answered steadily as Small Carm's eyes widened slightly. Penny turned toward me. "Hello Freddy Flowers. I'm so sorry to see you under these circumstances. I'm very worried about Dommy. When he went outside to look at the car, his face went kind of blank. After he helped me to the sidewalk, he just went and sat over there, where he is now. I asked him if he needed a doctor, and he shook his head. I asked him who we should call before we call the police, and he handed me his cellphone. I found the entry labeled 'home' so I pressed that one."

"You handled yourself beautifully," I said. I could hear the adrenaline causing my voice to rise in pitch. I could also feel my heart rate climbing.

"Dom used to get like this when he was younger, but it hasn't happened in a long time," Small Carm said. His voice sounded like it was coming up out of the sewer. "Usually he'd snap out of it in a few minutes. A few times it went a lot longer, but as I said that's not the norm."

"I guess this isn't normal, eh?" I said with an awkward

laugh to try and ease the tension. Small Carm shot me a look and finally asked me if I was in on this.

"Yeah, I helped him rent the car. But c'mon, Small Carm, Dom is a grown man. If he wants to — "

Just then, a police car announced itself with a loud double chirp as it stopped abruptly in front of us. Deborah had just come downstairs and walked over. She gave me a small wave and then ran over to Penny and hugged her tightly; their embrace was illuminated by a jerky red and blue lightshow. Taking charge, Small Carm approached the officers and told them who everyone was and what their roles were in this little drama. I could hear him explaining what was wrong with Dom, and that he'd bring him in for a statement when he was feeling better. A flatbed tow truck pulled up behind the police car and a skinny guy with greasy hair jumped out, a key ring jingling at his hip. He let out a low whistle as he shambled over to the smashed Ferrari. I looked over and Penny and a very worried-looking Deborah had crouched down in front of Dom. As Deborah put her hand on his unresponsive head, an officer pulled Penny away, still the calmest one out of all of us, to ask her some questions.

Well, Small Carm seemed pretty calm too, but I know him too well: I could tell that his blood was boiling beneath the surface.

CHAPTER X

☞ Falconi's Tractor ☜

I WOULD HAVE thought that destroying the front end of a Ferrari would rank pretty high on a person's Worst Day Ever list. But the *braciole* really hit the fan after Penny and Deborah had gone home and Small Carm and I finally escorted the mumbling, stumbling Dom into the Falconi building after a very silent drive up Spadina. I've seen Small Carm disappointed over the years and I've seen him quietly angry, but he just exploded, Mount Etna style.

"Do you have ANY IDEA what I've done for you two over the years? DO YOU?" He was pacing back and forth under the harsh florescent lights of the showroom as beads of sweat dotted his forehead. Out the window, late-night club-goers, washed in the orange of the streetlights, stopped and pointed at the three of us, completely surprised to see people and activity in the weird old building with the red tractor in the window. "I paid for your schooling, Freddy! I HELPED YOU BUY YOUR HOUSE!"

Dom was still in a semi-trance. He was slumped over in one of Dad's ridiculous, designer chairs, which have been scratched and faded for a while now. His eyes were beginning to focus as he blinked up at the bright lights and the one brown ceiling tile where there had been a leak a few months ago. Then he squinted at Small Carm and cocked his head in an effort to understand why he was yelling so loudly.

"And YOU," he said, thrusting a big beefy index finger in Dom's general direction, "I've taken care of you for the past TWENTY-THREE years. You've lived the life of Riley in here with your stupid model kits and your stupid pet squirrel while I get up EVERY DAY to work to keep food in the refrigerator! To keep the furnace and the AC running. To keep the lights on. HAVE YOU EVER HAD TO WORRY ABOUT MONEY, DOM?" Droplets of spit were flying from Small Carm's mouth. Shiny lines of sweat now framed his face.

"Hey, man, c'mon," I finally said. "The guy's been through a lot tonight. I mean, can't this wait until tomorrow, when we can call the rental company and see what's what?"

"You're right, Freddy, you're right," Small Carm said, his voice lowering. He stopped pacing. He stood still for a moment and looked out the window. Maybe this was the end of the tirade.

"The thing is, I took over the family because I had to," he said. "There was no one else. No one ... you understand?" His voice started to tremble. I'd never seen Small Carm cry before, so I wasn't sure if that's what I was witnessing. Was that sweat, spit, or tears on his cheek?

"What do you do when your entire future is decided in one second?" he asked, softly. "What would you have done if *you* were *me*?"

Silence for thirty seconds as Small Carm just stood there, breathing, his big salamis hanging limply at his sides. Dom didn't look confused any longer, but the silence had become too much for him. He started to fidget, so I spoke up. "We know what you did for this family, Small Carm."

Mount Etna again.

"DO YOU FREDDY? Because if you did you wouldn't have gone behind my back. You wouldn't have done something this STUPID. RENTING A FERRARI? DOM HASN'T DRIVEN A CAR IN FIFTEEN YEARS. BUT YOU KNOW THIS."

Finally, Dom cleared his throat and spoke: "I can drive a car. I'm not an idiot. Some *testa di cazzo* on a bike swerved in front of me."

"YOU'RE NOT AN IDIOT? Maybe, but you're no *rocket scientist* either, Dom. Where would you be without my protection? Without this roof over your head? What if I THREW YOU OUT? Could you live on your own? Could you support yourself? NO, YOU'D HAVE TO LIVE WITH YOUR OWN KIND: RETARDS. WITH AROUND-THE-CLOCK NURSES TO LOOK AFTER YOU. BECAUSE ONLY A RETARD WOULD DO SOMETHING LIKE THIS."

At that, Dom bolted out of his chair and charged Small Carm. His arms outstretched, the palms of both of his hands slammed into Small Carm's chest and pushed him backward with an incredible amount of force. One of his salami-arms flew up and backward and hit the big teak desk. It made a horrible, wet snapping noise. There was a subsonic thump as Small Carm's big body connected with the hard tile floor. His golf shirt wrinkled upward and exposed his hairy belly. The gold crucifix around his neck glued itself to the sweat on his forehead. His face was contorted and he was clearly seeing stars.

I was immobilized; I just stood there and watched the insanity unfold as if in slow motion.

Dom ran past Small Carm's splayed body and into his model-making room. He was making weird, laughing-grunting noises. "I'll show you what a RETARD does!" he yelled. I could hear the sounds of clattering metal from the old drafting studio.

Small Carm shook his head and stumbled as he tried to get to his feet. I offered my hand. He grabbed it with the hand attached to his one good arm. We entered Dom's model room just as Dom took the first swing with the big steel driver. A shower of plastic bits rained down on us as an entire division of tiny army tanks was turned instantly into shrapnel. Then, the history of Lamborghini, from the 350 GT to the Gallardo, was erased with another incredible swing. A dozen Ferraris, all red, were destroyed in a great crimson explosion. CRASH! SMASH! Holding the golf club like a bat, he beat down on the aircraft carriers and battleships like they were big, disgusting insects.

"I'M NOT FUCKING RETARDED," he screamed.

Like piñatas, Dom attacked a squadron of warplanes that dangled overhead. Tiny bits of plastic lodged in my hair, my eyes, and stuck to the perspiration on my cheek. *"YOU'RE* FUCKING RETARDED, POLISHING THAT FUCKING TRACTOR ALL THE TIME."

Dom ran past us, swinging the club wildly over his head. Instinctively, we both ducked as we heard the whoosh of air. He ran across the showroom. He stopped at the Falconi Finch in the window for a split second.

"HOW ABOUT *YOUR* FERRARI? HUH?" The club came down hard and pinged off the back fender, leaving a big dent and a divot of bare metal. Then he started hammering it — PING! PING! PING! PING! — but it wasn't doing enough damage, so he moved to the front. Each headlight shattered easily and loudly. The club went through the grille next. THOCK! He took a swipe at the engine, but the club got caught in the tangle of sparkplug wires, so he yanked it out quickly and rammed it into the louvered hood instead.

"YOU LOVE THIS FUCKING PIECE OF SHIT," he screamed. His voice was as ragged as the chunks of Ferrari he'd scattered across Queens Quay West an hour ago. Small Carm and I stood there, transfixed. If we moved too close, Dom's backswing would've brained one of us. After he'd repeatedly slammed the club into the big green rims and made them look as if someone had emptied a shotgun on them, he turned to the dashboard.

CRASH, TINKLE. The impact to the main instrument panel sent tiny fragments of glass into the air. A few caught Dom in the hands, so, within seconds, tiny dots of blood appeared on his skin. His roundhouse to the steering wheel was so powerful, it took a small chunk out of it.

His next blow was to the lower dashboard. A toggle switch went flipping through the air. Then the glove box —

"NOOOOOOOO, DOM, DON'T!" Small Carm screamed at the top of his lungs. His voice was so loud I think the windows rattled. Dom was startled into stillness. He turned around to face Small Carm; his cheeks were wet and red and his chest was heaving.

"*MOM* IS IN THERE!!!" Small Carm said. Dom stared at him for a full two seconds and then dropped the golf club with a clatter. He walked out the door and into the cool night air of Spadina Avenue.

∽

I left Small Carm standing there, face contorted, veins pulsing, good arm cradling his broken one, and rushed outside to chase after Dom. There are about fifteen buildings between the Falconi building and the first cross street, and he was walking so quickly he was already halfway to it. I ran to catch up. I grabbed the arm of his cream-coloured jacket, which was cuffed with a ring of blood.

"Dom, STOP."

He stopped. I let go. He started walking again, a bit slower. I came up beside him.

"What the fuck is Small Carm talking about, 'Mom's in there'?!?"

We were at Cecil Street. There was a crowd milling about and smoking outside of Grossman's Tavern. Must have been a blues band just finished their set.

"Come down here," Dom said, and pulled me in the direction of Cecil. We walked down the dimly lit street. A few seconds later, we were at the entrance to the alley that would deposit us at the Falconi building's familiar concrete pad and Black Locust tree. He walked quickly up the alley, navigating as much by muscle memory as by sight. It was suddenly very quiet; all I could hear were our dual footsteps echoing off of the multiple garage doors. Dom stopped and pressed his back against a concrete block wall covered in graffiti.

"Mom's ashes," he said, still out of breath.

"What?!?"

"He must've been keeping them in the glove box," he said, his voice raspy. A lone cricket was sawing away to the left of us. "I didn't know. All he said was that he'd taken care of it. He'd had her cremated."

He let his back slide down the wall until he was sitting on the asphalt, legs sticking straight out like a ventriloquist's dummy. I sat next to him. He started to make gasping noises. Hiccups, maybe? It took me a few seconds to realize he was crying. I'd never seen him cry before either.

"I don't want to go live in a group home, Freddy," he said. "I can't."

"You can live with me," I said as I put my arm around him.

"How could Small Carm *say* those things? We're blood. We're family."

"I know, bro, I know."

"I'm not retarded."

"I know that too."

"There's something you don't know," he said in a weird small voice, like a child telling a ghost story. "I don't wanna think about it, Freddy, but you should know the truth about The Incident."

"Are you sure you want to tell me right now?"

He didn't answer. "Her beautiful face was blue, Freddy. There were red veins all over it. Her tongue was sticking out," he said, gasping for air. I could feel his body convulsing. "She was hanging there when I found her. From the ceiling joist. Like a fucking ragdoll. Twirling and twirling."

"I — I had no idea," I stammered. My heart was beating so loudly, I couldn't hear the cricket anymore.

"She had FUCKING PISS AND SHIT DOWN HER LEG, Freddy. I still can't fucking believe it. When Small Carm came home, we went upstairs and cut her down."

I don't know how long we cried together, but it was a really long time.

༄

The next morning, Dom and I were crabby because we hadn't slept very well. He was sitting at my garbage-picked, chrome-and-Formica dining table complaining that my coffee was weak. I was telling him to go down to the Starbucks, then. He was saying that he let Penny down and she's never going to want to see him again. He was going on and on that Gina and I are his only friends in the world, and that he's supposed to call her to give a report on the big date, but he can't because he's too embarrassed. He was talking about anything but the alleyway last night, when he told me everything he could remember about The Incident. Then the phone rang: It was the exotic car place.

For obvious reasons, they said that they were not happy. They showed up to unlock their sad little door but instead found their six-month-old Ferrari ripped open at the front with a bum wheel and a business card from a random tow truck company under the windshield wiper. There was an emergency number we were supposed to call if anything happened, they said; I vaguely remember Mike telling us about this, but a lot happened in the twelve hours that followed, I argued back. They suggested that the deductible we'd have to pay was not going to be pretty. Then they threatened Dom with a civil suit. I finished by asking them to call back later when I could think straight.

With the cordless still in my hand, I offered to call Gina on Dom's behalf. He just grunted and said: "Just don't make me sound too stupid, bro." She was very sympathetic and understanding, and after a few minutes she asked to speak with Dom. He begrudgingly took the phone but walked out the front door and into my postage-stamp front yard. I could see him pacing back-and-forth along the tiny pathway between the flowerbeds.

When he came back inside a few minutes later, he looked slightly less pained, so I said: "Well, there's an elephant in the room and its name is Small Carm. Who's gonna call him, you or me?"

To my surprise, Dom said: "I'll do it. You were just a bystander, Freddy. Me and Small Carm freaked out on each other."

Dom hit the Falconi number on speed-dial. "It's ringing," he said. A few seconds went by. "It's the C. Falconi Investments message. I'll try his cell." Dom couldn't find it on my speed-dial, so he punched it in by memory.

I figured Small Carm picked up, because Dom said: "Hey bro, it's me." There was a five second pause as Dom listened. His mouth opened slightly and his eyes closed. He slowly lowered the phone from his ear.

"What did he say?" I asked.

"He said: 'You broke my fucking arm. Go find someplace else to live.' Then he hung up on me."

CHAPTER XI

☞ The Incident ☜

MY HEAD HAS been spinning since Small Carm hung up on Dom. I feel doubly betrayed by him: Not only did I not know the truth about my own mother, he's turned his back on Dom when Dom needs him the most. I also feel stupid. I fell for the story that Mom died of a broken heart, hook, line and sinker. I also went along with the whole missing person's thing because Small Carm said it was better for the honour of the family; plus that whole blood oath ceremony thing he made us do made a big, scary impression on me. I had nightmares with bloody hands reaching out to grab me for years because of it. I was nine, so that makes sense ... but I did grow up.

So why didn't I question things? Why didn't I ask Small Carm why Mom was "buried" in Sicily and not here in Canada? Good thing I never went to visit her grave. Why didn't I ask why we were giving Nonna Caporuscio, Aunt Anna and Aunt Candida false hope by making them think Rosa might come back one day? Because I believed my big brother. Because we'd lost touch with the Caporuscios after a dozen years. Because we, as a family, don't talk about The Incident very much.

The Incident is like the Falconi Black Hole: It's at the centre of all of our lives; it's supremely powerful, but if we cross the event horizon, we'll get sucked into it and be ripped apart. Like last night, when Dom freaked out with the golf club. So we all pussyfoot around and pretend like everything is fine. I went to the police because I was fed up. Everything is *not* fine.

∽

Our family is once again in panic-mode: Small Carm has been charged with second degree murder.

I'm not naïve, I knew the police would immediately arrest Small Carm when they went to the Falconi building. They told me they would do so within two hours. But after the way he'd treated Dom, I didn't have a choice. I was also worried he'd do something stupid, like destroy Mom's ashes or the suicide note Dom said must be in the tractor's glove box along with them. What I didn't expect was that he'd be charged with murder after the police conducted their interview with him.

It's not like Small Carm reached out to Dom and me to let us know. Once he was in custody, he called Gina. She was the least complicit in Operation Lucky Penny, so I guess she was the only one he figured he could turn to in a crisis; it helps, too, that brother-in-law Rocco has a cousin who's a criminal lawyer. Gina went down to the police station before he was interviewed, when the charges were just offering an indignity to a corpse and public mischief for filing the missing person's report in 1984. While Small Carm was allowed to wait until Rocco's cousin, Ed Petrucci, showed up before the cops started the interrogation, he didn't remain silent after that: He told the police everything that happened that day, despite Ed's coaching.

He said that, at the time, he was still under the impression the Catholic Church wouldn't give Mom a proper burial after a suicide. (Turns out he was close; the Catholic Church only reversed this decision in 1983.) Back before the internet, you couldn't get an answer to a question like that so quickly, I guess. So he was forced to take care of Mom's cremation on his own. He started going on about how suicide is the worst sin a person can commit. He quoted Article Five of St. Thomas Aquinas' *Summa Theologica*, where it's written that "suicide is always a mortal sin as being contrary to the natural law and to charity" and that "to bring death upon oneself in order to escape the other afflictions of this life, is to adopt a greater evil in order to avoid a lesser." This was why he filed the missing person's report; it was about the honour of the Falconi name, he said. The cops thought this was all very suspicious, like he was trying to throw them off the trail of a murder, so that's when they slapped the big charge on him.

I didn't know about the murder charge when I left the police station after giving my statement, of course. But I did tell Dom what I'd done, because I didn't want any more secrets in the family. He actually took it kind of well.

"It was about setting the record straight," I said. "There have been too many lies in this family."

"I understand," he said quietly. "Remember, I've been walking around with this for twenty-three years. You've only known the whole story for twenty-three hours."

"Well, maybe that's the problem," I said. "If you hold

onto something so surreal for so long, maybe it becomes sorta normal, like a part of you, and the urgency goes away."

Dom nodded.

"I just want Mom to rest," I said. "I want the few people in our extended family who still give a crap to be able to rest their *brains*, you know?"

Dom got up from his chair and started pacing the room. "Do you think Small Carm will go to jail, Freddy?"

"I don't know," I said, detecting a slight tremble in my voice. "It was a long time ago. He thought he was doing the right thing."

Dom was transformed into a silhouette as he paused in front of the living room window to watch two kids beat the snot out of each other in the alleyway across the street. "Do you think I'll get charged, Freddy? I mean, I'm the one who found her. I helped Small Carm wrap her up and put her in his car."

"Dom, you were seventeen. Plus you didn't know what he was going to do. He drove away that afternoon and took care of everything. You went back to school. He also went to file the missing person's report completely on his own."

I didn't have the heart to add that, with his Planet Xenon episodes and learning disability, no jury would ever convict him, even if he *was* guilty of anything.

Convincing Gina that I had done the right thing by ratting out Small Carm wasn't quite as easy. When Dom phoned her, she lost it and demanded he hand over the phone so she could give me a good chewing out. Dom refused. He went over what we had just talked about with her. I heard more tinny yelling on the other end. When Dom explained it again, tenderly, lovingly, calling her Gina-beana-bumbalina, she quieted down. But it wasn't her love for me that convinced her; it was her love for Dom.

∽

The Crown hasn't requested a preliminary inquiry. This has Gina, Dom and me worried because we take that to mean the prosecution feels it has a pretty strong case. Small Carm and Petrucci didn't bother applying for bail; he had no sureties and the Crown was going to suggest he was a flight risk like his hero, Big Carm. Through meetings with Petrucci at the Don Jail, Small Carm has made it quite clear that he wants nothing to do with Dom and me, so until the trial in Superior Court starts next week, all we know is what Gina tells us, and she's pretty busy helping Petrucci build his case. About all Dom and I know for sure at this point is that we're going to have to testify because we've already been subpoenaed, and we're pretty nervous about that.

I've taken an extended leave from work. They understand. And to keep myself distracted until next week, I'm going to make sure Dom gets in touch with Penny to let her know what's going on. Something tells me she'll stick by his side no matter what. Even when she finds out Small Carm belongs to a cult.

Gina told us about the cult angle because it's going to be a huge part of both the Crown's case and our own. The Crown is going to claim that Small Carm was under the influence of Opus Dei, a cult-like group within the Catholic Church, when he "murdered" Mom; the defence is going to claim that he wasn't a member in June of 1984, and, besides, it's a legitimate organization with altruistic aims. None of us knew about Small Carm's membership, by the way, but Gina says Small Carm keeps insisting it wasn't a secret. He says there are many scholarly books on the subject on the bookshelf behind his desk, in plain sight beside the super-boring *The Silence of Pius XII* by Carlo Falconi, which Small Carm gave me to read when I was a teenager (but I didn't) because Carlo was Nonno Joe's third cousin. There are even a few popular fiction titles including *The Death of Faith* by Donna Leon and the bestseller *The Da Vinci Code*, which both feature characters who belong to Opus Dei. These, he says, make his membership quite clear.

Depending on who you ask, Opus Dei, which means "Work of God" in Latin, is either a place for out-of-touch nutbars, or for Catholics who really want to do good things in the world. It's an institution of the Catholic Church that was founded in Spain in 1928 by a priest named Josemaría Escrivá, who has since been sainted. It was given the stamp of approval by the Church in 1950, and further strengthened by the very popular Pope John Paul II, who in the early 1980s, gave it additional status as a personal prelature. This means that the group is autonomous and doesn't have to answer to the local arm of the Church in the cities in which it operates. The official line of Opus Dei is that it's an organization that promotes being "a saint in everyday life." According to St. Josemaría, members should practice "divine filiation," which means carrying a "deep awareness" of "being children of God," that they perform "sanctifying work," whether that work is "outstanding or humble and hidden," and practice piety "such as prayer, daily Mass, sacramental confession, and reading and meditating on the Gospel." There is an additional blurb on their website that stresses members "act with freedom and personal responsibility, not involving the Church or Opus Dei in their decisions, nor presenting those decisions as the only Catholic solutions."

Critics say that last statement is malarkey. Since Opus Dei's inception, many people have described it as a dangerous cult that damages the aims of the Catholic Church. They say it's a highly secretive organization with questionable recruitment tactics, that it bullies its members, and it was, in its early days, supportive of Hitler and Mussolini — so much so that members were part of Francisco Franco's government in Spain. Influential members of the Catholic community, such as new, and very young owners of tractor companies for instance, are often targeted for membership and love-bombed until they are flattered into joining. Once they're locked in, they're forced to meet with a Spiritual Director once a week and pressured to reveal the most intimate details of their lives. It's rumoured that the twenty percent of Opus Dei members called Numeraries, who are celibate and live in residences run by the group, allow their mail to be opened and read, and willingly accept that certain books are banned. Small Carm, who joined as a Supernumerary (this is seventy percent of the membership, while the other ten percent are priests) shortly after Mom died, thankfully didn't enjoy these "privileges," as Supernumeraries are able to marry and have jobs, but they are expected to contribute financially. Some ex-members say they were forced to choose between their families and the group, however, and harassed if they chose the former.

And speaking of ex-members, a group called the Opus Dei Awareness Network was formed in 1991 to help people who have been adversely affected by the group. Their website has links to dozens of personal stories of escape, with articles such as "How Opus Dei is Cult-like," "I Was Shocked by Hidden Agendas" and "My Nightmarish Experience in Opus Dei."

Many Opus Dei members practice mortification of the flesh, which means that they either deny themselves certain pleasures or they punish themselves for being sinners. Apparently Small Carm does both. He fasts regularly, he sometimes sleeps on the floor, and when he's alone he'll open the windows in winter so that he's super cold and uncomfortable. He has also been wearing a discomfort-inducing device called a cilice, which is a metal chain with inward-pointing prongs, around his upper thigh for decades. Maybe that's why I've never seen him in shorts. He uses a personal whip, called a discipline, to strike his back and shoulder during prayer. I saw this self-flagellation just once, when I was nine years old, during our Falconi blood oath ceremony.

The Toronto chapter of Opus Dei is run out of Ernscliffe College, a nicely scaled Modernist building at 156 St. George Street on the University of Toronto grounds, although the university makes it quite clear that they are not affiliated with them in any way. There is a strict curfew at Ernscliffe, and residents aren't permitted to own stereos or TV sets. There is a separate entrance for female Numeraries, who are tasked with the cooking and cleaning. Computers in the basement lab block many websites. Opus Dei has occupied the building since 1994, and there are extensive records of Small Carm signing in for visits going all the way back to that year (it's a fifteen minute walk from the Falconi building) and of cheques he's made out to the Director.

I don't know whether to feel good or bad about this.

The trial is held at Old City Hall, that beautiful Richardsonian Romanesque building from 1899 across the street from our current, also beautiful, futuristic city hall. The last time I was in a courtroom was in Grade 12, when our law class sat and watched a trial in that very building. I thought it was an imposing place to be back then ...

When I am escorted in, the first thing I notice is the jury. All different colours, young and old, soft faces and hard. They look like they are acutely aware they have someone's life in their hands. Then I see Small Carm, who looks particularly small sitting all by himself in the little fishbowl where the prisoner sits. His shaved head is bowed, and his eyes are closed. Thankfully he is wearing a real suit, not an orange one. He may have a temper, but he's always been a patient, gentle person, especially with me, and I feel an overwhelming sense of remorse. I want to run over and tell him I'm sorry, that I didn't mean to cause all of this to happen, that if I could go back in time I'd just let the lie continue so we could all be friends again and live together at the lip of the black hole.

I want to sit in the public area every day to show Small Carm that I do care about what happens to him, that I *do* love him, but the lawyers don't want my story of The Incident to affect the way it is told by other witnesses, and vice versa. So, me and Dom and Gina have been barred, apart from giving our own testimony, from the courtroom during the trial and also sequestered at home. That means Dom has gone back to live at the Falconi building (since Small Carm is in custody) and Gina stays up in Woodbridge. We aren't allowed to phone each other for obvious reasons, and this is extremely difficult for me, as Dom is still my confidant. At least I found out he saw Penny again through the few spy notes we exchanged before he started seeing helicopters.

You want to know what is even more difficult than not seeing Dom? The day I have to look Small Carm in the eye as I point him out for the record.

It's when I'm in the witness box and I'm asked to identify him that he looks up at me. His eyes meet mine for exactly one second, and it's the longest second of my life. I thought I'd seen a look of disappointment when I told him I was dropping out of Trent University; well, that was a walk in the park. This time, his dark eyes under those big caterpillar eyebrows drill into me with the most piercing, most haunted, most intense look I've ever experienced. I don't know if it's hatred or emptiness in those eyes, but it shakes me to my core. I want to curl up into the foetal position right there in the jury box and cry. Instead, in a very shaky voice, I tell the court everything I know.

Thursday, June 28, 1984 started off a little differently than most days. Conversation at the breakfast table was more animated, more interesting. Mom was asking everyone all kinds of questions about their plans for the summer and listening intently to our little, meaningless answers. She'd been like this for most of the week, and the three of us were relieved, since she'd been pretty glum for a long time. Even the crying had seemed to stop. That morning, she'd got up extra early and had whipped up a big batch of pancakes for us, with blueberries inside the batter, and had put real maple syrup on the table. We never got real maple syrup. I remember Dom asking: "Whose birthday are we forgetting today, Ma?" and all of us looking around the table at each other like we'd won the lottery.

The psychologist who testified on Small Carm's behalf said that this is classic behaviour. When a severely depressed person has made the decision to end their life, they feel an immense burden lifted from their shoulders. They feel euphoric because they know their pain is going to end. They spend their remaining days savouring life, having intimate conversations with those close to them, trying new things and, sometimes, they even mend fences with their enemies.

Dom and Gina and I went to school as usual, and Small Carm went downstairs to work at Falconi. He had to go up to the farm to meet someone later in the morning, so he was trying to get some paperwork off of his plate first. Around 9:30 a.m., Small Carm went upstairs to tell Mom he was leaving. She was in the bathtub, singing to herself. He found it odd, since she always preferred showers at night before bed, but he told her through the door that he was about to go up to the farm. She said the following:

"Carmy, you take care with your driving, okay?"

"Sure, Ma, I always do."

"No, do not just say it; promise me you will take extra care. You have too much aggression when you drive."

"I promise. I'll see you around one or two, okay?"

"Yes. Take your time. Thank you, Carmy, for helping me care for the family. I love you, my big serious man."

"Uh, I love you too, Ma. This big serious man will see you soon, okay?"

It was a weird exchange, he thought, but he shrugged it off and went to take care of business.

At 11:30 p.m., Dom got out of class and realized he'd forgotten to bring lunch money, so he couldn't go to the cafeteria and goof around like he always did. He had a spare period after lunch, so he decided to walk the eighteen minutes to the Falconi building and eat at home, then dash back to school. Instead, he ended up vomiting out his breakfast when he saw Rosa dangling from one of the exposed rafters of the living room ceiling. The furniture had all been pushed to the walls so she'd have nothing to grab onto, and the stepladder she'd used to secure the noose (and presumably to get her neck into it) was lying flat on the floor beneath her.

Dom ran out the back door and down the metal staircase. He ran down the alleyway. He ran as far as Queen Street and stopped. Queen West and Spadina, in those days, wasn't the hip strip of retail shops, advertising firms and media outlets it is today. In 1984, it was a seedy, Bohemian neighbourhood where outcasts and artists lived. A place for punks and poets, halfway houses and heroin. A group of Goths, all dressed in black and with spikey hair, white faces and heavy eyeliner, were pointing and laughing at him, so he turned around and started running back to the Falconi building. When he got there, he went into the backyard and sat under the Black Locust tree. He knew that when Small Carm came home, he'd pull up onto the concrete parking pad first. Then he took his first extended trip to Planet Xenon. He says he doesn't remember anything until Small Carm tapped him on the shoulder around 1 p.m.

The urgency in his eyes as he grabbed Small Carm's

arm and pulled him to the staircase, saying "Just come with me, this is an emergency," was so great, Small Carm didn't protest. While Small Carm didn't vomit when he got to the living room, he did feel weak in the knees, so he went to sit down. That was when he saw the suicide note that had been placed on Nonno Joe's favourite chair. Before he read it, however, he convinced Dom that they had to cut Mom down and lay her on the bed. Dom just stood there with big eyes, so Small Carm went into the kitchen and returned with a massive carving knife. After he got Dom to help him with the stepladder, he asked him to hold Mom's legs so she wouldn't fall to the floor once he'd cut the rope. As Dom grabbed her around the waist, the feces and sticky urine on her legs soaked into his shirt.

Once they'd carried her into the bedroom, Small Carm opened the envelope. The handwriting was meticulous, neat. There was a lipstick kiss-print on the bottom. It read:

My dearest Carmelo, Luigina, Domenico and Alfredo,
    I love you all so much. My heart bursts with love for you, my beautiful children. So you will not understand why I am doing this, but I hope that maybe someday you will.
    My mind is in such a dark place. It is a place I have visited many times in my life, even when I was a little girl in Sicily, but this time it is like I am a permanent resident, just like my sister. I cannot shake it. When I look at the beautiful birds singing in the trees, I think of how they all must die. When I see a man is crossing the street, I wonder if a car will hit him. When I look at my hands, I see the bones

underneath. I cannot stop thinking about death. It walks beside me as my companion.

But instead of being afraid, I have decided it is a good thing. It is a way to become quiet and peaceful. I have not been at peace for a long time. I have made a mask that I wear for you, but underneath the mask is the face of a sad monster. If I were to choose life, to stay here with you, you would see this face soon, and it would scare you. I will not be a good mother with this face, with this soul.

I look at you Carmy, and I see strength. My big man who never smiles, who is so serious, but I am so proud. You are the one who should take care of this family, not me.

Domenic, my comedian, my artist. You can make such things with your hands. Will you become a mechanic? A sculptor? Maybe one day you will make better tractors?

Gina, my little beautiful girl. You are my music, my free-spirit, but sometimes I see such sadness in your eyes. I pray that you will not be sad like me. Promise me you will go and find your happiness.

My Flower Boy, Freddy, you are sunshine. What will you become? I wish I could see it. Will you make tall buildings? Houses? Promise me you will.

I know you do not believe me now, but all of your lives will be better when I am gone. I am too broken and cannot be repaired. I do not know what is real any longer, and what is false. Except for one thing.

Remember I will love you always,
Mamma.

Small Carm folded up the note and tucked it into his pocket. He asked Dom if he could be alone for a few minutes. Dom obliged. Strangely, that's when Dom went back into Mom's bedroom to see her again. He says he doesn't know why he did this, but that's when he saw the library book on her bedside table: *The Ashley Book of Knots*. He picked it up, brought it to his room, and hid it in the closet.

A few minutes later, Small Carm knocked at Dom's door.

"I have a plan," he said. "Can you help me get Mom down to the car? I'll take it from there."

Dom helped Small Carm wrap Mom up in her bedclothes and bring her downstairs. Dom says that, as he watched the Seville's taillights disappear down the alley, he felt a massive sense of relief. The body was gone and it was now Small Carm's problem. After he'd changed into a clean shirt, he went back to school because he didn't know what else to do.

Small Carm drove as carefully and as quickly as he could up to Falconi Farm. After he hid Mom in the barn, he drove a few minutes more to visit Dad's old friend Paul "Whitey" Whiteway, now head of Whiteway Cremation Services. As one of Dad's few confidants, Whiteway wasn't too surprised to learn that Rosa had killed herself. He was surprised, however, when Small Carm asked if he could use one of his cremation chambers. I have no idea how Small Carm convinced him to help, but help he did. Small Carm claims his argument that the Catholic Church wouldn't bury her, plus the loyalty he felt toward Big Carm, was all it took. Whiteway says he was coerced and threatened by the strapping, six-foot-two, muscular kid with the dark, piercing eyes. That's for another jury to decide, since Whiteway will face his own trial in a few weeks.

Small Carm didn't have time to wait for the cremation process to be completed, so he made arrangements to pick up Mom's ashes the next day. He drove back down to the Falconi building just in time to intercept Gina and me as we came home from school.

The morning after the blood oath ceremony, Small Carm called the police station — the same one I would go to twenty-three years later — to file the missing person's report. Looking back now, it was crazy, but when the officer arrived to interview us, we had all been coached to act upset and pretend that we had woken up that morning to find our mother gone without a trace. We had to sit around the dining table while he searched the house for clues. Small Carm kept getting up and shadowing him to ask if he needed help; I think he was paranoid he'd forgotten to clean up something. To get me involved, the officer asked me to find a few different photographs of my mom that he could borrow and take down to the station. After about a half hour, another officer showed up and the two of them told us they were going to go interview the neighbours. When they left, Small Carm asked Dom, privately, if he had noticed anyone in the alley when they brought Mom down to the car.

It became even more surreal when Small Carm contacted everyone in Italy. Nonna Ines, who was then a widow of seventy-five, immediately made arrangements to fly to Toronto to help with the search. The paralyzed Nonna Serafina and heavily medicated Aunt Anna couldn't come for obvious reasons, but Aunt Candida also flew in. For a whole week, we all had to walk Spadina, College, Dundas, Queen and pretend to look for Rosabella for hours and hours. We made photocopied posters with a bunch of detachable phone numbers at the bottom and stapled them to wooden telephone poles, which were still around back then. We did the same thing in the east end Little Sicily where the Caporuscios had lived in the 1960s. We got crank calls. We visited a few of Mom's old friends on Milverton Boulevard to tell them; they told us the police had already been there and questioned them.

Whiteway said in court that he kept Small Carm's activities secret, but I'm not sure if I believe him. He and Big Carm were *really* close pals; wouldn't you call your buddy if his son showed up with such a bizarre and illegal request? In any case, back in 1984 Toronto police had located Big Carm in Rancho Cordova outside of Sacramento and interviewed him also; if he knew about Rosa being dead or cremated, he didn't say anything about it to them. Our cops then contacted the police department there to check the motels and hotels to see if Rosa was stalking Big Carm, but they came up with nothing.

I felt strange about all of this, even at nine years old. I felt guilty seeing the looks of pain on the faces of my grandmother and my auntie. How all of our friends on Spadina allowed us to tape the "HAVE YOU SEEN THIS WOMAN?" poster in their windows. I thought about all of these cops doing all of this searching for nothing. One night, I asked Small Carm why we were lying to everyone.

"I agree that lying is wrong, but much bigger wrongs have happened, ones that make this little lie okay. Plus, you made a promise to the family, Freddy. Besides, think of how sad everyone would be if they knew Mom had died, right? It's better this way, trust me."

I did trust him. For twenty-three years. So did Gina; she didn't know it was a suicide either, or that Mom's ashes had been unceremoniously stuffed into the Finch's glove box.

After about two weeks, the police told us that they had absolutely no leads and no bodies had turned up in any of Toronto's many ravines or floating in Lake Ontario, so my Nonna Ines and Aunt Candida went back home. Small Carm, however, had to talk with them on the telephone every week after that for the next six months, and then twice a month for the next few years. No wonder he looked so serious all the time.

Under cross-examination, the Crown attorney keeps asking me why I didn't go to the police sooner, why I was okay keeping this kind of a secret for so long. I don't know how to answer that one, so I just keep saying to her: "I guess it's an Italian thing." Or: "Well, I know this is a weird example, but you know when you've been working with someone for a long time, and you still can't remember their name, but it's too late to ask them because you don't want to offend them? Well, it's kind of like that." I don't want to sound flippant, but it really was like that; by the time I was a teenager and I could really question it, it was what it was, and it would have been too awkward to change it. Crazy as it may sound, the black hole was familiar, you know?

The Crown takes it easy on me when it comes to questions on Mom's mental illness, since she knows I wouldn't have been witness to much of that. Both lawyers ask me if Mom had ever talked about death, and I say no, she hadn't. I make sure to mention that Mom was a big library user, and that comes in handy when the defence brings up the library book on knot-tying that Mom had taken out. Dom still had it, and he gave it to Petrucci for evidence: It still had a due date of July 5, 1984 stamped onto the little card tucked into the tan pocket on the back cover.

The really good evidence that Mom had mental issues comes via video-link. Nonna Serafina, now in her eighties, sits in her wheelchair and, between crying jags, tells the court about her daughter's struggles with depression and about her other daughter, Anna, who now lives full-time in a psychiatric hospital. She thinks the whole situation is her fault.

The Crown asks me if I think it's strange that there was no funeral, that I believed Rosabella was buried in Sicily. I tell her what Small Carm told me all those years ago: That's what she wanted. I also tell her that a lot of strange things, like our grandfather dying in a car crash and our father leaving our family without saying goodbye, had also happened, so this was just one more thing, you know? She asks me why I never wanted to see my mother's grave. I tell her that travel wasn't a consideration for me after our company went bankrupt, and that my panic attacks and obsession with my own mortality in my twenties didn't put my mother's grave very high up on my travel list. Besides, when I was ten, Small Carm had shown me a photograph of a tombstone with a big FALCONI on it, and that was enough.

Both the Crown and the defence, Petrucci, ask me a lot of questions about Small Carm's personal religious practices, but all I can tell them is what I'd personally witnessed over the years, and that isn't very much. Obviously, I know it's very, very important to him, but I don't know how many times he goes to church in a week (turns out it's four) or what he does behind closed doors. They ask me if I've ever seen him do anything bizarre. I say: "That depends on your definition of bizarre." I can tell the Crown wants me to give her something juicy, but all I have is the blood oath ceremony, when Small Carm turned himself into a stigmatic by cutting his hands open, which I'd already told both of them about, and that I'd seen him coming out of his room wearing the Brown Scapular on a few occasions after that. The Scapular is a necklace with two small square panels; one panel has a picture of Our Lady of Mount Carmel (a.k.a. the Virgin Mary), and the other has text that reads: "Whoever dies clothed in this Scapular shall not suffer eternal fire." You need a priest to enrol you into a confraternity that gives you permission to wear it.

I'm not there to see it, but the Crown calls a witness who is an expert on cults who tries to suggest that Small Carm had killed Mom while performing some kind of bizarre ritual. The defence counters with representatives of Opus Dei who paint a very different picture of the organization. The Crown also has a star witness take the stand. This is Donald Yan, who owned the building two doors to the south of the Falconi building back in 1984. Yan swears he saw Rosa and Small Carm in the alleyway screaming like crazy and pushing and shoving each other just a few weeks before Small Carm filed the missing person's report and then knocked on his door to ask him to put a sign in his restaurant window.

That's when the defence calls on *their* surprise witness, Big Carm, or "my dad the cad" as I now call him. It turns out *he* was the one in the alleyway, pushing and shoving and screaming. He'd flown back to Toronto one last time to try to save his marriage, but it turned into a big, violent mess. He was wearing a hat and sunglasses, so his face was fairly obscured and, since Small Carm had always looked older than his years, Yan's confusion makes sense. Anyhow, Petrucci tells me that Big Carm, now sixty-six years old, has completely grey hair receding at the temples (but still styled like ol' Dino), a deeply lined and tanned beef jerky face from living in California for the past two decades, and tubes going up his nose to supply his lungs with oxygen. A smoker all his life, he has advanced emphysema: He walks slowly; he pauses for breath when he speaks; and he often coughs blood into a handkerchief. But he flew up here because he knew his testimony would help his son and former best buddy.

I'm pretty sure this is one of the main things that saves Small Carm from going to jail for a long time.

༄

I don't see my father while he's up here. He just flies in and does his duty on the stand and then he flies back south again. But he finds out where I live and slips a note under my front door while I'm sleeping. I'm trembling when I open it and realize who it is from.

Dear Alfredo,

I am a cad. And I will not call myself your dad, since I gave up that privilege a long time ago. I will not ask for your forgiveness, either, since I don't deserve it. I have heard from a few people that you've grown up to be a good man, and that's what I would expect with someone like Carmelo Jr. acting as your father.

I'm not the best with words, so I'm not going to try and explain the reasons I left. For one thing, you probably don't give a crap and, for another, I think you can put two and two together considering your mother left from your life even more dramatically than I did. I know you and your mother had a special relationship — in fact, I can tell you that she was at her best when she was with you, Freddy. She loved you so much! Sometimes I envied the attention you got from her because it reminded me of the way things used to be for us when we first got married and up until your brothers were little. Just know that when I left, I was at my wit's end, and that I have thought about all of you kids every day since — I'm being serious here.

Look, I know there's nothing I can say to make you like me. I will say that if you ever want to talk, even to rip into me, I'd love to hear your voice. Crazy, I don't even know what it sounds like. I've put my phone number at the bottom of the page. You may want to hurry up, though, because I'm not in the best of health. And no, I didn't write that for pity.

Carmelo.

Small Carm is lucky. He is found *not* guilty of second degree murder by the jury. To add to the defence's case, a handwriting expert was brought in to analyze the suicide note and compare it with samples of Mom's writing and they determined that it was, indeed, written by Rosabella in 1984. (The Crown had tried to suggest the note was a forgery.) Thankfully, Small Carm hadn't done anything drastic with the note and the ashes when the police came to arrest him; the ashes were sitting in the cheap urn on his desk in the Falconi office, and the yellowed note was spread out beside it as if he'd been reading it after Dom's freak-out.

Small Carm had admitted his guilt for indignity to a corpse and public mischief at the beginning of the trial, so the judge reminded the jury of this during her summation and cautioned them on some of the Crown's tenuous claims about Opus Dei. She reminded them that Small Carm had led a clean life since his misguided actions on that day and had no criminal record. She also stressed that he'd taken on great responsibility in raising his siblings.

So Small Carm was convicted of those two, lesser charges and sentenced to one year of house arrest, since the judge decided he posed no danger to the community. He does have to wear a wireless ankle bracelet, and I've been told he has to pay some of the costs associated with it. He's only allowed to leave the Falconi building for medical appointments and Mass, and he gets a couple of hours per week to go grocery shopping. He's not allowed to travel and he's got to report to a supervisor every two weeks. So, basically, his life won't be very different than before.

Dom's life isn't very different, either. After moving back to my house when Gina warned us she was about to drive Small Carm home to start his sentence, she calls again a day later.

"Dom, Small Carm says he's sorry and wants you back at home," she tells him. "He's got you down as a registered resident at the Falconi building. He's also allowed to have visitors, so tell Freddy I'm going to work on getting the two of them talking again."

Dom is crying happy tears when he hangs up the phone.

It takes less than a week for Gina to build a bridge between Small Carm and me. Yes, he felt betrayed, but the trial forced him to reconsider a lot of things. Like how his excessive religious zeal must have scared a small boy who had just lost both his parents. Like how holding onto a lie for almost a quarter century was tough, but that his little brother had done it out of love and loyalty. Like how the Ferrari accident, combined with watching one brother break the other brother's arm, and then finding out his mother had hanged herself, must've been a lot for a person to take in one night. And, finally, like how maybe his little brother might have been suffering with his own anxieties and wrestling with his own demons. (I'm finally on medication for them, and doing much better, thank you.)

So, I'm on my way to the Falconi building right now, and, truth be told, I'm nervous as hell. My big brother — my father, really — now has a criminal record, and I'm the one responsible for it. As I approach the big shop window, I notice that the tractor's dents have been hammered out and there's touch-up paint where Dom's golf club whacked away that nice Ferrari red and Italian flag green. The broken headlights and front grille have been replaced with ones from the basement. Small Carm is waiting at the door to the old showroom, holding it open for me. He tries to smile, but fails and looks like a chimpanzee.

"Come inside, brother," he says, and then steps aside to let me in. The minute I'm through the door, he gives me a big bear hug, cast and all.

"I'm the Christian, yet I didn't forgive you," he says into my ear.

"That's okay, Small Carm, I shouldn't have — "

"Don't finish that. You did what you needed to do. I respect you for that." He steps back and looks into my eyes. Those two dark beads under the caterpillars actually don't freak me out for once. They're warm.

"Dom and Gina are upstairs and we want to show you something," he says quietly. "You're the smart one, so we need your input. We're working on a proper funeral for Mom."

Black Into Red

As much as I hate cemeteries, it's nice to know where Rosabella Maria Falconi rests for eternity. Just like an expensive ruby, she's locked inside a little glass case in the Queen of Heaven Catholic Cemetery columbarium. Her home is a swirly, red marble urn that matches her hair. And she's a ten-minute drive from Gina and Rocco's place.

It's been one year since the funeral service and the placing of the ashes, so we've gathered here to pay our respects. I never know what to do in these situations, so I'm fiddling with the zipper on my windbreaker and looking out the window at the orderly, gray tombstones below. My fiancé, Penny's cousin Charlotte, walks over and puts a hand on my shoulder.

"You okay, babe?" she asks.

"Yeah, I just hate thinking about this mortality stuff," I say. "Plus, I've got a lot of work to do."

I've got a big assignment due at the end of the week and I'm behind the eight ball, big time. But I'm not complaining: Studying architecture at the University of Toronto is absolutely thrilling, despite my being fifteen years older than most of my classmates. It's partly thanks to the architect of Gina's home, Jerry Markson, that I got accepted. We met a few more times and had some long and fruitful conversations, and despite his joking that I'd be miserable as an architect, he wrote a glowing letter of recommendation to the Dean, who happens to be an old classmate of his. Markson even says he'll let me intern at the office "if" I'm good enough. I'm pretty sure he's joking.

Until he got into the columbarium, Dom was dancing around like he had ants in his pants, which was causing Penny to giggle quite a bit. Then again, as of last week, he's done paying off the ten grand he owed to Speed Kingz Exotics, so he's in a particularly good mood. Oh, and he's been the proud owner of a TTC Metropass for almost a year now. Penny already had one, so the two lovebirds have been using the streetcar and subway on their dates. They're doing this thing where they get off at a different subway stop each week and then challenge themselves to find a good restaurant within a five-minute walk and at least one other interesting thing to do. "Good luck when you get to Kennedy station," I keep telling them. If Dom's got any money left over after he's purchased the engagement ring he showed me, he says he'd like to take a course to get his motorcycle licence. But he's not interested in a big, smelly Harley-Davidson; he wants to get a cool little Vespa. Small Carm says he'll even help him out with the purchase *if* he promises to ride only during daylight hours.

Small Carm, by the way, has turned over a new leaf. Once his ankle bracelet was off, he made it quite clear that he was going to start doing things outside the Falconi building that have nothing to do with Catholicism. And because he got a little flabby from sitting around for a year, one of those things is a membership with an indoor beach volleyball team. Weird, I know, but I'll bet it's a great way to meet chicks. He's been slowly moving away from Opus Dei, too. We keep telling him we'll love him no matter what, but I think he's decided that too much religion can take the focus off other things, like family.

Speaking of which, our little redheaded nephew Joe is turning into quite the artist. And Millie, well, she takes after her mother. She's so good on top of a horse, we think she might be able to compete as an equestrian in the 2020 or 2024 summer Olympics.

And as for Big Carm, I did get out his letter and pick up the phone, finally, a few weeks ago. His calendar girl, Linda Larson, answered. I asked for him. She said, in a very sombre tone, that he had just passed away. I told her I was an old business associate looking to touch base, and that I hadn't seen him in decades.

☛ Acknowledgements ☚

The excerpt from *Winter Night* by Liborio Lattoni (1935) comes from *The Anthology of Italian-Canadian Writing*, edited by Joseph Pivato (Guernica Editions, 1998).

Chapter II would not have been possible without the kind tutelage of the very patient Mike Freeman, who spent an afternoon showing me (and letting me drive) his 1963 J. I. Case "Case-O-Matic" tractor on his beautiful property near Lake Scugog. What I know about Massey-Harris' history and their products comes from various web searches and the following book: *The Big Book of Massey Tractors* by Robert N. Pripps (Voyager Press, 2006).

While there are many sources on Mussolini's New Towns, I found this paper to be quite helpful: https://www.researchgate.net/publication/222671674_Destructive_creation_fascist_urban_planning_architecture_and_New_Towns_in_the_Pontine_Marshes

The information on Liborio Lattoni comes from the following sources: http://spectrum.library.concordia.ca/6882/1/salvatore_italian_canadiana.pdf and pages 57–63 of

Filippo Salvatore's *Ancient Memories, Modern Identities* (Guernica Editions, 1999).

The Legend of Heliodorus in Chapter V comes from a Google Books scan of *Duffy's Fireside Magazine*, Number XI, September 1851.

For everything I know about Spadina Avenue that's not already in my own head, the book on the street's history by Rosemary Donegan, *Spadina Avenue* (Douglas & McIntyre, 1985) was indispensable, as was a 1971 *Globe & Mail* article, "Spadina — Home of the Needle Trade" by Jack Batten. The Toronto Archives on Spadina Road was also of great assistance with additional information on Spadina's building stock.

Books on Italians in Toronto I consulted: *Italians in Toronto: Development of a National Identity 1875 — 1935* by John E. Zucchi (McGill-Queens University Press, 1988) and *Eh, Paesan! Being Italian in Toronto* by Nicholas DeMaria Harney (University of Toronto Press, 1998). My own little "Rat Pack" in Montreal, John Trivisonno and Fred Sarli, helped by reading an early draft and assisting me with nuances of Italian language, although both insist that I am already an "honorary Italian."

Non-Falconi news stories I refer to are authentic, including the fatal fire at the Phillips Garment Co. in 1950, and were accessed using the Toronto Public Library's archive of *Globe & Mail* and *Toronto Star* newspapers.

For the brief history on Kensington Market outlined in Chapter VII, I owe a debt to Jean Cochrane for *Kensington* (Boston Mills Press, 2000).

A treasure-trove of information on pre-1950 Canadian architects can be found at architect Robert Hill's Biographical

Dictionary of Architects in Canada: dictionaryofarchitectsincanada.org

For Chapter VIII, I listened to *Captain Stormfield's Visit to Heaven* by Mark Twain (as read by Kevin LaVergne) here: https://archive.org/details/cptstormfield_kl_librivox

The 2007 Ferrari F430 I drove for exactly a half hour was rented from Ultimate Exotics in Stoney Creek, Ontario. If you must know, it cost me $200 for the privilege and I enjoyed driving the Case-O-Matic tractor more.

Edward D. Prutschi, a lawyer with Adler Bytensky Prutschi Shikhman in Toronto, helped with deciding Small Carm's fate, and engineer-extraordinaire Dave Bowick of Blackwell came through with a laptop when I desperately needed one.

The book you are holding would not have been possible without the support of the fantastic folks at Guernica Editions: to Michael Mirolla and Connie McParland, my deepest thanks for believing in my work enough to take it from dream to reality. To Julie Roorda, you made the process of tightening and editing my words as painless as possible, so thank you.

I would be remiss if I didn't thank the love of my life, Shauntelle, for supporting me, encouraging me, and proofreading many versions. A nod to literary agent Hilary McMahon of Westwood Creative Artists; she read an early version of the book and offered some much-needed, constructive criticism.

All of the thoughts about Toronto architecture come from my own time serving as the *Globe & Mail's* weekly "Architourist" columnist; just like Freddy Flowers, I've been obsessed with Toronto's built heritage since I was a little kid, but, unlike him, I never did become an architect.

☞ About the Author ☜

Dave LeBlanc has been writing weekly as the *Globe & Mail*'s "Architourist" since 2004. In 2014-15, Dave hosted a pop culture web/television series *Where Cool Came From,* and in 2017 he appeared on HGTV's *Great Canadian Homes.* He has acted as juror for both the Ontario Association of Architects and the City of Toronto, which, when one considers how much he liked to draw significant Toronto buildings as a child, is a dream come true. Dave lives and works in Toronto and enjoys cooking, mixology, refinishing Mid-century Modern furniture for his wife's store, and riding his motorcycle in his spare time. *Falconi's Tractor* is his first novel, and he sincerely hopes that you enjoyed it.